DIE BEHIND THE WHEEL

DIE BEHIND THE WHEEL

Crime Fiction Inspired by the Music of Steely Dan

EDITED BY BRIAN THORNTON

Compilation copyright © 2019 Brian Thornton
Story copyrights © 2019 by Individual Authors

All rights reserved. No part of the book may be reproduced in any form or by any electronic or mechanical means, including information storage and retrieval systems, without permission in writing from the publisher, except by a reviewer who may quote brief passages in a review.

Down & Out Books
3959 Van Dyke Road, Suite 265
Lutz, FL 33558
DownAndOutBooks.com

The characters and events in this book are fictitious. Any similarity to real persons, living or dead, is coincidental and not intended by the author.

Cover design by Damonza

ISBN: 1-64396-016-4
ISBN-13: 978-1-64396-016-6

CONTENTS

Foreword — 1
Jeffrey Weber

Introduction — 5
Brian Thornton

Dirty Work — 9
Cornelia Read

Your Gold Teeth — 23
Nick Feldman

Home At Last — 43
Sam Wiebe

Haitian Divorce — 57
Simon Wood

Black Cow — 77
Linda Joffe Hull

Pretzel Logic — 93
dbschlosser

Green Earrings — 117
Bill Fitzhugh

Josie — 133
Stacy Robinson

Do You Have A Dark Spot On Your Past? — 153
David Corbett

On Your Knees Tomorrow — 165
R.T. Lawton

Harley Quinn Is Dead — 181
James W. Ziskin

Show Biz Kids — 195
Brian Thornton

FOREWORD
Jeffrey Weber

Desire, then envy. Those are the two emotions that occur when Los Angeles musicians learn that Steely Dan will be recording their next project in town.

Known for their meticulous production, Walter Becker and Donald Fagen had a history of selecting the finest musicians on the planet to contribute to their endlessly fascinating work. Playing or singing on their albums was as much a validation as a tribute. Yet, Walter and Donald had an inner sense of precision and perfection and often asked their musicians to record up to forty takes on each track. On at least one of their albums, they spent over a year in the studio.

Weary of the road in their early years, Steely Dan became a studio only band for quite a while. It was difficult to get studio musicians to go on the road then, and Donald, because of an intermittent panic disorder, was reluctant to sing live so they retreated to the studio. It became their home.

As a music producer for forty years, I too, take great care in hand-picking the finest musicians I can find to complement the artist and the music that I am recording. I have used a great number of the same musicians as Walter and Donald did to perform on my recordings. (Special musical gratitude to Michael McDonald, Jeff Porcaro, Dean Parks, Jeff "Skunk"

FOREWORD

Baxter, Victor Feldman, Larry Carlton, Lee Ritenour and Pete Christlieb.) These session musicians, as they are often called, are my insurance policy. They perform at a staggeringly high level. As a producer, if you're smart, you'll sit back and let them do what they do. They represent the highest level of artistry in music. Actually, they make producers like me look like a damn genius.

In addition to music production, I am a collector of signed, first edition, crime fiction. Reading was, and is, more than a simple passion. For countless years, it was an addiction so all-encompassing that as my library grew and grew, I had to negotiate with my wife for floor space for my collection. Many of the authors in this anthology have resided on my shelves for decades and brought me immeasurable hours of enjoyment.

It was clear to me that Walter and Donald were readers with the same degree of exploration and passion that I had. It guided them as they hand-picked the musicians that would deliver just the right tone of their music to their eager audience. To Walter—guitars, bass, background vocals—and Donald—keyboards, lead vocals—these stunning players were an integral part of the equation.

For about ten years, they blended jazz, pop—as we knew it then—and R&B with thematic lyrics that were cryptic, ironic and open to intense interpretation. That might have been obvious had you known that Walter and Donald named the band after a series of strap-on dildos mentioned in the William S. Burroughs novel, *Naked Lunch*.

Their lyrics have been the subject of speculation for years. Some have said that Steely Dan never created a heartfelt love song. Some believe that their songs deal with personal passion in the guise of a destructive obsession or a delusion. Populated by victims, derelicts, bottom feeders and failed dreamers, their lyrics feature disturbing twists on various realities such as love, prejudice and poverty. And then there are even darker themes exploring incest, pornography and prostitution. Perfect for this anthology!

In Los Angeles, they often recorded at Producer's Workshop, a small, cinderblock studio, completely hidden behind a well-known mastering studio, in the thick of Hollywood. Right smack on Hollywood Boulevard, no less. As is the case with most recording studios, if you know about it, you'll find it. If you don't, you won't. Producer's Workshop had its own notable history in that Pink Floyd's *The Wall* was recorded there along with projects by Alice Cooper, Ringo, Neil Diamond, Carly Simon, Fleetwood Mac—*Rumours*—and, of course, *Aja*. I recorded a few of my own projects there, too. Back then, the studio was co-owned by Liberace. Who knew? It's still there today, and that well-known mastering studio in front of it is now "The Museum of Death." Only in Hollywood.

Besides having a celebrated history of success on the charts and at the Grammy Awards, Steely Dan's music was coveted by a niche of music enthusiasts known as audiophiles. Audiophiles search the world for music that has the exuberance of extreme dynamics. If the bass doesn't whip your clothing and shake the lighting fixtures, then that recording is tossed. If the mids and the highs are clean and tight without being strident, then that disc may be a keeper. It wasn't so much the message as it was the purity and punch of the sound. And Steely Dan's recordings really delivered.

But for the rest of us, the grateful and enduring fans, the release of a new Steely Dan recording was cause for celebration. We looked forward to discovering the pleasures of the complex arrangements. The tightness of the production. The richness of the harmonies. The crispness of each instrument as it was carefully yet effortlessly brought to life in the mix. And then there were the lyrics. We could use our imagination to dig deep as we interpreted each lyric's cinematic script. Sometimes whimsical, sometimes dark, sometimes fanciful, sometimes dangerous, but always stimulating. Always thought provoking.

FOREWORD

Time and again, Steely Dan displayed the finest in the recording arts. Their music proved to me that, as a producer, I needed to up my game. Their music allowed me a glimpse of what could be done. But, more importantly, their music provided insight as to what must be done.

I'm getting there.

INTRODUCTION
Brian Thornton

Donald Fagen and Walter Becker were responsible for some of the most subversively slick pop hits of the 1970s. The two were jazz lovers who met while undergraduates at Bard College, toured as part of Jay and the Americans, and then parlayed jobs as staff writers for ABC records—where they wrote, among other songs, "I Mean to Shine," later recorded by Barbra Streisand—into a recording deal with the type of creative control most artists only dream of.

The result was a string of jazz albums masquerading as pop-rock albums, possessed of sterling production values, sharp, enigmatic lyrics, and chops executed by some of the best studio players ever to record. Starting in 1972 with *Can't Buy a Thrill* and running through 1980's *Gaucho*—as well as two more albums and countless tours since reuniting in the early '90s—Fagen and Becker wrote cynical, often wry lyrics which owed a considerable debt to the tropes of crime fiction.

Songs about whorehouses, "Here at the Western World;" the "colorful" parts of town, "Pearl of the Quarter;" smoking heroin and the toll it takes, "Time Out of Mind;" and failed relationships, "Everything You Did," "Reelin' in the Years," "Dirty Work," "My Old School," just to name a few; vied with titles like "Don't Take Me Alive," songs like "Kid Char-

INTRODUCTION

lemagne"—based in part on the life of Owsley Stanley, the first drug chef to whip up LSD and sell it in mass quantities—and whole albums such as their bleak, gorgeous masterwork *Aja*, to paint a desolate world populated by noir heroes, sometimes successful, just as often not.

A number of years back I had the idea that it might be interesting to take something by Steely Dan and use it as the inspiration for a story. After all, there was already a crime fiction connection there. Fagen even included a song entitled "The Goodbye Look" on his first solo album, *The Nightfly*—a title lifted from a book by hard-boiled/noir master Ross MacDonald—to whom the song is intended as an homage.

I quickly came up with a plot, wrote half a draft, and then shelved it when my son was born. And there it languished until September 2017. Specifically, the day Walter Becker died. (The finished product, "Show Biz Kids," is included in this collection.) I wrote a tribute on my blog, including in part: "I've often said that the music of Steely Dan would lend itself to a themed anthology of the type recently collected by Joe Clifford, and centered around the music of Johnny Cash."

And then my wife, who is my first reader and perennial wisest counsel, asked me, "Why don't you do it?" Turns out she soon had company. Several friends asked the same thing after reading that piece.

The idea sold itself. I approached Down & Out Books publisher Eric Campbell about it, and we quickly worked out a deal. And there was such an enthusiastic response to my request for stories inspired by the music of Steely Dan that our planned collection quickly ballooned in size.

That single anthology "morphed" into *two* companion anthologies, you could even say, "It changed, it grew, and everybody knew….": the one you're currently holding and *The Hangman Isn't Hangin': Crime Fiction Inspired by the Music of Steely Dan*, which will be out later this year. Note that there is no "Volume 1" or "Volume 2." These anthologies are thematically linked, yet truly stand alone.

It has been genuinely humbling working with the terrific crew of writers whose efforts populate these pages. Their creativity, their flexibility, their bonhomie suffuses this anthology, and has rendered this collection the better for their collective presence. I thank each and every one of you from the bottom of my heart for giving so freely of your time and of yourselves. You have done great work!

I would also like to take a moment to thank Eric Campbell and the crew at Down & Out Books. They have been incredibly supportive and helped make the process of collecting and editing this group of stories a relatively painless endeavor.

I owe a further debt of thanks to Jim Thomsen, Stacy Robinson and David B. Schlosser, for their terrific proofreading and tireless editorial assistance. Thanks, you three. Fresh eyes are a must when working with stuff like this. Talented ones are a bonus.

Lastly, thanks to my wife, Robyn Thornton: first reader and final editor. For the support in myriad ways, and for pushing me to commit to this idea in the first place. Love you, honey!

DIRTY WORK
Cornelia Read

Lonergan kicked me off the hay truck around noon.

It's dirty work. Shards of alfalfa chuff off the baler and catch in the sweat that forever streams down your back by late summer. They prickle and chafe and pretty soon you've got a thousand tiny nicks everywhere: itching, wet, and salty in August's miserable stillness of leaden heat.

Field hands used to knock back cold stoneware pitchers of a drink they called "switchel." It was an ersatz lemonade, with cider vinegar mixed into the chilled maple-sugared water in lieu of citrus.

Turns out if you're overworked and dehydrated in the high-noon sun, switchel can stop your heart.

We might have tried it if Van Wyck Durant had been a farmer.

Sadly for all concerned, the smug old bastard taught semiotics at Bard, and I owed him a hundred more pages of my undergrad thesis on The Meaning of Meaning before he'd deign to let me graduate.

Wyck knew full well I didn't have the money to stick around for the summer without a job.

"You got yourself into this, Tommy," he'd said, leaning back in the leather chair behind his campus desk. "You're bright, but you're a lazy little fuck for a boy who thought he'd just breeze through this place on a full ride."

"I suppose that's right, sir."

"And I *suppose* you expect my help, but you're shy three credits and without my say-so on this piece of shit you're calling a thesis...."

He was a big guy and handsome, a Ted Hughes who'd have preferred the rugby scrum to verse.

You wouldn't think to look at him that he was the sole heir to gobs of money, or that he'd never had to work a day in his life unless it amused him. Not unless you looked at his hands.

My mother was home alone in Allentown, no doubt ginning herself up to work her second shift at the Econo-Lodge.

I sat up straighter. "Sir?"

It was late afternoon on the day I should have graduated. Giddy familial congratulations echoed across the verdant expanse of Bard College, outside Wyck's leaded windows. We were on the eastern bank of the Hudson River, her waters cobalt and stately as they rolled out with the tide.

Durant let me swing for another long moment, as though deciding whether to temper my fate with a soupçon of noblesse oblige.

We both knew he would, but that he'd make me pay.

"I could use another hand at the farm," he said.

"Certainly."

"Ask for Lonergan at the barn, tomorrow at six." He tore the end off a sheet of foolscap and scrawled the address.

"Excuse me, sir, but, ah…what's the going rate?"

"Three hots and a cot until I approve your thesis for the panel. That'll light a fire under your ass."

"I expect so, sir."

"You're welcome," he called after me, as I started down the darkened hallway.

* * *

I started fucking Durant's wife halfway through June, but I hadn't wanted to kill him. Not at first.

The old story: Holly'd been one of his students, a Botticelli redhead with long legs, no tits, and an ass like a choirboy.

Mrs. Durant the First bowed out with grace, her long-ordained departure sweetened with a large check and two villas in the Azores.

I knew who Holly was, of course, and she first saw me when she'd come in from an early-morning gallop along the river on her big gray hunter.

The day was already steamy, though it wasn't yet eight o'clock. I'd been mucking out stalls for Lonergan in a sweat-dark T-shirt, stinking of horse shit.

I'd stumbled back out into the sunlight, blinking, when I heard Holly clatter to a halt beside the mounting block.

I guess she still liked what she saw. Ten minutes later we were rutting like minks in the hayloft while her gelding, abandoned, whickered at a hitching post.

Six weeks after that, Durant was away at a conference in Chicago, and I watched Holly lock the last door behind their old cook Gladys for what seemed like the thousandth time.

She led me upstairs to where she'd lit a few dozen candles in the master bedroom, fat squat little things that perfumed the summer night with the scent of linden trees in full blossom.

I roped her long red hair around my fist, leaning in to kiss the side of her neck. Her silken shirt slid off that shoulder to reveal smudges of bruise marring the tender skim-milk perfection of her collarbone.

"It's nothing," she said, but he'd spoiled what was mine and we both knew he had to go.

I took her from behind.

* * *

As we lay across the tangled sheets of their marital bed, her head light on my chest, Holly started talking.

"He doesn't do it all the time," she whispered.

"What?"

"Hurt me."

"Once is too much."

"It's mostly when he's bored. Like a tantrum. It passes."

"Leave."

"I won't give him the satisfaction, and he knows it. I'm not going out on the street so he can sweep up his next possession. Someone younger, more vulnerable."

"I'm picturing an airtight pre-nup."

"More of a chokehold," she said.

"There's always the traditionally obvious way around that kind of paperwork."

She laughed. "Don't think I haven't considered it."

"Should be easy enough. In fact I think I'd rather enjoy taking care of it for you."

"There's a catch."

"Do tell," I said, stroking her hair.

"In the case of his demise, his daughter gets everything. Tricky to set things up that way, but with fawning lawyers and a few shell corporations, he managed."

"Wow," I said. "You think he sat them down and said, 'So here's the thing, boys…I need to make sure I won't be murdered in my sleep by my beloved wife'?"

Holly ran her fingernails down the hair on my belly. Then she took my nipple in her teeth.

"The way forward seems clear," I said. "We take out the daughter, too."

Holly raised her head and smiled, teeth glowing in the candlelight. "She's coming for two weeks on Friday."

I flipped her onto her back, scissoring between her long legs while I reached to pin her arms above her head.

She stuck the tip of her tongue into my ear, then whispered, "And the little bitch can't swim."

Friday at dawn, Lonergan pulled the old International up in front of the grooms' house. He had the baler hitched behind it, and four of us followed him up to a northern field in the hay truck.

He let the tractor idle while he got down to check the belts and chains, then gave each fitting four pumps of grease. He stepped around the baler on one side, lowering the pickup wheel.

"Rained last night," I said.

He grinned at me. "Worried the bales'll be too heavy, are you?"

I shrugged. "You might want to drop those wheels lower."

Lonergan squinted. "Done this before?"

"My uncle's farm, out past Wilkes-Barre. Every summer from the age of five."

"Have at it," he said.

I made the adjustment to his satisfaction. He got back up into the cab and throttled all the way back before he turned on the PTO.

I saw him lean his head out, and he motioned me up toward him.

"You're to be picking up young Miss Durant from Rhinecliff station," he yelled, over the engine noise. "The twelve-fifty-eight. Shower first and yer man'll give you the keys to the Volvo."

"Sure," I said.

"I hear you've said more than 'Good afternoon, miss,' you'll be shoveling shit till New Year's, you follow?"

I gave him a snappy salute, walking backwards to the wagon behind his baler.

* * *

Holly stood in the grooms' bathroom when I stepped out of the shower.

I must have jumped back three feet. "Jesus H. *Christ*, woman."

She dangled the Volvo keys, nonplussed. "I've been thinking it over."

"Which part?"

She sidled up against me. "You may have to fuck her."

"How do you figure?"

"We've got to get them out on the boat together, with both of us."

"I can't see Wyckie plumping for that—taking the help out for a spin on his sloop?"

Holly raised the tip of her index finger to my lips. "That's why it has to be her idea."

She shifted her pelvis into mine. I pulled her closer, then leaned forward so she was pressed against the tiled wall.

I licked her neck. "You're putting an awful lot of faith in my looks and charm."

"Wyck made her do a summer session at her boarding school," she said. "All girls. Tell her you want to be a pirate. She'll do it just to piss him off."

"And how will I get it up for anyone but you, light of my life, fire of my loins?"

"Close your eyes and think of England."

"Rule, Brittania," I said, rocking my hips into her.

Holly ducked out from my arms and strode from the room, throwing the car keys back over her shoulder without turning to look.

I caught them one-handed, feeling like a giant idiot with my towel on the floor and a raging hard-on.

"Hey," I said, "so what's her name?"

Holly's disdain could have blistered the paint in the stairwell. "Lavinia."

I stood at attention beside the Volvo wagon at Rhinecliff Station, my khakis and blue button-down shirt rapidly losing their starch.

I'd arrived fifteen minutes early. The train, being Amtrak, was a good hour late.

Friday's heat had built to a hideous crescendo from sunrise onward. Tar oozed from the parking lot's patched asphalt, and a low brown haze obscured the Hudson.

Every ten minutes or so, I got back in the car and started her up for a few treasured moments. I hoped the A/C would keep my sweat at bay, and understood that few things make a young girl's fancy less inclined to thoughts of love than hot leather upholstery on a muggy afternoon.

I figured Lavinia would recognize the car, if not me. Her father's initials were emblazoned on its aptly named vanity plates, then repeated in nautical code-flag stickers just above the handle of each front door.

Rhinecliff is rather a dumpy little footnote to the old Dutch village of Rhinebeck. Tourists often wonder why the bluffs with the best river view are crammed with the wan old cottages of an almost-completely vestigial servant class. Even the grand old piles of the Vanderbilts and Roosevelts are set well back from the water.

Old Cornelius could have told you this was because of his railroad, whose steam engines ran on coal until the mid-fifties. Even back when Edith Wharton came up to visit her cousins, these hillsides were choked and stinking with cinders and ash, often catching fire if the summer rains weren't steady. The ticky-tacky houses of butchers and bakers and parlor maids had provided a comfortable buffer between the rich and the New York Central.

And as I was smugly pondering that, I heard the low moan of the so-called 1:52 express. I gave myself one last blast of blessed air conditioning and left the car running as I resumed my place by the rear passenger door.

The newly arrived crowd began meandering out into walloping heat. I wondered what Lavinia might look like.

She could well be blonde. I'd more than once heard Holly refer to Wyck's starter wife as "the feckless flaxen-haired cow." (At this juncture I confess I pictured a simpering Charlene Tilton, squat and neckless *avec* tip-tilted nose.)

She could instead take after her father: his leonine dark looks made coarse in the form of a brutish field-hockey captain, forever lumbering about in search of her misplaced shin guards.

As people and cars slowly ebbed away, I began to wonder whether Lavinia would show up at all.

It was only as the very last taxi pulled free of the stand that she emerged from the station doors.

She clocked the Volvo and walked toward me, her skin and hair seemingly poured from the same ewer of honey-gold. She was nearly my height, floating coolly across the pavement in a froth of white eyelet skirts and a wide-brimmed straw hat, through the open weave of which tiny spangles of sunlight danced across the perfection of her face.

She carried no purse, just a small leather grip that looked like something Annie Oakley or Nellie Bly might have taken around the world.

She stopped a pace away from me.

I couldn't for the life of me think of what to say. My mouth was dry and a deluge of flop sweat raced down my chest.

I would have given anything to drop to my knees, to bury my face in homage at the high juncture of her perfect thighs.

Lavinia glanced at her watch.

"Dude," she said, bored already, "you're supposed to open the fucking door."

"Of course, Miss Durant."

I reached for the chromed back handle and took her bag.

She only caught me staring at her twice in the rearview mirror.

The second time, she smiled.

I went up to my tiny room under the eaves just after dark that night. Not that I wanted to sleep. My window faced the big house, and I thought if I turned off my lights I might catch a glimpse of Lavinia through the dozen gold-paned French doors of the dining room, or as she climbed the great front staircase toward her own bed.

Instead I saw Gladys perch in the kitchen window to sneak a cigarette, once she'd served the soup over which Mr. and Mrs. Durant ignored one another from opposite ends of their long mahogany table.

Holly was dressed exquisitely, as always, her thick red hair caught up on a low chignon at the nape of her graceful neck.

Remarkable, I thought, that the woman I'd wanted to ravish on a tiled bathroom floor only that morning should now evoke nothing, not even pity.

Holly slipped into my bed naked around 3:00 a.m. She went down on me when I didn't respond, and still nothing happened until I closed my eyes to call forth the image of Lavinia's head, bobbing up and down in her stepmother's place.

I nearly called out the wrong name at the end, catching myself just in time to moan "*lover*," instead.

She curled up alongside me, draping one leg across my thighs. "Cat got your tongue?"

"No cats, sheer pleasure," I replied, kissing the top of her head.

Her hair felt rough against my lips; her perfume's musk cloying at the back of my throat.

"I told Lavinia we'd go for a ride tomorrow morning,"

Holly purred. "Seven o'clock."

"I'll be there with bells on. And a pitchfork."

"Good. I'll stand her up. Give the two of you a chance to chat."

On the strength of that, I found myself ready for an encore.

Lonergan had a pair of horses tacked up and spit-polished by six forty-five. He left them tethered to the rail beside the mounting block.

At seven sharp, Lavinia walked up to the bay mare and pulled the stirrups down their leathers, then checked the girth.

"May I give you a hand?" I set my pitchfork against the barn wall.

"No," she said, up in a flash.

Her sundress had made me want to take both knees. In breeches and boots she was murder.

The mare pranced beneath her, restless. Lavinia tucked her ass down in the saddle. "Cut the shit, Princess."

The horse stilled, obedient.

Lavinia looked back toward the big house, muttering "that lazy bitch" under her breath.

I picked up the pitchfork just as she turned the mare neatly toward me.

"What's your name, stable guy?" she asked.

"Tommy."

"Can you ride a horse, Tommy?"

"I fell off some old Shetland ponies as a kid. Mostly I suck at it."

"Get yourself a helmet from the tack room," she said. "I'll wait."

I was barely in the saddle when she grabbed my reins, cracked my horse's ass cheek with her crop, set us both off into the woods at an all-out hand gallop.

Half an hour later, on the mossy green floor of a gem-like

grove, Lavinia was riding me.

If I could've died the moment she straddled me, I'd have lived a full and perfect life.

"So," she said, suiting up once we'd finished. "How long have you been fucking my stepmother?"

"Wait, what?"

She laughed. "Oh, please. The hot stable boy? I bet she jumped you before you were halfway out of bed the first morning."

I looked away. "Since June."

Lavinia laughed again. "I'll tell Gladys we'll be four at dinner. Should be fun."

She was back on the mare and away before I'd located my boxers in a clump of poison ivy.

Holly beamed at me from the end of the table as dinner wound down to its excruciating denouement. "How's your crème brulée, Tommy?"

"Delicious, Mrs. Durant," I said, resisting the temptation to add *rather like Stalingrad, circa February of 1943*.

Lavinia chose this moment to briefly graze my fly with her bare toes, and I think I covered the resultant choking fit rather well, considering.

Wyck had spent the meal silent, glowering, and knocking back what must have been a fifth of single-malt—waving away another untouched plate at the end of each course as Gladys fussed over him.

"Gladys was Daddy's nurse," confided Lavinia. "She's been with the family since practically the dawn of time."

Her father closed his eyes. "Lavinia, I'll thank you not to be unkind."

"Oh for God's *sake*, Wyckie," snapped his wife. "The woman's been deaf as a post since the Tet Offensive."

Lavinia reached down the table, laying her hand across her

father's. "I'm sorry, Daddy. You're absolutely right. She's always been lovely to me."

"Apology accepted," he said.

"What do we all have planned for tomorrow?" asked Holly, trying to mimic their affectionate tone. "It's supposed to be perfect, not a jot over seventy degrees with a *lovely* breeze…"

"I've got a full desk that needs tackling," said Wyck. "And young Tom here has a solid day's work ahead of him."

Lavinia gave his fist a squeeze. "For goodness sake, Daddy, have you given him a day off all summer? How do you expect him to *ever* finish that thesis?"

Holly clapped her hands together.

"I know," she said. "We'll have a picnic! Out on the boat!"

The boat was a thirty-foot sloop with a small cabin below, and the day was indeed glorious.

Holly whispered "just leave it to me" as we pulled away from the dock, and all I could do was try to figure a way out of this whole ridiculous plan.

Our picnic consisted of lobster salad on crusty baguettes, and Holly had pressed Gladys to pack not one but three thermoses of Bloody Marys, which she poured out for us all with generous abandon.

After lunch, Lavinia went up to the foredeck to sun herself in a white bikini. She'd refused to put on the life jacket I tried to insist she wear.

"Don't be ridiculous," she'd said, laughing as she pushed it away. "The tan lines would be appalling."

Wyck, meanwhile, had gotten chummier with every glass he drained. "Thirsty work, sailing!"

By the time we'd passed West Point, he was so lit I was amazed we hadn't capsized when the wake of a tug boat and barge hit us broadside.

"You're not a bad man on the water, Tommy," he said, as

Holly twined her arms around his neck. "Admirable, for a boy from Wilkes-Barre."

"My father was in the Coast Guard," I said.

He nodded. "Admirable."

"*Admiral*," crooned Holly, winking at me as she raised her glass. "Admiral Tommy."

"Hear hear!" said Wyck, tossing his umpteenth bloody down the hatch after lifting it toward me in toast.

A tanker was chugging upriver, a hundred yards away.

"Take the tiller for a moment, sweetie," said Wyck to Holly, giving her a peck on the cheek. "I'm going below to hit the head."

She waited until he'd climbed down the gangway and turned toward the bow.

"Lavinia, don't you want another cocktail?"

"Now that you mention it," said Lavinia, raising herself up from the deck.

She got to her feet and started nimbly picking her way back toward the cockpit.

"Jesus," she said, on tiptoe now, "this deck's hot as *shit*."

The tanker was closing on us.

"Holly," I said. "You see that boat, right?"

"We've got right-of-way, Tommy. We're under sail."

"Even so..." I said.

"Don't worry, Tommy," said Lavinia. "Holly's an old hand at this."

She leaned just a little on the word *old*, dragging it out.

Holly laughed. "Just for you, Tommy, I'll give it a wide berth."

Lavinia mouthed "pussy" at me.

"Ready about?" asked Holly.

"Ready," said Lavinia.

"Hard a lee," said Holly, cranking the wheel toward the boom.

We turned away from the tanker, mainsail luffing.

Lavinia loosed the jib sheet on the downwind grinder, then pulled its twin taut on the other side so we picked up speed again on a broad reach heading for shore.

"Sweetie," said Holly, tilting her glass toward her stepdaughter, "would you mind giving me a re-up?"

Lavinia stood, reaching back toward the glass, slightly off balance.

"Jibe ho," said Holly under her breath, cranking the wheel hard and fast in the other direction.

The boom snapped hard, catching Lavinia across the side of the head. It came away bloodied.

Holly stood to give her stepdaughter a shove overboard, then pulled the mainsheet taut—all in one motion—just as we hit the tanker's wake.

She took the roll with her knees, shoving an oar against the hatch as we capsized.

I crawled over the side and onto the keel as the sloop's sails slapped down hard on the water.

"Tommy," shrieked Holly, grabbing at my legs. "What are you *doing*?"

I tried to kick her off but somehow she'd managed to get one hand wrapped in my belt.

"Stop it," she said. "Tommy, you're not thinking…"

The side of the boat was wet, surprisingly cold. I couldn't get a handhold on the slick wood.

"Let me go," I said.

"It's all perfect now," she said, gripping my belt with her second hand. "We'll get it all. We'll have *everything*."

I kicked her in the face with all the force I could manage.

"Half right," I said. "*I'll* have it."

I kicked her again, feeling something essential break with the force. She slumped down, arms now limp.

I used Holly's shoulder for leverage, pushing off hard with both feet to hasten my dive toward Lavinia.

YOUR GOLD TEETH
Nick Feldman

Got a feeling I've been here before. Couldn't say for sure. Deep enough into a run like this, all the felt starts to look alike. Not like the casinos with their branded tables and uniformed dealers. Those tables look like they're telling you a story. These ones are just telling you where your money goes.

Mine mostly goes away. Sometimes it comes back. Sometimes even with friends. They never seem to stay long, though. That's okay...my friends don't stay long, either. Nobody likes to stand too close to a gambler.

Or so I tell myself, as I look out across the killing floor covered in gamblers with women standing very close to them. For now, I think, and I make it almost a full second before I catch myself in the lie; I've been around enough, I've seen a lot of these faces before, and plenty of them always have the same face next to theirs. So I switch to a better lie, that it's all about the money.

Once upon a time it was for me, too, wasn't it? Or for her. Who can remember? She's gone now, along with most of the money. Bad luck, good riddance. I'll never fall for another girl in a game again.

Of course, soon as I think that, she walks in. Not her. New she. Looks less like a gambler, more like a lottery. The prize, not the ticket. Those are sold out.

Black hair, gold streaks, and lots of both. But it's what's underneath that's got every eye in the room and most of the oxygen. Bright blue eyes, dark brown skin. Mae Young makeup, Nicki Minaj motif. Soft red lips, solid-gold grill. Old Hollywood hip-hop.

The neck starts with a chain and ends maybe a quarter-mile later when it ducks behind a long scarlet dress that reaches all the way to her left foot and her right thigh. That's not to say the right leg goes uncovered; she's inked to the ankle, mostly black-and-silver Cantonese characters. No idea what they say, but I've got a sudden urge to find out.

Pretty sure I'm not the only one, either. Wish I'd had time to put money on it, as by the time she's made it to her table half of the mutts in this kennel have slurped their tongues off the floor enough to start barking up her tree. I haven't moved, myself. Begging for treats doesn't work when you're already playing dead.

I go on with my business, that being losing at blackjack, while six tables over she starts taking people's money on the river, often enough that I think the dealer might be helping her fish. Probably just my imagination; girl like that, every time she wins at anything, every man in the room thinks the fix is in. Every man in the room is wrong, though; playing fixed, she'd at least have the decency to lose a few hands first for appearances.

She doesn't lose for a couple hours. I do, but that's not news these days. Lucky for me, I'm running a tab. Even luckier, I'm playing low-stakes tonight. Mostly because, luckiest of all, I'm about ten grand of the way through that fifteen-grand trip to another broken thumb or two. Plenty of time for my luck to change.

Around 2:00 a.m., it finally does. I get hot, end up about six grand up from when I came in, which puts my tab back in the manageable "nobody's knocking on my door if I don't show up for a week" range...though I'll still show up for the week.

Normally somebody'd notice a streak like mine. People like to sit next to a winner. Still true tonight, so long as the winner isn't me.

Or maybe not. Her luck's changing. She's been at the table too long, the guys who know what they're doing have had enough time to shake off her shock-and-awe. They're finally looking at her tells instead of her tits.

She's still not bad. Losing slowly, mostly on folds or bad math. But she's still losing. The longer it goes, the more it shifts. They've got her now, and with enough sharks at the table, even when she outsmarts one of 'em the others are waiting to take her money.

She's halfway back to where she started when I sit next to her. Dealer shoots me the eyes, telling me I'm not supposed to. That's fine, I'm not staying.

"Stop. They've got you made. You'll win more anywhere else." I say it softly enough that only she can hear me, and probably buy myself a little trouble down the road if the other mugs at the table assume she's my player. It'll serve me right for playing Lancelot. Just call me the sucker Samaritan.

She looks at me out of the side of that viper's eye of hers, but she doesn't say a damn thing. Fair enough. I've got nothing else to say myself, so I hit the bricks, the road, and the sack, in that order.

I don't like to think of myself as a sucker—Samaritan or otherwise—but I would have bet on never seeing her again after that night, and boy, does that turn out to be a sucker bet. Three, four nights a week she pops up where I do. Never playing the same game that I am, by coincidence or design.

I see her in Marty's basement on Tuesday, shooting craps while I bet the playoffs. On Thursday, she's playing blackjack at Sammy's when I walk in to pay off my bookie and lose a few hands of hold 'em. Saturday, I decide to put some distance between myself and my natural habitat—and yeah, the foxy new apex predator that's fucking up my ecosystem—and head out of the city, to the Wandering Rains Indian Casino. Nice and legal and classy and damned if she isn't here, too, playing poker again, losing with a smile that even I can't prove is a lie.

Nicer places like this, I only play poker. House is too smart to let you win enough at anything that's their money, and there're a lot more suckers out here in the light than in the jungles back in town.

I take my own table, give her plenty of space. I've got a bunch of drunk businessmen and their expensive dates, and they're paying off my tab good and fast. Shoulda done this weeks ago.

She smells the smoke from all that money they're burning, and it isn't long before she's sitting next to me. I tell myself I tried to avoid this, but I'm too good a poker player to buy a bluff that bad.

"Hey, stranger," she says to me with a not-quite-wink that may as well have spiked my drink, "...and stranger, and stranger, and even stranger." She's nodding to every other sucker at the table in turn and making each one of 'em even dumber than they were when I walked in. And they were already pretty dumb.

"I'd like to cash out," I tell the dealer, even though, for the moment and most of the night, I'm poppa big stack.

"Ah, don't tell me I scare you, stranger?" She leans just an inch or two my way. Exactly enough for the perfume to reach me like a soft jasmine jab...and the pheromones to hit me like a Sugar Ray roundhouse. Time to throw in the towel.

"I'm no good at bluffing. You scare me," I tell her, taking my chips and going home. I tell myself I'll avoid her entirely next time. I really am no good at bluffing.

She is, though, and it's two weeks of me staring at doorways, just starting to suspect I've seen the last of her, before our paths cross again.

I'm down big in a bad place, too deep to the wrong people. Shouldn't have come here, damn sure shouldn't have stayed. I've still got three grand in chips left to me, but the three bulldogs across the table from me have got at least ten apiece, and they'll bully me into bust. I'm tabbed out to forty grand I don't have. This could be the end of me.

Except she apparates over me, dropping twenty grand in chips on the table like my guardian angel while her other hand takes a devil's rest on my shoulder.

"Sorry I'm late with your stake, sweetie. Can you ever forgive me?" she purrs.

"Guess I have to," I grunt.

As for the bulldogs, she's thrown them off their game; they're good players, but in dank dark dens of iniquity like this one, you don't see a ton of women like her. Well, you don't see too many women like her period, here or elsewhere, but the point stands. Before too long I'm back up to even... minus her twenty. My knees are saved for the evening, but I owe her now and that can't be any good for my head.

Out of the frying pan and into the center of the sun. At least the view is nice.

She insists on a drink after the rescue, and being a chivalrous gentleman type who also happens to owe her twenty large, I oblige. She says her name is Naomi, but she says it like she's lying and wants me to know it. I tell her my name is Joe, and I say it like it's true. It isn't.

"Nice to meet you, Jack," she says. This time she's not lying, and that's even more bad news, though I admit it sounds pretty good on her broadcast.

"Nice to meet you, whoever you are," I say right back, and she's just kind enough to let those gold teeth peek through those lips. Guess she thinks I'm funny.

The bar doesn't have much to offer—that'll happen when you're playing in a boiler room—but we make do. I'm sipping cheap whiskey that's been open too long, she's tickling a glass of champagne that's probably closer to a bottom-shelf white with some seltzer in it. Cheap, but dressed up to look nice. Wonder if she's trying to tell me something.

"I've been watching you, Jack," she purrs through her bubbly. "I think you're just the kind of rube I could get along with." I don't like to think I'm any kind of rube, personally, but then my person has proved me wrong enough on that point I can't make too much of a stink over it.

"Yeah, well, everybody thinks that at first. Then they taste my cooking."

She smirks, looks me over, and leans back. She produces a cigarette—an expensive one—and perches it on those lips. She doesn't wait for me to offer a light, slipping a little golden pistol lighter out of her handbag and lighting up. Then she uncrosses her legs and says, "Guess we'll just have to eat out then."

I know what she's doing. I've seen this dance before. Doesn't mean I'm not tempted, but in my old age I've grown weary of fraternizing with my debtors, and I just manage to avoid taking the bait.

"Nah, I'm on a diet. Gotta watch my heart."

That one scores me a raised eyebrow, but she doesn't force the issue. She knows she doesn't have to; she's lived long enough to know that if she just stands next to a fella long enough, he'll tie the noose himself sooner or later.

"You know, Jack," she says, changing the subject as she ashes her smoke, "I think you and I could make a little money together."

"Maybe, but I think you make a little money just fine without me."

"Well, maybe a little more than a little, then."

"Say, twenty grand more than a little?"

She smiles, glad I'm keeping up. "A little more than that, even, Jack. Enough for you to pay your debts...and mine."

"Oh? And how big is yours?" I cringe as I say it, knowing I've set myself up for another round of innuendo and come-hither glances, but she surprises me with a straight answer, dropping the mask just enough to sell it.

"Two hundred fifty. In the wrong places."

I know better than to ask this question. "Where?"

"Benny Tops."

She wasn't kidding.

Benny Tops runs a couple mean underground joints around the city, risky enough that even I don't bet there. He gives out big lines of credit, but they come with East Jersey loan-shark vigs...and South Philly loan shark consequences if you don't pay up.

Things start clicking; why I keep seeing her out where I've been seeing her. She's trying to piece the money together without running into Benny's boys; anywhere she could make real money, they'd spot her. Benny keeps an eye on anywhere with a real bank. I'm guessing she's overdue, and that makes our run-in at the Wandering Rains anything but a coincidence; it's the one place I've seen her where Benny'd know to look. That was a gambler's risk. She's still perched on two kneecaps, so I guess she won the hand.

"You don't wanna owe Benny Tops," I tell her, like she doesn't already know. "And Benny Tops doesn't want people to owe him, either."

"Au contraire, mon frère. There's nothing Benny wants more than to keep me in the hole until I have to find some other way to pay." There's an edge in her voice now, an honest one. I'm talking to a woman now instead of a gambler. Benny's a creep. Worse, he's a creep with power.

"Don't like paying in trade, eh?" It slips out of my mouth before I can catch it. Figure I've got a slap coming, but I figure wrong. If she's wounded, she doesn't show it.

"Nah, I like to keep my business and pleasure separate." She doesn't bother with which is which, but we both know.

I let it sit for a moment. I owe her, sure, and her act—if it is an act—is working on me. But I'm too old and too cowardly to play hero.

"Of course, if someone's kind to me, business can be a pleasure, too," she says to sweeten the pot.

"Don't," I say. "I'm not Benny."

"Exactly," she replies, a twinkle in her eyes, "that's why I like you."

"You mean that's why you picked me."

She shrugs, sips her drink, and turns back to the bar. "Maybe I just like betting on the good guys."

"I'm not—"

She cuts me off. "At least they always pay their tabs, right?"

Dammit.

Three days later and here I am, walking into the backroom at Sinatra Lounge, a Rat Pack-themed rat hole that exists only to clean Benny's money and house Benny's hustles. There's an empty bar out front, with a lone bartender and cook there to serve any civilians slowly enough to make sure they never come back for seconds. It's just clean enough to pass health inspection, but unpleasant enough to make sure the inspector hurries.

The back, though, is a two-room ordeal in red felt and bad lighting. Benny likes his gamblers off-balance, so while the drinks are free, and strong, nobody can ever quite relax. Music's too loud, too.

There's a couple poker tables. Naomi's playing draw, because our plan works better without the river fucking us up. There's also a couple craps tables, and a single blackjack table. All no-limit, which'd usually be dangerous for an off-booker like Benny, but people know not to win too much from him. They tend not to come back when they do, whether or not they were planning to.

Naomi apparently didn't get that memo, though, as she's planning on cleaning him out tonight. She's already here, in a blue dress this time with her hair up in one of those chopstick buns; playing to Benny's tastes, I'd wager. Girl knows how to use every advantage, gotta give her that. Her plan's not awful, either, minus the part where if it works, Benny'll be coming for her...and maybe me.

Speaking of Benny, he's here tonight, leaning against the bar and staring at her with one of those lecherous grins that only a couple decades of authentic, practiced misogyny can generate. He's a handsome thug in his fifties, strong leading-man features and dignified salt-and-pepper on top, all of it bound up in an expensive suit he thinks makes him look like the Chairman, but no amount of handsome can keep him from oozing sleaze. Not that he's ashamed of it; man in his position's got no need to hide his sin.

He knows the odds; she walked in here with thirty grand; no chance she can stay hot at the table long enough to turn that into what she owes him. What he doesn't know is that I'm here to help break the odds.

That's our first big risk; we've only been seen at the same table twice, but both times we were helping each other out. There's a good to great chance nobody noticed, or at least that nobody noticed both, or at the very least nobody who noticed both whispered it all the way back to Benny...but people have been wrong about those kinda chances before, and those people don't come around anymore.

Benny doesn't know me, because I don't gamble here, but he's probably heard my name. Bookies and bankers tend to gossip about us degenerates, and I've been degenerating long enough to be talked about. The hope here is that my rep, such as it is, doesn't peg me for a patsy. It shouldn't, especially after how badly things went for me with a certain lady of fortune a few years back. Ever since, I haven't been seen with anybody'd who'd constitute a "known associate" and I always seem to pay my tab, if maybe a little late sometimes.

I'm old, broken down, and totally bereft of ambition. I'm the last guy who'd be dumb enough to think he could take Benny's money. That's on our side.

On the other hand, Benny and everyone else in the building knows that if she's playing here to try and pay him back, she thinks she's going to win. Once she starts winning, he's gonna get suspicious, and here I am, a new face at the table where his money keeps marching into her purse. If he smells a rat, he'll cook one, too.

Too soon to worry about all that, though. First she has to win. She's doing okay so far. She's only been here an hour or two, and her flirtatious-femme-fatale routine is still keeping them guessing. A spot opens—she's cleaned out some five-foot-nothing pile of beer belly and male-pattern baldness—and it's show time.

I sit down at the table, pay my stake on credit. It's another unnecessary extra risk on an already risky plan, but she didn't have—or didn't admit to having—the bank to stake me herself. Everybody nods, including her, and I nod back. She's been winning, so now she loses a few hands-on purpose. I win two of them, getting some chips to toss around.

But I'm not here to win. I'm here to make other people lose. We've got no signals between us. They'd sniff that out in a minute. She's betting on the two of us being good enough—and different enough—gamblers that between us we can bully anybody else off the table and keep the cash flowing. And slide each other chips when we have to.

The other trick is keeping the table populated; one of our stacks gets big enough, who's buying in? In another hall, maybe, but you don't want to risk going too deep in the red in Benny's, lest you never come back out. But if we stay roughly even with each other, well, a good gambler can talk himself into playing us against each other. Neither of us, in theory, can bully the table with the other one lurking there to call.

That means we can't just clean people out, either; we have to take big losses sometimes—and sell being less than thrilled about it—to keep things "honest." None of that necessarily means that Benny won't eventually notice that we're the only ones making any long-term gains.

The endgame is to frustrate Benny enough that he sits down at the table himself. Otherwise we're just milking his customers, which is fine for Naomi's debt, but won't serve her vengeful streak. Once he does sit down, everyone else will bail; nobody's dumb enough to play a crooked house at poker. Except us.

The million-dollar question at that point is whether or not he tries to cheat. His dealer's probably good enough to do it, but I might be good enough to spot it, and Benny's old-school enough that he won't want to take the hit to his rep if he gets outed playing dirty...especially if he gets caught doing it to beat a woman half his age.

So, yeah, it's a good plan with bad odds. Plenty of gamblers have died by that mantra.

First hour it's her, me, a corporate suit who's had too much to drink but knows it and isn't betting shit because of it, a burly dockworker who's probably dirty given that he's playing at this table, a couple salesmen out of their depth who will be bust inside of twenty, and two Japanese tourists in expensive silk button-ups and sunglasses who know what they're doing; only big-time gamblers go to places like this when they're on the road. Heck, they might be running the same scam we are.

Sure enough, thirty minutes in our businessman has cashed out and the stevedore's gone bust, serenading the table with lyrical profanity only a union man can muster as he leaves. Nobody else buying in yet. Not great for our long-term prospects.

As for the Japanese, they're keeping about even with us. Naomi keeps trying to strike up a conversation with them, but they're not biting. These guys are here to gamble, and there's nobody pretty enough to sugar them off that path. They're smart bettors and they know the numbers. One of 'em can bluff and one of 'em's got a decent eye, but luckily we've been able to figure out which one's which. They also don't seem to be on the same side, but maybe they're just hiding it better than we are.

Naomi keeps winning nickel-and-dime hands with three of a kind or two-pair. I'm betting conservatively and watching the tourists, trying to figure out which one we can break first. Neither wants to get greedy, and they're too patient to bite whenever Naomi puts real money on the table. We can whittle them down with folds if I get a little more aggressive, but if she folds every time I do—or vice versa—it might send up more smoke than we'd like this early in the evening.

Hour two rolls around without much changing. Benny's stopped watching for now, and is chatting up some poor thing at the craps table. We've all got about a quarter of the total pot right now—seventy grand apiece, not bad given the buy-in was only twenty (meaning plenty of money got dropped on the table before either of us sat down).

Naomi's usual tricks aren't working, though, and she's getting too aggressive. They're starting to siphon off her chips, and I'm either going to have to start taking theirs or feeding her mine. We're careful not to lock eyes too much, and I remain paranoid about doing anything that could be construed as a sign, so there's no way for me to tell her to back off except with my cards.

I bully her the next four hands, even when I've got nothing. I win three of 'em; one of the tourists takes the other, and of course it's the one that went the highest. I figure she'll back off but she actually leans in, losing as fast as she can, but mostly to me.

Takes me maybe a hand too long to figure what she's working at, but it's not a bad play; my stack grows to one-twenty and I start beating up on the tourists, over-betting on everything and chipping away at the war chest of the one with no eye, though I'm feeding his buddy more than I'd like. She's sitting back now, calling only when she has something worth calling over.

We've got No-Eyes just about bust, but he buys back. Perfect. More money on the table is exactly what we need to attract new fish. Sure enough, Naomi pouting over her shrinking stack attracts a knight in shining rayon to wander over and offer to stake her another five grand. She sugars him off but invites him to join so she can win his money "honestly... and buy you a drink with it for your generosity." He buys that line for all it's worth and the second he sits down she's got her edge back; he's exactly her kind of mark and she uses him to pick on our tourist friends; he's so hooked she may as well be playing his hands for him. She can read him like a book—though so can the tourist with the eye—and knows just how to slump her shoulders or twitter her eyelashes to get him to spend more or less on a given hand.

Thanks to that trick, it's basically three on two now, and we're siphoning chips his way to keep Benny guessing. That risks him cashing out, but he can't do that until she goes bust without giving up whatever shot he thinks he has. He looks like Guy Fieri's disappointing nephew, so I can't imagine he's drowning in women who look like Naomi, I don't care how rich he is.

Hour three rolls around, and Benny's back to paying attention, but still from across the room. One of our tourists is getting frustrated—No-Eyes—but he buys back in again and starts playing angry. Good. Flavortown's still trying to impress Naomi with endless patter about his trust fund—of course it's a trust fund—and she's still letting him think it's working. The other tourist is holding his own, but since he can't bluff for shit he's having a hard time making any real money with both Flavortown and I playing aggressively.

We also get a new arrival, a stockbroker. Young one, too, who spends money on cologne. These guys are my favorite; they always think they're fifty percent sharper than they are. They're great at numbers and shit at people, but they're surrounded by people who pretend differently.

He falls right into Naomi's trap too, and all of a sudden her stack's looking healthy again without me having to feed her, or letting Flavortown bust out too early. She's got to divide her attention a little more carefully now, has to play them off each other. She makes jokes that call back to things Flavortown said earlier, and he's not used to people paying attention to him, so he drinks it up. Meanwhile, she's combative verbally with the stockbroker, but she punctuates it all with dancing eyebrows and half-smiles that make him think they're playing cat-and-mouse...without realizing I'm the wolf on his flank, picking away at his chips whenever I want. He's betting hard to show her he's brave, but he doesn't have the cards for it nine times out of ten. She doesn't take too much of his money for fear of pissing him off, but she teases him when I do.

Hour four. Now it's getting good. Our table finally fills out as we get an old pro—that's bad—and an almost-definitely mobster—actually good. Both tourists have to buy back in, and I think that's probably the last of their money that's going to hit the table, but Flavortown and I are heavy enough now we should be able to take every cent of it. Mafia Man is drunk and cheerful and goes all-in five hands in, losing it all, and buying back in with a hearty laugh and a slap on Flavortown's shoulder. Things must be going well in the insurance business.

Meanwhile, Naomi's carefully kept herself from catching up to Flavortown or myself, staying competitive without making things obvious. I'm getting too hot and Benny's noticing—he's stopped paying attention to anything but this game, meaning if he's gonna make a move it'll be soon—so I lose a few hands to Flavortown, who at this point is basically our bank.

The stockbroker is getting antsy after two buy-ins, but he's got money to burn and pride on the line. Naomi folds a hand I'm almost sure she could have won to double his stack and give him some confidence. Mafia Man busts again, buys in again, but he's not laughing anymore.

Flavortown's getting bored with winning. The problem with rich kids: this kinda money don't mean shit to them. He was just in it for the game, but his attention span's run out. He's ready to take Naomi back to his yacht or whatever already, and he starts losing focus and money.

She picks up on it, and almost flirts him into an all-in that'd give her about forty percent of the total money on the table but the old pro—an African American septuagenarian in a bowler hat that only men his age can get away with—cuts in.

"Kid, she's playing you. Been playing you all night. You go all-in this hand, she's taking every cent, and you're going home alone."

Table goes silent. Nearby, Benny grins. Flavortown takes a few seconds to wipe the deer-in-headlights off his face, then speaks.

"No way. You're just trying to get in my head," he says, unwilling to let go of the fantasy of a woman like her finding him remotely compelling.

"No, son, I'm trying to win your money. Lot easier to do it bit by bit from you than to try and take it from her if she puts your chips on top of hers and starts throwing her weight around."

Silence again. Everyone else is already out on the hand, so it's down to him. Naomi takes matters into her own hands.

"Sweetheart, you believe what you wanna believe…but all I've got's on the table. If you've got the cards to take it, I won't even have cab fare home…unless, you know, you're still feeling generous." She bats her eyelashes and it's transparent to the point of being nearly sarcastic, but the kid is dumb and desperate and he's making the mistake of looking the basilisk in the eyes, so he calls her fake bluff and his full house loses to her four of a kind.

She's nice enough about it to slide him a few chips for his trouble, and kisses him on the cheek as she declines his offer to close out and hit the town.

From there it's almost academic; she's got the firepower now and she gets mean with it, especially with me making the occasional dramatic call or fold to complicate things. The tourists, Mafia Man, and stockbroker fall in short order, even with a couple buy-backs from who you'd expect, and she siphons enough chips off to me and the old pro to keep it honest. She starts getting combative with me, but it's all an act. Benny buys it, but the pro doesn't. A few more hands and he cashes out for good, taking about double what he came in with but not sticking around to swim in these sharky waters.

Now it's just her and me, and Benny glaring at that stack she's got that's more than plenty to pay him off. Between her and I, we've got almost half a million. We could quit now and come out ahead. But she wants to push it, so she looks him right in the eye and pokes the bear.

"Well, Benny, you just gonna let me take all your customers' money? Or do you think you can cool me off?"

"Sweetheart, you can't be that dumb. I own the joint; you really think you can beat me on my own table?" He's dangerously close to figuring he's been set up, and it's made him cautious, but he's hiding it behind bluster. Now's where I come in.

"Only reason she's still winning with the marks all gone is she's got the stack. Being the house and all, you could take that edge away from her...so long as you're not a mark, too. Of course, you'd also have to beat me, and I'm not having a bad night either." People don't talk to people like Benny like that. He doesn't like it. Now he wants to take my money, too.

But he's too smart to play angry, and he throws a curveball.

"Nah, bad look for me to play in my own house. But I do want those chips, so I got a proposal for ya. I deal, and Nigel here—" he gestures to his dealer, "—takes my seat at the table. A proxy, ya know?"

Nigel's exactly what you'd expect in a place like this: quiet, slimy professionalism. I've barely noticed him all night. Thick black mustache, beady black eyes. He's probably a decent card player, but there's no chance he's better than Naomi and I; if he were, he'd be more than a dealer.

That means Benny's planning to cheat. Naomi sniffs it out, too, and cuts him off at the pass.

"Sure, Benny, but no way in hell I let you deal. We pass the deck each hand, like the top-shelf hustlers we are." She pauses and looks at me. "Well, you and I, anyhow. Not sure about Baby Stack over here."

This time Benny takes the bait, and we're off. Benny stakes Nigel a full five hundred in house money—more than what's on the table—and expects to bulldoze. Every time it's Nigel's deal he's going to win, and we both know it, but between the two of us it's pretty easy to make sure those other two hands don't go his way.

Plus, I'm a better cheater than he is, and every time I deal, she wins. So I'm bleeding chips at least two out of three hands, but they're mostly going one direction and it's only an hour before she's got a bigger stack than Nigel. Benny's sweating and seething, but I'm personally relieved; enough money on the table to piss him off, but not enough to get us killed. I hope.

I have to switch to a more conservative style as my coffers dwindle, but I still pounce when I've got a good hand, and Naomi's got the sense to recognize it, so she never loses much to me.

Nigel's going to lose, and he knows it. Benny knows it too. Naomi knows it, and keeps reminding Benny. Once Nigel gets down to a hundred grand, Benny kills the game.

"Enough of this shit. Nigel, you're a bum. And, Naomi, if you know what's good for you, you will get the fuck away from my table right now and you will never, ever play a cent in my house again. I don't know how you fucked me but I know when I'm being fucked." He may still kill her, but it'd be bad for business after that little speech. If he'd let her go all the way, it would have been one thing, but now that it's obviously personal—and there's still a good dozen witnesses here that know it—he probably can't do it without getting more attention than he'd like.

Gotta admit, she played it perfectly, and she's walking out with just over four hundred large after she pays him off. I could cash out, too, and leave with over two hundred grand of his money if I wanted to, but hey, my luck's due to change after losing so many hands to her, right?

So she makes her exit, wisely resisting the urge to aggravate Benny any further, and all I give her is a nod. Then I move over to the craps table and give Benny almost all that money back; hang on to just forty-five or so. That takes about an hour. I close out, thank the host—he just grunts at me, happy to have the money back but still pissed about Naomi—and I head for home.

I'm actually a decent craps player, but I don't want to be on Benny's radar. He might not be able to hit Naomi after his outburst, but nobody'd notice if I stopped showing up for the Friday game at Ronnie's.

Naomi's waiting for me, all Cheshire smiles.

"Where you been, Jack?"

"Oh, just losing my ill-gotten gains. Down to forty...which reminds me." I peel off the twenty I owe her and offer it. She doesn't take it.

"Baby, you've more than paid your debt...and besides, we're gonna make way more than that when we hit Atlantic City." She leans in for a kiss, like she's riding high on the victory adrenaline and it's not premeditated at all, and hey, maybe it's not...but I pull back.

"I don't do Atlantic City."

She laughs. "Well, we can negotiate about our next game...

in the morning."

She leans in again, and I don't have it in me to step back again. She's smart and gorgeous and irresistibly herself, and worse, she knows it. She's a world-class gambler and an even better woman. Kisses like she means it, too. If sincerity had a flavor, that's what she'd taste like. This could be the perfect end to a pretty good night, really keep the good times going into tomorrow, and next week, and maybe even into Atlantic City. Feels like I could roll sevens the rest of my life with her.

But hot streaks don't last forever. I step back again. "Take the money, Naomi. We're square."

This time she doesn't laugh. "Jack, we maybe got a real thing here. We made enough tonight to live fat off at least a year. Fuck-off money. And we can make it again any time we want. But even besides the Benjamins...I kinda like having you around."

"Yeah...feeling's more than mutual, Naomi. But I don't like playing dirty, and I like it even less when it comes back around. Something tells me when your cold streaks hit, they hit hard. You end up owing a man like Benny, and I just don't have the cards for it."

"I don't owe Benny a damn thing anymore, Jack, and you don't owe me. All that's at stake here is two people with a whole lot of money who make a whole lot of sense, and might have a whole lot of fun. That kinda luck doesn't come around twice."

"Yeah, I know. It's the smart bet. But if I was the kinda guy who makes the smart bets, you'd never have been able to buy me in the first place. If you were the kinda girl who won smart bets, you wouldn't have needed to. How long you think it is before one of us fucks up and you have to throw out those gold teeth to cover? What happens if they're not enough? When do you need a newer Jack, one nobody knows, to climb out of the hole we dug? The one I end up buried in? Don't answer, I don't wanna know."

She starts to argue, but I just turn and walk. She doesn't insult me with fake tears, but I can feel those baby blues of hers glaring daggers through my back. She thought she'd found her partner in crime, her way out, her happily-ever-after. Maybe. If she did, it's a damn dumb thing I'm doing turning my back on her. Odds are even maybe on her side on that one. But…I looked in her eyes, and I didn't see a mark. And when you can't see the mark…well, you know the rest.

Sure, maybe this time there is no mark. Sure, I might be walking away from the best thing that's ever gonna happen to me, just because I'm too big a coward to place a bet that counts. And sure, she could get any other man in the world, and they'd be lucky to have her, but for tonight at least all she wants is me. That's a million-to-one shot at any book you can find, and here I am tearing up the ticket. I might wake up every night the rest of my life kicking myself for doing it. Shit, smart money says I will. I should turn around, go back, bet on myself for a change. Bet on her. Ride that hot streak till it burns out, at the very least. Or just ride it to Atlantic City, and make enough to quit the grind, live out the rest of my days fat and happy with her, or even without, if it comes to it. Maybe life calls my bluff and none of it works out that way, but the smart thing to do is to chase that dream. Any sucker or Samaritan could tell you that much. Yeah, I should go back.

But I'm a gambler, and I've got enough money in my pocket to really do some damage, so I think I'll go do that instead.

HOME AT LAST
Sam Wiebe

You should know certain things about your best friend. What they want done with their body, for instance. Cremation or sky burial or burial at sea, or trucked back home to the family plot in Lewisburg. Or Allentown, or Waukegan. Sioux City in Nick's case. If you don't—if after all your late-night philosophizing, your pot- and loss- and Rolling Rock-fueled sessions after both striking out at the tables, watching for the first bloody slice of dawn before starting the car and trying for home—well, that speaks to the depth and nature of your friendship.

It's not like death wasn't a common subject for us, either. I knew how Nick wanted to die—horse riding accident, the nag at full gallop, a loose stirrup, a backwards fall from the saddle. The world upturns, you flip straight back, and your last thought as your neck snaps is, "This is exhilarating."

"Unless you survive," I remember telling him.

"But I wouldn't." Nick wasn't interested in my critiques.

"Ideally not, but how do you know? You could hold out for weeks. Comatose, vegetative. A medical miracle."

"Dan," Nick said, with the patience of a substitute teacher entirely uninvested in the student he's chiding. "Daniel. That's how I want to go."

HOME AT LAST

"I'm just saying, it's not foolproof."

"No," he agreed. "That's the drawback to a lot of perfect deaths."

A minute passed silently as we further minimized the roach Nick had discovered in the ashtray of my Cadillac Brougham. I adjusted the radio dial with a safecracker's touch, searching for the all-night jazz station coming up from a college in Oregon. All I found was a scratchy evangelist preaching the End Times.

"That'd be mine," I told Nick. "My choice. Final Judgment. To be there at the end. Then you'd *know*, right?"

He'd shrugged and pried apart the roach, and began removing any unburnt shake, adding it to the Zig-Zag he'd smoothed atop the Brougham's dash.

"Knowing's overrated," Nick had said.

His death hadn't been that spectacular, nor so dependent on the vagaries of fate. In the end, they'd taken him out back of the casino and thrown him in the alley.

Three hours later, once I'd been bounced from the semifinals of a pai gow tournament, I'd walked outside for a smoke in the fresh air and seen the paramedics load something into an ambulance, drive off, not bothering with the sirens. And I'd known.

Nick's death didn't signal the End Times. Just the End of Good Times.

I took him home in a plastic sack wedged into a cardboard receptacle. The grains of him shifted inside the sack, and the sack shifted inside the box. I left him by the sink atop the stack of empties. I sat on the couch, wishing for a drink, then noticing, as if conjured, a tumbler of rum and Coke amidst the TV table clutter. Nick's, left over from three nights ago, when we'd come back here, the beach being too cold to pass out on this time of year. The surface of the drink was black and perfectly still. A gift from beyond.

I lit an American Spirit and drank the tepid booze and wondered what I actually knew about Nick Selway, and what to do next.

All across the Pacific Northwest there are casinos like the Skookum Chuck. Ugly beige boxes, usually a joint enterprise between a foreign conglomerate and a local First Nation. You take an exit off the superhighway, drive through a small collection of bungalows and a 7-Eleven, skitter along the promenade of a rock beach, dark grey and stinking of chemical runoff. The casino is skirted by parking lot, always three quarters empty. The place collects riff-raff the way junk mail builds in the threshold of an abandoned home.

I washed up in the Chuck four years ago, buoyed by my divorce settlement, blood money I was determined to get rid of. My third novel had bombed spectacularly, earning the kind of notices that would cause a more sensitive soul to swig a pint of hemlock. My teaching job had hinged on my being married to the department chair, and a willingness to exaggerate my students' talent and publishing prospects. When divorce and a half-assed breakdown made both impossible, I borrowed every book on poker from the college library, converted my assets to one bank account, and set off in search of dissolution, miracles, and uproar.

Nick was already a casino regular, part of a small group of fellows with nicknames like Skip, the Doc, El Cid and Badger. For the first few months he was garish ornamentation, a memorable bit player in my tragicomic struggle on the casino floor. He cadged cigarettes, lost loudly at table games, and dispensed questionable advice with an authority unattested to by his own outcomes.

Our friendship was cemented during one of my rare runs. I was up thirty grand, playing blackjack at the big kids' table. The dealer was a woman named Evie. I liked to think she goosed me along, though she swore she didn't. My luck was never that good.

She'd dealt herself an ace of clubs and asked if I wanted insurance. With eight in front of me, I'd shrugged and said might as well. I shunted a further two hundred into the pot.

"Sucker move," I heard from my left shoulder.

Nick stood watching, sucking some sort of tropical drink from a blue straw shaped like a treble clef.

I hit a four, a three, thought about standing.

"Queers the play," Nick was saying. "Insurance goes against the entire purpose of the exercise."

"Uh huh." I tapped the table and was dealt a three. The dealer flipped, showing a seven. Hit on four. Took my money.

"You're new to this game, aren't you?" Nick said. "Only amateurs take insurance."

"I won off the insurance," I said.

"Immaterial," Nick said.

I told him that was news to me.

"No it's not. Got a smoke?" He helped himself to the pack in my breast pocket. Lit it with a match, which he dropped into the pile of ice left in his drink.

I played another hand, won, then lost two and told myself it was because of Nick's chatter. I cashed out, took the little barcoded slip of paper from the dispenser.

"You have to ask yourself certain things," Nick said. "Like what profiteth a man to win if he disrespecteth the rules."

"That from Psalms?"

"Just reminding you what you're here for."

"You're throwing off my card counting," I told him, earning a smile from Evie.

"I need to take my medicine. Let's grab a coffee."

We sat at the counter of the restaurant, watching the line for the buffet parade past us. Suckers with plates of cold fried chicken and angry yellow rice pilaf. Nick tapped out some orange pills, chased them with a solution of aspartame, coffee, and cream.

"You strike me as a guy who's halfway smart," Nick said. "Meaning, unlike the chicken brigade, you know you're not here to win."

"Just to lose as slowly as possible, that what you mean?"

"No," he said severely. "To lose gracefully. To lose with élan."

I held up the slip with the digital numbers that signified twenty-eight thousand and change.

"I'm not leaving here with any of this," I told him.

"Brother," he said, "you're not even leaving."

After I'd finished my miracle booze, and smoked the last of my cigarettes, I left Nick's ashes in the apartment and wandered the beach. The salt sting off the little cove felt good, even with the eggy stench of industrial waste. I was alone, able to kick driftwood and sea cucumbers out of my path.

Nick's death felt halfway toward a million things, and nothing in itself. You think there'd be some last request, a final task that needed to be checked off. Revenge, or amends, or something purposeful. I could find who killed him, but that would be ridiculous. He'd earned his death, probably knew going in that cheating the casino would end with something like this.

The death certificate, which was still in my pocket, attributed Nicholas Selway's demise to heart failure brought on by extreme trauma. Death by misadventure. They'd beaten him up a little too well. Maybe someone had been overzealous, or maybe, more likely, the accumulation of abuses had worn his resistance down.

In any case, it wasn't the kind of death that would get the cops worked up. Not with the town running off the casino's fumes.

So whose fault was it? No one person's. The pit boss had

followed the unwritten protocol of the casino. The security guard had done his job. The manager, whoever had told the others what to do, had issued the same order dozens of times before.

Was it Nick's fault, a sort of suicide, with the shadow machinery of the gambling establishment serving as his vial of Seconal or plugged exhaust pipe? That required Nick possessing both foresight and shame, two things he'd never shown to me.

And his friend, who'd had his own game to run, and hadn't been part of this last quixotic struggle—what portion of blame did I take for myself?

I thought long and hard about buying a gun. Then decided against it. Too expensive, too messy, and it was far too late for me to become some kind of marksman. My talents lay in destructions of a different sort.

Becoming best friends had taken longer, had required a few other people to drop off the map. Nick's pal Doc had been running some sort of interstate prescription med scheme. For a while Nick was making the runs with him, until Doc was caught wrong with an underage companion and given six years in Snake River. He sold out a lot of people, Doc, but Nick hadn't been one of them.

Months later Nick had asked if I wanted to help him re-establish the route.

"I did the run enough to know who Doc dealt with, roughly," he said. "A couple days asking around Barstow, we could probably fix it up again."

I told him I'd pass. My ex had finally sold our place, and I was busy running through my half of the proceeds. The money had come when I'd most needed it, when Evie wouldn't lend me another hundred, a few weeks after I'd been forced to sell my driver's license and passport. I could finally cut the landlord a check for another year's loafing, and focus on my new fascination: the casino's racing feed from Hong Kong. Handicapping seemed a more stylish means of blowing money, with new rules and a new jargon to learn. I was going to will myself into hitting a trifecta, and work my way up from there.

We busied ourselves with our respective schemes. We'd see each other around the casino, or at the beach during off-hours in the summer. He'd sometimes crash with me, bringing over whatever pills he couldn't sell. We'd swill them down with rum and Coke or his favorite, Grandad and Ginger, and talk about jazz rhythm sections or James M. Cain, or the best movie drunks—Dorothy Malone, *Written on the Wind*, hands down.

Once he told me he'd read my novel.

"The first one," he said. His expression was both drunk and scholarly. I prepared myself for the critical drubbing every writer fears is around the conversational corner.

"It sucked," I said pre-emptively. "It's okay, I know it."

"It didn't suck, exactly." Nick's eyes searched upward, chasing the correct words. "I'd call it a noble failure."

"The book, or the author?"

He didn't smile. Criticism was serious business for him.

"The idea of a modern epic isn't bad in itself. It's been done before, and done well before."

"By Joyce," I said.

"I meant that film *The Warriors*, but yeah, him too. In your case I'd say your viewpoint was wrong. There's no immediacy, narrating from on high. First person would've been better. Kind of a Lew Archer amidst the armies of Cyrus, maybe add a little Woolfian interiority. But it wasn't bad as is, Dan. It shouldn't've been remaindered that quickly. I certainly felt I got my two bucks' worth."

"Might set the next one at the track," I said. "Some of the characters I've met, you wouldn't believe."

He'd nodded, but his expression had carried a pronouncement. I'd never write another. He was as sure of it as I was.

Not a gun, but dynamite. Between construction projects and general misbehavior, there was always some around town.

A check-cashing place had gone in across the street from the casino—a coincidence, I'm sure. I sent a message to my ex asking for seven hundred dollars. The response came in ten minutes flat. *Why would I ever deign to send you another dollar?*

Last time I'll ask, I wrote back. *Ever. Swear on the souls of the kids we didn't have.*

Armed with the money, I bypassed the welcoming mouth of the Skookum Chuck, and caught a ride to the home of Liz. If Nick had ever had a steady gal, it had been her.

Liz had been a nurse at one point, and lost her job helping Nick with, or out of, some scam. Now she was married to Jake, an ex-soldier who did the odd construction job and hoarded illegal weaponry. Explosives included. Jake was prepared for the Ottoman Threat, or whatever uprising would eventually send him into the hills.

Liz stood on the other side of the screen door, blowing essence of Kools at me through the mesh. Gray hair and still looking good. She wore a black T-shirt and loose black slacks, which was probably as close as any friend of Nick's would get to mourning garb.

"Sure I could get you a few sticks, Dan," she said. "Question is what for?"

On my way to her place I'd wisely divided my money into two piles, three and four hundred. That way I could present part of my funds as all the money I had. But looking at her, knowing she was the only other person that felt anything about Nick's demise, I smashed the two piles together and held them out for her.

"He wanted you to have this," I said.

Liz probably believed that even less than I did. But she'd always been big on role play, and grieving widow was a part too choice to pass up. Forget that Nick wasn't her husband, that they hadn't seen each other in months, that their relationship had been mostly drug and business based. She'd enjoyed playing bad girl with him, till they were busted. Then she'd enjoyed giving him the tearful kiss-off. I sometimes wondered if her marital health was sustained by telling her old friends how happy she was, now that she'd been airlifted out of the rat race.

"He was a great man, in his way," she said through tears.

"A prince," I agreed. "We shall not look upon his like again."

She blubbered a bit and dried her eyes, then told me to wait while she looked around. I heard clangs and shuffles from the garage, Liz no doubt hunting through her husband's junk to find the explosives.

What finally entwined our fates, and further clinched our friendship, was a phone call from McQueen's Bail Bonds. The bondswoman told me someone named Daniel Starkings had said I'd front the money for his bail.

"That's funny," I said. "That's my name."

The bondswoman said yeah, in a voice that held no faith in a universe that favored coincidence.

The bail was ten thousand, which meant a grand was needed up front before this other Daniel Starkings could be released. I didn't have nearly that much, my exercise in handicapping having turned out the way I'd expected. So I headed onto the casino floor, determined to let fate decide.

Fate decided I'd win, sporadically but cumulatively, until I had more than enough for my doppelganger's bail. But we didn't stop there, Fate and I. We took our two hundred and change up to three grand. By the time I'd dropped it to fourteen hundred, it was almost the end of the work day. I cabbed to the office and entreated the bondswoman to process the money and bail the other Starkings out.

Of course it was Nick. He'd taken a fall for some minor drug charge, having ditched most of the load in what he painted as a thrilling *Thunder Road*-style pursuit. When he was pulled over he'd not only used my name, but produced my driver's license.

It had been late, the cop was someone's son, and these things happen.

"Some coincidence," I said.

"Couldn't be helped, brother. We'll beat these charges, though. You won't have a record for long."

A court date had been set, and I'd showed up, verified that I was Dan Starkings. The cop who'd pulled Nick over pointed me out in court, causing me a moment of Dostoevskyan panic. Confronted with his error, he tried his best to aid the judge in imagining why my face and prints didn't match the arrest sheet. His creativity sunk him.

I'd returned to the casino expecting—something. Nick was having dinner with Skip and the others in the lounge, and nodded at me when I came in as if the court appearance hadn't been a favor, but a personal appointment I was now free from.

"Still need your license?" he asked.

When the Romans conquered Greece, so the legend goes, they angered the subjugated people by looting their local wines. The Greek citizenry, in spite or desperation, began sealing their casks with pine resin. Theoretically the seal would keep the wine better in hiding, and if found, the funky taste would put the Romans off. In later years it became a popular drink all its own, the resin more subtle, added only for flavor.

I don't know if any of that is true. But I like the story. The practical origins of the mythopoeic, everyday activities which linger past their usefulness and are then done reflexively, evolving into custom. Spite and taste and habit all wrapped up together. It speaks to my experience of this world.

One of Nick's connections at the casino, a bellhop named Leon, had dropped Nick's name to the pit boss. A guest had suffered a very public freak-out, and questions had to be asked. Where had the stuff come from? Nick was warned about peddling his wares on the premises.

A joke—Nick didn't exactly deal. He offloaded his cargo at what I took to be below market rates, clearing only enough to cover his markers and a few tries at the tables.

I was now into Chinese games of chance. Big Two, Heaven and Nine. Nick had forsaken games entirely, investing his time and meager funds in what he called "sure things."

"I know more about the staff here than the bosses do," he confided. "All you need to do is figure out who's taking what, when it wears off, and clock what shifts they're working. You see?"

I didn't. He was happy to explain.

"Say Evie's working eight to four. She takes a little something to keep awake, right? If it's gak, it'll last days, but if it's Dex or Adderall—see what I'm saying? Wait out the four to six hours, then they're at their least effective."

"For what? Card counting?" I scoffed and flipped pages in my English-to-Mandarin phrasebook. "You're not a savant, Nick."

"But I am," he said. "I know people. It's become very clear to me. I can anticipate how all this will go."

It was either a lie or a dark admission on his part. For months Nick either lost, or caught a beating, or both. He shrugged it off, the cost of working miracles.

Once he was dead I could easily trace the decline. But only then. You run alongside someone, blithe and unencumbered, rarely glancing sideways or gauging their progression. Why would you? Then all at once you're alone, and you put together that, come to think of it, he *had* been slowing down a bit recently, his breathing getting ragged. But so had yours. It hadn't seemed unusual at the time. Just two running, best they could.

Nick's ashes out of the cardboard carton looked like a bag of gray ground coffee. I wore my rain coat with the deep interior pockets, placing Nick in one and the dynamite in the other. The sticks looked like they did in the movies, only the red was richer, that deep Double Happiness red. The fuse was green, not black, and coated with a slow-burning lacquer. Three sticks fit in my right pocket. I put the Zippo on Nick's side, just to be safe.

My plan was inchoate. At first I thought I'd wait till dark, give him a beachfront send-off. But Nick hated the beach. He'd once confided that he only came down there because it seemed the thing to do, and that he'd as soon the casino was airlifted to Phoenix or Tehran. The town had a small park, but he liked that even less. Any time he slept out there he'd complain about the dog shit on his shoes, used condoms left in the mulch by summering college kids.

In the end, I went back to the casino.

I had three bucks in change, and handed it to the teller with all the dignity I could muster. I plunked my chit into the first machine of a row of nickel slots, Classical themed, the Aeolian Harps. Someone had left three quarters of a smoke in the ashtray atop the machine.

A hit, a very palpable hit. I walked away from the screeching machine with seventy dollars more than I'd sat down with.

I bet half my stake at the blackjack table. When the dealer showed an ace, I pondered buying insurance. Nick didn't know shit about blackjack. Riding out a bad hand for probity's sake was ignorant. If I was betting for him now, and I guess that's what this was, there was no need to bet stupidly just because he would have.

I'd given no indication, and the hand moved on, uninsured. And sure enough the dealer had a queen. Blackjack, first hand, is a good indicator that it's not going to be your night.

I lost the second hand, a cautious ten-dollar bet, then won the next and the next, and pushed, and grew less timid and bet it all and won. Ninety dollars. I lit a smoke and rode out a few iffy deals, waited for a good feeling, then doubled my money. Nick's money. I played slow, smart, and drove my number up to three hundred.

If I break a thousand, or if I go bust, I'll excuse myself. Go to the washroom and run a faucet-dampened hand over my face. Ask my reflection if I mean this. If the bastard tells me yes, then I'll light the fuse and wait a few seconds till it burns partway down. Then walk out to the casino floor. There's a row of defunct slots and patchy carpet that hasn't been in use since I've been here. Away from everyone, I'll hold my jacket close, and probably have second thoughts, and tell myself it might not go the way I think, old dynamite not known for being reliable. But if it does?

If it does, then hoo-boy.

HAITIAN DIVORCE
Simon Wood

Barbara knew her marriage was over the second the FBI stormed her home. The feds fired tear gas through the windows of her ranch. She watched black-clad figures flood into her home from behind binoculars on a ridgeline a mile from the raid. She'd miss the place, the horses and the peace of living in the country, but Will had sold her out.

"Clean Willie strikes again," she said to herself.

She hated the nickname that had attached itself to her husband. It was an ugly reminder of what he was capable of when push came to shove. He always got away clean...even when it was at the expense of his own crew. This time the son of a bitch was burning her to save his own ass. The brilliance of his ruthlessness had blinded her, but over the years, as he sold out crew members then friends and now her, she saw it for what it was—the instincts of someone who didn't give a shit about anyone other than himself.

She'd seen this day coming and she'd prepped for it. She turned her back on her beloved home and got behind the wheel of her the car.

"No tears. No remorse," she said to herself. That was the way she had to think. The way Will thought.

Speeding down the hillside, she cursed Will for his impulsive nature. If he'd listened to her, they wouldn't be in this shit, but he had to go for the next shiny object no matter how far out on a limb it was. She'd been happy with the art scams, the bogus property deals, and the investment boiler rooms that had earned them millions, but that wasn't good enough for Will. He had to go for the big one, the one where the downside outweighed the upside, the one that got people killed.

Will's Holy Grail was the U.S. Treasury. You didn't take on the federal government and not expect them to come back at you. She could cut her own deal with the feds, but it would mean jail time. The public and the politicians would demand it. Besides, considering that the FBI were kicking in her door, Will had already cut a deal. He wouldn't abide by it. He was just using her to slip out the back door.

She grabbed the cell phone from the car's center console and hit speed dial.

After three rings, a voice said, "Yes."

"Give me Papa."

"There's no Papa here, lady."

"Tell him it's Babs, Clean Willie's woman."

If Will's moniker didn't get her in, nothing would. Will had screwed Papa over for years and it had cost him five years of his life. Helping her would square accounts.

"What you want, Babs?" Papa's voice was thick from decades of smoking cigars.

"I told you I'd be calling."

A slow, dirty laugh filled the line. Barbara pictured Papa's teeth, big enough to challenge any Osmond family member. He'd make her squirm, but as long as she got what she wanted, she'd squirm.

"So things have come to a head with Clean Willie?"

"Yeah."

She wondered what bill of goods he'd sold the FBI and what story he'd concocted about her. Knowing her husband, it would be a colorful one and there'd be a paper trail to back it up. It was sad to think her life up until this moment was over. She'd get over it. She'd live. Even if the legendary Clean Willie didn't.

"Irreconcilably. I want it done."

"Want what?"

This was Papa making her squirm.

"If you can't say it, you can't have it."

If she hadn't needed Papa, she would've kicked the son of a bitch in the balls. That would kill that smile. "I want a Haitian Divorce."

"Good. Good. You're on your way to being a free woman. You'll need to see the Haitian yourself. He'll want to be paid in person."

She could have bitched about having to travel to Haiti, but being out of the country for a while sounded good.

"You got money? A clean passport? You can travel, right?"

"I can travel. I have his money."

"Get yourself to Port-au-Prince, then call me."

"Will do."

"Just don't forget Papa needs his co-pay before you leave."

"You'll get your money," she said and hung up.

Barbara drove the forty or so miles to Colorado Springs to her unit in a crappy, public storage facility. Will didn't know about the unit. It was under a fake identity, after all. She'd only kept it as a last resort.

Inside she kept all the things she'd ever need—cash, a clean identity, clothes, a gun (that she sadly couldn't take with her) and a boring-as-can-be Honda. Inside the safe was close to two hundred and fifty grand. She took fifty. It was all she needed for now. Ten for Papa. Twenty-five for the Haitian. The remainder was for expenses. She put the money in a roller bag with enough clothes to last her a week. She'd buy more if she needed them.

She ditched her ID, credit cards, jewelry and anything that identified her as Barbara. She was now Linda Miller. A wave of sadness draped itself over her shoulders. She liked being Barbara, but even once she had her Haitian Divorce, she could never be Barbara again. That saddened her more than she expected. She hoped she'd get to like Linda just as much.

Barbara stared at her wedding ring sitting in her palm. Will had given her that after their first big score. It hadn't been off her finger since. She'd considered it unlucky to take the ring off. Her luck had run out regardless. Screw superstition, she thought, but she couldn't bring herself to sling the ring in with the rest of her jewelry in the safe. She slipped the ornate band back on. She'd give it back to Will at the divorce. That thought put a smile on her face. Not a joyous one. But a fuck-you one.

Swapping her Audi for the Honda, she left her old identity there in that storage unit to gather dust. Once on US 24, she settled in for a long drive. Denver airport was right on her doorstep, but she wasn't taking any chances on her name being flagged, even with her rock-solid Linda Miller identity. No, she'd drive to Miami and catch a flight to Haiti from there.

There was no way she'd reach Miami in one shot, so she checked into a motel in St. Louis. Once in her room, she dyed her blonde hair to match Linda's red hair on the driver's license and passport, put Papa's ten grand in a FedEx envelope, and booked her flight to Haiti.

Hitting the road the next morning, a single thought distracted her—she wasn't headline news. At the very least, she expected some FBI alert saying there was a manhunt in progress and asking people to call some tip line. But there was nothing on the national or local news. She didn't know what to make of that. Either the feds knew exactly where to find her or she wasn't important to their case. Either way, they wouldn't be waiting for her in South Florida.

She spent the night in a hotel in Coral Gables, not twenty minutes from Miami International. The following morning, she checked into her flight with thirty grand stashed in her clothes, which was all the cash she was taking to Haiti. She'd stowed the remaining cash under the Honda's spare wheel.

Security wasn't a problem. Her flight was around two-thirds full. She was pleased to see plenty of white faces on the plane. The last thing she needed was to stick out more like a sore thumb than necessary.

Port-au-Prince's cloying heat hit her like a fist. The humidity enveloped her the moment she left the air-conditioned cool of the aircraft. She shuffled along with her fellow passengers into the airport as they chattered away. French and English flew over her head. She didn't talk to anyone. It was the way she wanted it. She'd kept to herself on the flight, shooting down anyone's attempts to chat. Now she regretted that. A lone tourist stuck out. She needed decoys and fast.

She scanned the crowd and locked onto a chatty pair of American couples a dozen people behind her. She let other people drift ahead of her until they caught up to her, then stepped on one of their toes "by accident" to kick off a conversation. She sold them a line about traveling alone on account of a friend canceling her trip at the last moment. Taking pity on her, they welcomed her into their fold. Now they were a group of five. After blowing through customs and immigration with her disposable friends, she passed through and out of the terminal, ghosting them.

Cab drivers descended upon her. French hailed down upon her from all directions. She didn't understand a word, but she understood the subtext—you're white, which means you have money and we want it. She hated hustlers, hypocritical under the circumstances, but it was more to do with small-time hustlers. Their desperation disgusted her. Black or white, she respected hustlers with cool. Hustlers like herself and Clean Willie. Hustlers like the broad-shouldered guy staring directly at her, leaning against an aged Toyota sedan with his arms crossed against his chest. This guy knew tourists spooked easily and that playing it cool won the day. She pointed at Mr. Cool.

He shoved his competition aside and grabbed her roller bag. The second the competition knew they'd lost out, they pounced on the next set of tourists.

Her driver opened a rear door for her to get in and put her roller in the trunk. The car sank a couple of inches when the driver dropped into his seat.

"Where to?"

She handed him a scrap of paper with an address she'd gotten from Papa.

The cabbie frowned. "What is your name?"

Barbara's neck muscles tightened. "Linda."

"You do not want to go here, Linda."

She didn't buckle under the weight of the man's concern. "I do."

"I know this place. People go there for one purpose. It's not for you. It's not for anyone. Whatever your problems are, they can be solved another way."

She leaned forward in her seat. "What's your name?"

"Maurice."

"Maurice, if I had any other way of resolving this issue, I would do it, but I don't, so please take me to this address."

Maurice sighed and turned away from her.

Port-au-Prince changed as they left the modern feel of the airport for the city streets. Bad roads were packed to capacity with vehicles. Mopeds cut in and out of traffic and seemed to be the smartest form of transportation if you wanted to get somewhere fast. Buildings and homes were packed tight and not well. This was a city of hard living. She'd known tough times but, dollars to donuts, these people knew harder.

Maurice didn't talk to her during the ride. She'd disappointed him. That or he pitied her. She'd wait for another time to be embarrassed. She just wanted to get this done and move on with her life.

Their journey ended on a narrow dirt road. Stucco sided

homes without a single architectural feature rose up on both sides to exaggerate the claustrophobic street.

Maurice pointed at a rundown bar on a street corner. "That's the place you want. Don't go in the front. You want that door on the side."

Barbara reached for her wallet.

"I will wait here."

"Won't be necessary," she said pulling out a twenty.

"It will. You will want a friend when you come out."

"And you're my friend?"

"In Haiti, I am."

She smiled. She guessed she was flattered by how Maurice perceived her. He saw her as some desperate American rich bitch looking for a way to get out from under—not a ruthless con artist. She should be flattered by that. She held out the twenty.

"That's a gift for my friend. See you in a while."

Maurice offered no smile in return but took the money.

The door Maurice had pointed out wasn't locked, so she let herself in. An unlit stairwell greeted her. Before she reached the top, a wiry guy tall enough to be in the NBA emerged from the darkness holding a .45.

"You're in the wrong place, bitch. Fuck off." His accent turned the word "bitch" into "beech."

Unfazed by either the gun or the slur, she said, "I'm here to see the Haitian."

He laughed. "We are all Haitian here, beech."

You listen to too much hip-hop, she thought. "Yeah, but you aren't *thee* Haitian."

A voice from the shadows said, "Let her up. She's Papa's girl."

One thing she wasn't was Papa's girl, but she let it slide. Mr. NBA held back a curtain that stood in for a proper door.

The room on the upper floor stank. It was a heady cocktail of booze, weed, sweat, decay and men who didn't give a shit.

Just her type. The Haitian rose from a leather club chair against the far wall with a mini-fridge humming loudly on one side and a gaming console on the other. A TV sitting on a coffee table covered in empty beer bottles was in front.

Children in men's clothing, she thought. Again, just her type.

The Haitian was a cute, baby-faced guy in his thirties, although he carried too much weight around his waist. That weight would catch up with those good looks one of these days. He offered a hand to her and they shook.

"You are Barbara, yes?"

He spoke with a faint French accent that made her wonder if he'd spent time in the States.

"Yes," she replied.

"Enchanté. Do you 'ave everything I need?"

She removed an envelope with pictures and information on Clean Willie. The Haitian took the envelope and walked it over to a desk by a shuttered window. He sat on the corner of the desk and gave the contents scant examination before tossing it to Mr. NBA.

"The money?" he asked with far more interest.

She pulled twenty-five grand from her purse. The Haitian's face lit up as she dropped the neatly packed bundles on the desk. He tossed one to Mr. NBA, who sniffed it like it was a Michelin star meal. There was no hiding what was of interest to these guys.

Putting the money aside, the Haitian said, "So what is it you want?"

Fun and games, really? She'd been hoping for a smooth transaction. "You know what I want."

"I do, but you 'ave to say it."

"What for?"

"The contract. There's no paper, so you 'ave say it."

She'd jumped through bigger hoops. "I want a Haitian Divorce."

"Again."

She sighed. "I want a Haitian Divorce."

"Again."

"I want a Haitian Divorce."

The Haitian grinned. "Now we 'ave a contract."

She wasn't sure if this guy was screwing with her but she remembered some factoids about having to say, "I divorce you" three times before getting your divorce decree. She guessed the Haitian was a stickler for tradition.

"When can I expect it done?"

The Haitian and Mr. NBA looked at each other and laughed.

"You really do not know 'ow this works, do you?" the Haitian said.

She couldn't believe she'd screwed up. Papa had fucked her over. She knew she couldn't trust that slimy son of a bitch. Well, fuck these guys. She was out of here. She reached for her money and didn't even get close.

Mr. NBA shot out one of his stick-thin arms and latched it around her throat before pressing the .45 against her temple. She grabbed his wrist to pull it away but there was real strength in his wiry frame. He spat French at her as he marched her backwards across the room until she connected with the sofa and he tumbled on top of her. Maurice's warning to her echoed loud in her mind. She should've listened to her cabbie.

The Haitian opened a desk drawer and pulled out a .38 revolver half wrapped in a dirty rag. He balanced it on his palm. "Let her alone, Emmanuel. I think she 'as got the message."

Mr. NBA released Barbara and got to his feet. He stood close with his finger tight on the trigger of his .45.

The Haitian crossed over to her with the revolver still balanced on his palm. "Let me educate you on a Haitian Divorce, the kind of Haitian Divorce I deal in."

He sat down next to her. "I am what you call a facilitator.

I provide an environment for your divorce but when it comes to the divorce itself," he smiled his smooth smile, "that is down to you, ma chérie."

He held the gun out to her. She took it, rag *et al.*

"The problem with you people," the Haitian said, "is you think because we are poor people from a shithole country that we'll do anything for your almighty dollar. You overestimate your importance and underestimate our desperation."

"Then what am I getting for my money?"

"My expertise. Because this is a shithole country, things can 'appen 'ere that can't in other countries. People 'ere are hungry. They want things from life that you take for granted so they will do things for a little money. Your husband can 'ave a bullet between the eyes, but I can have a death certificate saying he died of a 'eart attack and his body was cremated as per 'is written request."

"I don't want anything official. I want him to simply disappear."

The Haitian's seductive smile reappeared. "I can make that 'appen...or never 'appen as it were. Reality is whatever I say it is. That's what you are paying for, Barbara."

It was all nicely pitched, but the Haitian had forgotten one important detail. "My husband is in the U.S."

"Not for long. He knows you are 'ere. I will mislead 'im to get 'im 'ere and I will give you 'is location so you can serve 'im a lead filled divorce. Then you return to America a single woman...oui?"

Goddamn this asshole for his games. Goddamn Papa for bullshitting her. Goddamn Clean Willie for screwing her over. Goddamn this country for being an armpit that allowed itself to get reamed by the rest of the world for three hundred years.

She tightened her grip on the revolver. "Yes, I'll be free woman."

* * *

Maurice stopped his taxi in front of her hotel, Le Merengue. She didn't know where she was other than the hotel was on the coast and the drive had been long. The place was idyllic, a postcard paradise come to life, but it was background noise to the gun in her purse and what she had to do with it.

It took a moment to realize Maurice was talking to her.

"I'm sorry. I didn't catch that."

"I said you don't have to go through with it. I can take you back to the airport. You can fly home. Forget this."

It sounded easy but it wasn't. "I can't."

"Because of the money? Fuck the money. Consider it the price of coming to your senses."

"It's not the money." Her words sounded so faint and distant. She'd been looking down. She looked up, making eye contact with Maurice.

"Linda, be smart."

She generally was, except in one respect—Clean Willie. Falling for that son of a bitch was the dumbest thing she'd ever done and he would bring her down one way or the other. Maybe there was a way out of this but she needed a sounding board.

"Come in with me. Talk to me."

"I can't."

"I'll pay for your time."

He shook his head. "I am not your friend, Linda. I won't get involved. But I don't want you to make a mistake. Leave before it's too late."

It was good advice. She pulled five twenties from her purse and handed them to Maurice. "Thank you."

He took the money and retrieved her bag from the trunk. He drove off without another word. He'd made his pitch and it was down to her to heed his warning. She turned around and entered the hotel.

***

Barbara broke the seals on the last two mini-bottles of rum and dumped them into her glass before covered them up with Coke. She'd cleaned out her hotel room mini-bar in the time it took to have a shower. She stirred her cocktail with her finger and rewrapped her towel around her body.

She stared at the gun still sitting on the bed where she'd left it after checking into her room. She didn't want to touch it. She was far from squeamish when it came to guns, but the thought of killing Clean Willie turned her stomach. She shot back the drink, letting the alcohol singe her throat.

Tossing the glass on the bed, she picked up the gun. The revolver was heavy and solid in her grip. As technology went, it wasn't complicated. It was a simple device for a complicated purpose—taking a life.

She snapped open the cylinder and spun it. Each chamber was filled with a round. Only one bullet was needed for her Haitian Divorce.

Christ, she'd been stupid. She should've known it was never going to be simple.

Maurice had told her to go home. It wasn't such a bad idea.

Barbara tossed the gun on the bed before crashing onto the bed herself. A four-rum head rush overwhelmed her during the fall but a thought solidified in her mind—why the hell was she was feeling guilty? Will had sold her out. A lead-fueled Haitian Divorce to the back of the skull was more than he deserved for his snitching ass. So what if she had to do the killing? She was the trigger man regardless if she fired the gun or the Haitian did. Picking up the gun, she realized it felt good in her grasp this time. She snapped the cylinder in place and aimed it at the ceiling and Clean Willie was transposed there by her mind's eye.

"With this gun, I thee divorce."

***

Night brought an onshore breeze that helped kill the heat and keep the humidity in check. Barbara put on summer dress that was light and airy. Anything to help that breeze kiss her skin. She checked her appearance in the mirror. The dress was a little young for her but she could still pull it off.

"Look at what you're losing, Clean Willie."

She followed the sound of the house band to the bar. It was a hotel's typical attempt to make it look like an authentic Haitian bar. She didn't know what that was and neither did the hotel judging by the décor. It felt more tiki bar than anything, but it opened up onto the private beach and she liked that.

The place was busy. Just about everybody staying at the hotel was here experiencing the staged Haitian nightlife. She guessed most of them wouldn't venture outside the resort. Not that there was much worth venturing out for.

She took a seat at the bar and a bartender with a silky French accent welcomed her.

"Rum and Coke."

"Want to see a menu?"

Barbara had drunk a lot but hadn't eaten since before the flight. "Sure."

As she looked over the menu while she drank, a Haitian appeared at her shoulder. He smiled at her and she smiled back. A character weakness of hers at times like these. At well over six feet with smooth, chiseled features, he looked like he'd stepped out of the pages of *Vogue*.

"Is anyone sitting there?" he said in an American accent.

"No."

He thanked her and sat on the stool next to her. His sheer size filled his space and encroached into hers. Her shoulder rubbed against his arm.

"Nice to meet a fellow American. I've been stumbling over my nonexistent French all day."

The bartender came over and he asked for a Crémasse in

perfect French. He laughed when he noticed her staring at him.

"Impressive."

He laughed. "My parents are from here so French was what we spoke at home."

"Here visiting family?"

"No," he said, the bright smile fading. "Both my parents have passed and I came to see where I came from."

"And it's not quite what you were expecting."

"This place is hardly an island paradise—" he indicated to their surroundings, "—unless you can afford it."

"I'm sorry the trip isn't turning out to be what you hoped."

"Yeah, well."

The bartender delivered the Crémasse, which looked like a White Russian.

"What is that?"

He held it up. "This is the Haitian national drink, creamed coconut, sweetened condensed milk and a shot of rum. Don't tell me you haven't had one of these?"

"No."

"Have mine," he said and asked the bartender for another.

Barbara tried the drink. It was sweet but the rum gave it a bite. He preference was rum and Coke but when in Haiti, do as the hot Haitian sitting next to you does.

"I'm Charles," he said raising his glass to her.

"Linda," she said.

"You know why I'm here. What brought you to Haiti?"

"My husband."

Charles's expression froze while his stare went to her ring finger. She realized she hadn't taken off her wedding ring.

"He betrayed me." She twisted the ring off and dropped it on the bar. "It's over now."

Charles went into reflective bullshit along the lines of there are more fish in the sea, but she zoned him out. Her focus was on her ring finger. It was pale and wasted away from over a decade of wearing the rings. Her hand felt lighter without them, significantly more than the scant weight of the rings. Her marriage had weight. It kept her grounded. It kept her sharp. Now that it was over, she felt cut adrift. Alone and lost. A tear welled up and she palmed it away before it could embarrass her by rolling down her face. She wouldn't give Will the satisfaction.

She interrupted Charles mid-eulogy. "You like me?"

"I do."

"Cool. You want to get out of here?"

His face lit up. "Yeah."

"Good."

She grabbed his hand and pulled him from his stool.

"What about your rings?" he asked.

"They're no good to me now."

Barbara dragged him through the bar and onto the beach. A handful of couples stood at the water's edge staring the moon and its distorted image on the water. She pulled him down the beach away from the people, the hotel and even the moonlight. Only the music from the band reached them.

Charles jerked her to a stop. "Slow down, girl."

Swaying to the music, she slipped her hands around his waist. He picked up her vibe and swayed with her. She pressed her body against his. He didn't pull away.

"Am I a rebound?"

Barbara laughed.

"Just because you've got some shit with your man don't think you can put me between you."

"He and I are finished. Tonight made me realize I don't have to keep on doing what I've always done. I can do whatever I like with whomever I like...and I like you."

Charles smiled.

"So you want to fuck?"

His smile turned into a grin. "I thought you'd never ask."

Pushing her into the tree line edging the beach, he kissed

her every step of the way. She bumped her head against tree as he pressed his body against hers and she felt a rush of heat throughout her body. He lifted her dress and tugged her panties down, then spun her around. She braced herself against the tree as he entered her from behind.

Barbara grinned as he pounded her again and again. She couldn't remember the last time she'd been this spontaneous. With Clean Willie, everything was calculated and planned. It had been her way of life for so long, but now the bond was broken and she could go with the flow. This underlined her liberation. Tonight had been about getting wrecked. Instead she was being plowed up against a tree. Freedom was feeling pretty damn good.

When Charles was finished, they carried the party to her room. They showed off, pulling out all their various party pieces to impress each other. Raw and sated, sleep took them before neighbors on either side of her room could complain.

Barbara awoke to the sound of her cell phone ringing. Its shrill tone dragged its fingers down her hangover. The other side of the bed was empty. Charles was nowhere to be seen. That was fine by her. There were plenty of Charleses to go around. Grabbing the phone, she mumbled something down the line.

"It's me." It was the Haitian.
"What do you want?"
"Clean Willie is 'ere."
Her heart rate quickened. "Where?"

Barbara strode down the beach while doing her best to appear normal. Her racing heart rate did nothing for the hangover occupying her skull. She released a long breath to uncoil the anxiety knotted in her chest. Her hand went to the gun in her purse hanging off her shoulder. She was getting close.

It turned out she didn't have far to go to find Clean Willie.

He was staying one resort over from hers. The Haitian had left a duplicate room cardkey in an envelope with the front desk. She'd decided to hit him there and then. If she gave herself the luxury of time and clarity, she'd cut and run. That was where the hangover played to her advantage. It made clear thought impossible.

Hitting him now made sense too. It wasn't even 8:00 a.m., so witnesses were scarce. She'd only seen one guest and a smattering of hotel staff so far. Also, Clean Willie wasn't a morning person. Her plan was simple—go to his room, let herself in, grab a pillow, use it as a silencer and put a bullet through her scumbag of a husband's skull.

His hotel came into view. It wasn't all that different from her own. She entered the place via the pool entrance and followed the signs to the lobby, then took the elevators to the third floor. Luck played on her side. Maids weren't working this floor yet.

Barbara stopped in front of his room. Her fingers tightened around the gun and the trigger as she slipped the cardkey into the slot. Her heart pounded in her chest and her breaths came hard. She eased the door open.

She didn't think, just acted. She slipped inside the room and closed the door, then marched towards the mess of bedclothes with the gun outstretched. Within two steps, it was obvious Clean Willie wasn't there.

The tension within her burst, turning to panic. She rushed to the bathroom, but he wasn't there either. The closet was also empty.

A flood of relief overwhelmed her. She dropped onto the corner of the bed, the gun slipping from her grasp. She was shaking. Her mind had been psyched up to kill her husband and that unresolved intensity took it out on her body.

"Shit," she murmured. She'd have to do this all over again. She dropped her head in her hands.

As stressful as this dry run had been, it proved one thing—

she could do this. She'd simply come back in dead of night, and she'd be more prepared next time. She could manufacture a silencer using a plastic bottle and cotton balls. She picked up the revolver, dropped it back into her purse and let herself out of the room.

Heading back across the beach, a twisted thought entered her head. Something that could derail everything. What if the feds had Will? As their stoolpigeon, he would likely be their star witness. If so, there was no way they'd let him leave the country with them coming along too. There was no way she could get past them. Some Haitian Divorce this was turning out to be.

With her mind on Will, her reactions were slow. She sensed him before she saw him walking towards her. They both came to a stop in front of each other.

He smiled. She didn't. She was working all the angles. He was alone. No FBI babysitters in sight. No tourists nearby. To do this here would be messy and fraught with issues but this wasn't the States. She could do him now, here on the beach. Her hand went to her purse and found the gun.

"I'm glad they didn't catch you, baby."

She hated it when he called her baby. "You son of a bitch. You sold me out. Why?"

"I didn't have a choice."

"Bullshit. Anything to save your own ass. It's the Clean Willie way."

"Babs, it wasn't like that. They knew everything."

More bullshit. How could he lie to her? Goddamn the man.

"Where are your FBI playmates?"

"I'm alone. I gave them the slip. Just like you."

"Liar."

"No, seriously. The FBI is big and slow. I'm quick and nimble like a cat. The bigger question is why are you here?"

"Duh, because you sold me out."

"Haiti isn't a non-extradition country, Babs."

They were talking too much. Making too much noise. Drawing too much attention. Will was buying time. She needed to get this done.

"Just a stepping stone."

He grinned. "You haven't filed for a Haitian Divorce by any chance, have you?"

Before she could say no, he reached behind him, pulled out a pistol and fired. There hadn't been a moment's hesitation. Will, her husband, her cohort for over fifteen years, had shot at her without a second thought. She was no different than any other problem in his life. When it had to go, it had to go. So be it. Divorce proceedings were now in motion. She fired back through her purse.

Both shots went wild. Will dove to the sand. She bolted for the tree line, wanting something solid between her and the next bullet.

"Sneaky minds think alike, eh, baby?" he yelled. "That's why I love ya."

She didn't answer, instead pulling the heavy revolver free from the purse, now replete with a fresh bullet hole. It was ruined but it wasn't worthless. She hurled the bag away. Will took the bait and fired at the flying purse. She used that moment's advantage to come out from behind the tree. On his knees, he was a big fat target. Like him, she didn't hesitate and squeezed the trigger. She'd aimed for his head but the bullet punched a hole in his shoulder. He yelled out and fell on his back.

She wouldn't get a second chance. She charged towards him, her gun arm outstretched. Clean Willie writhed on the sand. He tried to raise his arm, the pistol now loose in his grip. She squeezed out two shots, both hitting Will in the chest. He was finished.

"Our marriage is now dissolved, Clean Willie."

She grabbed Will's pistol and twisted it to wrench it from

his grasp. But the weapon remained tight in his hand. Worse, it twisted back toward her. She caught a cruel smile breaking out across Will's face before the gun fired.

The bullet, such a tiny thing when you thought about it, felt like a cannonball. She tried to take a breath but it got stuck. Staggering backward, she pressed her hand to the epicenter of the pain radiating throughout her body just below her ribcage. The pain skyrocketed. It went from white hot to impossible to comprehend. She took another step back before collapsing. She dragged herself over to a downed tree and propped herself up.

Will was talking, but she couldn't make out what he was saying. The pain in her chest was speaking louder.

A commotion behind her caught her attention. The Haitian, Emmanuel and Charles appeared. She looked at Charles, but he ignored her. She shook her head in confusion.

"Get everything off him," the Haitian ordered and Emmanuel and Charles descended upon Will like vultures.

The Haitian dropped to his knees at Barbara's side.

"Is he dead?"

"He will be." He patted her down. She yelled out in pain.

"I need a hospital."

"No. No doctor for you. Where's your purse?"

"Over there someplace. Are you screwing me?"

The Haitian laughed. "No. I'm honoring your deal, but I am honoring his deal too."

No, this couldn't be happening.

"You asked for a Haitian Divorce, but so did he. I always give my clients what they want."

She couldn't keep her head up any longer and rested it against the tree. As the Haitian stripped her of her necklace and bracelet, she looked up at the morning sun breaking through the clouds.

The Haitian leaned in. "Congratulations, this is your Haitian Divorce."

BLACK COW
Linda Joffe Hull

"I can't cry anymore," Debra says, dabbing her eyes.

But she can, and she will, if the last hour is any indication.

You know her name is Debra, not Deb or Debbie because that's how she introduced herself. It's a name you've always disliked, despite the fact it contains the word *bra*.

Which you do like.

For the record, her bra is black, lacy, and adorned with a little gold heart between her tits. You know this because it peeks out from the gap between the buttons of her blouse when she lifts her drink, which is often, and when she gesticulates wildly while talking about Kenny, her *adulterous bastard of a husband*, which is even more often.

She's just your type.

Certainly for tonight, which is Monday Margarita Madness and, you can't help but note, all-you-can-eat taco night at Rudy's.

Debra is blonde with a quarter-inch of telltale gray at the roots. She is a little bunny-faced, but in a good way. Plus, the one time she stops going on about Kenny and excuses herself to the ladies' room, you are able to confirm that she has not been exaggerating her repeated claim of "I work out every day. I mean, what more can he ask for?"

You picture Debra in the yoga pants she undoubtedly paints on most mornings before tooling around town doing errands, and you get a little hard. Hard enough that you are—semi—glad to endure another round of her heartbroken rant in the hopes she'll go a last round with you in the back of the luxury SUV or minivan she undoubtedly drives.

You assume this because, as you offer Debra your shoulder to cry on while she spills her secrets and brags about her attributes, all of which should have kept Kenny toeing the marital line, she repeatedly slurs, *we have everything.*

Had everything...

You should be asking yourself why you're willing to exploit a woman in such a fragile state, but instead find yourself wondering how Cheatin' Kenny makes bank.

Kenny, whose name is again on Debra's plum-colored mouth, her lipstick freshly reapplied, as she settles back onto her barstool. She takes a sip of the skinny margarita you sampled while she was gone. You wonder, but don't ask, how it could possibly differ from the full-calorie version. Especially after multiple refills.

"How could I have been so naïve?" Debra asks.

"You shouldn't be so hard on yourself," you say, settling in with your Tecate while she continues to unpack the duffel bag of dirty laundry that is her marriage.

"Did I tell you we were high-school sweethearts?"

She did.

"And that after I caught him with his hand up Mary Mullaney's shirt at a homecoming after-party, he swore he'd never cheat again?"

Once a cheater...you definitely don't say.

"I believed our marriage was built on a foundation of trust," she says. "We're Christians, for God's sake."

You shake your head in disgust practically in unison with her.

"I mean, would you believe he insisted we write our own

wedding vows? He told the whole church the only thing he'd ever need, besides me, was a sports car or maybe a boat."

Good one, you can't help but think.

"And every baby came with a push present in a little blue box."

You don't need to ask what she means by *push present* or *little blue box* to know the dude has game, even if he is a cheating asshole.

"If only he hadn't left his phone on the counter, by his keys." She drops her face into her hands. "How could I *not* look at a message from a contact named *Kenny's Remedy?*"

"I'd have looked, too," you assure her, liking that her fingernails are painted a sparkly, fuck-me shade of silver.

"At first, I thought he had a secret drug problem or something."

"It happens," you say.

"I had every intention of standing behind him while he got sober," she says, reaching for her drink. "Until I called the number and found out *Kenny's Remedy* was Heather, our twenty-three-year-old dog groomer."

You give her a sympathetic pat on the thigh. It's toned and taut.

"Would you believe he told me that he meant to type in *Monty's* Remedy, as in Monty, our dog?"

"Heather could be a dog groomer *and* a drug dealer."

"I almost wish she was," Debra said, reaching for her phone. "But I went through his text history and found *this.*"

The next thing you know, you're looking at a naked redhead in an unbuttoned smock, dog clippers in hand, and a smirk on her face.

"That's Monty in the cage behind her," Debra says with a sniffle.

You hadn't noticed the dog because Heather is anything but.

"What an asshole," you say, blotting the enormous tear

glistening on her cheek. "You deserve better."

"Talking it out with you is helpful," she says.

"I'm glad," you say, looking into her big eyes, their color indeterminate in the low light of Rudy's.

"You're sweet," she says, now putting her hand on your leg. As in *game on*?

"I should probably go," she says.

"I'll walk you to your car," you say.

"I'd like that," she says.

If this were a movie, you'd wink at the bartender as you escort a wobbly Debra out of the restaurant and into the stifling Midwestern July night. But it's not, and you're not that big a douche, so you ignore his knowing smirk.

Once outside, Debra stops in front of a shiny, black, tricked-out truck.

"Wow," you say. It isn't what you expected.

"Kenny is out of town so I took his car," Debra says. "I call it the Big Black Cow."

"Clever," you say.

Then you, so mercenary you've listened to the sad ramblings of a betrayed housewife in the hope of getting laid, are suddenly struck by an inability to execute that all-important first move. But you don't have to, because Debra leans in and kisses you with all the force and insistence you've been imagining since you caught your first glimpse of black lace.

The next thing you know, you are inside the fancy truck, which is roomy and smells like leather and Kenny's aftershave. From there it is all hands and tongues, and then she's unbuttoning your jeans.

"A lipstick," she suddenly says, stopping to clutch a silver tube on the floor of the passenger side instead of your similarly-shaped-but-not-sized item. "But it's not mine."

And then she is ugly crying. Again.

You hold her in your arms until she regains her composure.

"You can't drive home," you finally say, realizing she's as

drunk as she is upset. "You'll crash."

"I hope so," she says. "He loves this stupid truck more than he loves me."

"I'll call an Uber for you."

"No," she says, her lips suddenly on yours again. "You drive me. In Kenny's truck."

You shouldn't drive either, but with the renewed promise of her intentions, you agree and take the keys from Debra.

Soon, you're heading to her place.

The address is in Valley Estates in the suburbs, on the tony East Side. It's a good thing you know roughly where it is, because Debra has closed her eyes and you don't want to be the one who wrecks Kenny's truck trying to figure out the navigation system.

As you exit the highway and make your way toward the columned entrance, Debra awakens. She is sober enough to guide you down Valley Parkway, right onto Valley Avenue, left on Valley Way, and finally right again onto Valley Street.

She points to the third McMansion on the left.

"What a place," you say, curving around the circular driveway of the massive colonial house.

"Everything is in his name," she says with a sigh. "Pull up there."

You stop where she has instructed, between doors two and three of the *five* garage doors along the north side of the house.

You are startled when a floodlight clicks on.

"Motion sensor," she says.

And then, without warning, she's all over you again.

"You did say Kenny's out of town, right?" you manage, but she is already undoing the last two buttons on your jeans. And then you forget about everything but the fact that you are receiving what may be the finest blow job you've ever had. Certainly, the best you've ever gotten in another man's truck. In his driveway. From his wife.

Thankfully, there's no sign of Kenny before, during, or after.

"Thank you," she says, before you do. "I wish we'd met under different circumstances."

"Are you going to be okay?" you ask, wondering how to gracefully end this evening.

"Hard to know," she says, opening the passenger side door.

You get out of the truck and hug her goodbye, blinking under the overly bright lights, which stayed on, due to the motion, for your whole encounter.

"I'm here if you need me," you say, wishing you had a better exit line.

"I'll keep that in mind," she says, climbing into the driver's seat. She fires up the engine and disappears into her fraught world via garage stall number three.

You walk to the street and call an Uber to take you back to your car, still parked at Rudy's.

Which is where you should have left things.

You know you're never going to see her again, but when you arrive at your townhouse—which you can't help but note would fit inside Debra's garage, with room to spare—you're hungry and wired.

And your computer's still awake.

Grabbing a bag of Doritos—to maintain the evening's south-of-the-border theme—you type in *Debra* and *Kenny* and *11025 Valley Street*.

It's almost too easy.

Within seconds, you know they are Debra and Kenny Sampson. And that Kenny is, naturally, in financial services. He could lose twenty or thirty pounds and looks, at least to you, like a character from *The Sopranos*.

The thought gives you pause, but not enough that you resist the impulse to keep snooping. You read every Google search result mentioning either of them, rifle through all the public posts and photos on their Facebook pages, check out Kenny's LinkedIn profile and Debra's Instagram pictures, and browse every online image you can find.

You now know Debra and Kenny are forty-one. They have three children, whose names, pictures, and social media you've done your best to ignore, because that would be weird. Kenny has acquired both the boat and a Porsche in addition to the Big Black Cow—all of which he likes to pose beside.

The last thing you see is a link on page five of Kenny's Google results for a place called *Bark Tenders*. You click on the link and find yourself staring at Kenny smiling lasciviously at Heather, though this time her smock is fully buttoned, as the unwitting but all-knowing Monty endures a promotional grooming for the sake of a website photo.

You fall asleep that evening thinking about the mournful way Debra kept repeating.

We have everything.

Had everything...

Because FirmFit Training posts a list of members who meet and—in Debra's case—beat their monthly workout goals, you know she goes to the Valley Commons location. After driving by once or maybe twice, you also know she frequents the Starbucks next door and the Whole Foods at First and Grant. You don't accidentally run into her at either because you are not a creep.

You tell yourself you're just concerned about her well-being.

You aren't trying to hook up with her, even if you're not trying not to.

And Monday Madness at Rudy's is a thing. Lots of people go regularly, including you.

The next time you do, you sit at the opposite end of the bar from where you sat with her. You watch the game on

TV—and not the door, which is also in view—while you eat, drink, and don't expect to see her at all.

And you don't.

Noticing you aren't the only dude that seems to be lurking and alone, you pay the bill and leave.

You're halfway to your car when you see someone who looks very much like Debra across the parking lot. Of course, she can't be Debra, because that would be too easy. Also, she's not wearing the tight, short, black dress she was wearing in the Facebook post you keep looking at, the one you dream she'd be wearing if you did run into her again.

She waves.

You walk over to her and note that she looks just as good in a red tank top and short denim skirt.

"I was hoping I'd find you here," Debra says, her voice trembling. "I need you."

You do a quick count of the beers you drank because you wonder if you might be dreaming, and, in case you aren't, she needs you to drive her home again.

There is fury in her eyes as she hands you her phone. "Kenny has at least two other remedies: Bethany, his personal trainer and Chloe, *my* massage therapist."

You don't mind being ambushed, but you're too startled to come up with exactly the right words.

"What are you going to do?" you mumble.

"You," she says.

Your first thought is that you are definitely dreaming. The second is you're glad you have a condom in your wallet, given the depth and breadth of Kenny's wanderings. You also have a fleeting concern about inviting her to your down-market townhouse. "Where should we—?"

"Right here," she says, opening the door to a white Range Rover. "Right now."

On the one hand, you're glad you didn't have to offer your place, which you fear would kill whatever moment you're about to have. On the other, you're not thrilled about doing it in a vehicle again.

Not that you're going to say no.

You do wish she wouldn't keep saying *that fucker,* and *fucking Kenny,* while her tears dampen your chest hair. After you finish simultaneously—really!—she returns to the ugly crying that caused last week's rain delay.

"You should leave him," you say, the postcoital glow once again enhanced by the street light her vehicle is parked beneath.

"I can't," she says. "We have to think of the kids."

Seeing as their mother's skirt is still around her waist, you'd rather not.

"Besides, Kenny controls every dime I spend, what I do, and wear…I mean, I can only get away like this when he's out of town."

"But he's the one who's cheating," you say before you can think better of it.

"He was," she says with a giggle that might just inspire you enough for another round. "Now, I have my own remedy."

She kisses you deeply and passionately, which definitely arouses your interest again.

"I have to go," she says, grabbing her cell phone. "Give me your number."

I don't think that's a good idea, you should say. Or, *Maybe you need to get some clarity on your marital issues.* Or even, *This can't be good for the kids.*

Instead, you enter the digits in her phone.

Not that you're keeping track, but a week goes by. A week in which you remind yourself that she is, or was, a no-strings-attached hook-up. You think about texting her, but she has told you not to, so you don't.

You do, however, circle the parking lot of FirmFit once or twice on Tuesday.

Then again on Wednesday.
And Thursday.
You give up by Friday. She texts Friday night.
Are you free tomorrow?
You should wait an hour or so before you respond.
What time and where? you write back immediately.
10 p.m. 55 Green Street.
I'll be there, you reply, and then spend the next almost twenty-four hours gloating that you have officially received your first booty call.

You gloat that much more when Debra answers the door wearing a lavender bustier and matching panties.
 "Outrageous," you say.
 She pulls you inside the house.
 "Whose place is this, anyway?" you ask as she leads you toward the stairs.
 "Don't worry, we're alone," she says, not that you were.
 She opens the door to a guest bedroom where, once again, lights on—the way she seems to like it—you provide the anti dote, as you've decided to think of yourself, to the poison that is Kenny.
 Twice.
 Nearly three times.

It is Monday and you are parked across the street from the offices of Kenneth Sampson and Associates. You already know Kenny is richer than you, more successful, drives a nicer car, and is bored with the woman who occupies far too much of your mental bandwidth. You tell yourself that, after hooking up with Debra at her friend's house—which, you've learned, is one of a few places she can go without being questioned—you just need to see this asshole in real life. Your abilities may extend only to sexual healing and a limited ability to empathize, and you know you can't make everything right, but Kenny is a cheating, controlling, narcissistic fuck who needs to be confronted by someone.

You imagine yourself speaking using only your fists.

The thing is, as you exit your car, feed the meter, and cross the street, your heart is already pounding. You are dripping sweat by the time you enter the ice-cold lobby and confirm the suite number, which you already know. You feel short of breath as the elevator opens and whisks you to the eighth floor.

You get off expecting a hallway of office suites, only to discover that Sampson and Associates spans the entire floor.

"Welcome," says the—predictably—attractive blonde at the reception desk. "Can I help you?"

"Uh," you say, wondering what it is you think you're going to do next—tell her you have an appointment? Barge past her toward the corner office? Shout *Kenny* in your most threatening voice?

You hear the familiar swish of a bathroom door opening behind you. As you turn, the occupant emerges. He's the perfect cliché of taller, broader, and more likely to have started off his customer-service career as a bouncer than any of his internet photos revealed.

He is, undoubtedly, Kenny.

With the element of surprise on your side, you could whale on the guy and probably get one or two quick punches in before he totally flattens you.

"Mornin," he says, and then smiles at you with familiarity, like you are an old friend or a coworker.

You kind of are, in a manner of speaking. Which is why you absolutely need to get the fuck out of there.

"Wrong floor," you proclaim, turning for the still-open elevator. "My bad."

***

You, the Great White Knight, do not say a word to Debra about your wussy non-confrontation the next time you see her, all of her, in a meeting room she has reserved for the two of you at the Valley Estates Clubhouse.

"This is where Kenny likes to have his business meetings," she explains. "So, I do too."

You can't say you love being a revenge fuck, but given her enthusiasm, you're also not inclined to question her coping techniques.

"Isn't it kind of weird for us to be meeting here?" you ask.

"Not if you're a tennis coach I'm meeting to discuss private lessons," she says.

"Sounds like a bad porn scenario," you say.

"Exactly," she says.

Which you then begin to reenact.

As you do, her phone, which is on the table next to her tennis skirt, begins to buzz.

"It's just Kenny," she says, reaching over to decline the call. "No big deal."

By now, you've heard his name so often you don't even lose your groove. When he texts a few seconds later and she ignores it, you are okay too. Everything is cool.

That is, until you happen to glance through a misaligned slat in the otherwise pristine vertical blinds covering a nearby window.

You stop immediately. "Shit!"

"What is it?" she asks, a hint of irritation in her voice.

You point at the big black truck stopped at the light near the clubhouse parking lot.

Debra looks out the window and her eyes grow huge.

You are already hauling your pants up and tossing your shirt over your head.

"It's no use," she says, as the truck turns and rolls into the lot. "He knows where I am. He's going to kill us."

"I won't let him," you say, grabbing her pile of clothes and handing her everything but the phone.

"What are you—?"

"I've got this," you say, returning Kenny's text of *on my way* with a message of your own: *Out by the pool.*

"What did you say?"

"I bought us some time to sneak out."

"And go where?" she asks, finally slipping into her skirt and top.

"Thirty-two Westgate Drive, Unit Three."

Confusion clouds her face. "Your place?"

There is no time to explain to her that you are no Kenny, not in the wallet anyway, but you are there for here. "I'll tell you when the coast is clear, and you'll go."

You watch Kenny enter the building.

"What about you?" she asks.

"I'll drop your phone somewhere that will delay him more and be right behind you."

"This isn't how this was supposed to go," she says weakly as you crack open the door to the meeting room in time to see Kenny clear the front desk and head for the pool area.

"Run!" you say. "I'll see you at my place."

She does.

As you take a deep breath in preparation for your mission, you notice that Debra has left her panties on the floor underneath a chair. You grab them, stuff them into your pocket, and say a little prayer.

Kenny is on the opposite side of the pool as you slip outside behind the snack bar, toss the phone into a nearby bush, and hightail it out of the clubhouse.

Maybe it's because you chickened out last time, or maybe because you are scared shitless, but on the way to your car, you sneak over to the Big Black Cow. You take the pocketknife on your key ring, flip up the blade, and attempt to twist it into the thick, knobby front passenger tire. You're fairly sure you haven't penetrated the rubber more than enough to cause a slow leak so you jab the rear tire once. This time, the small blade breaks off in the tread.

You rush over to the safety of your car and head home feeling pretty gangster, even if your ride is a 2006 Honda Civic.

Until you get inside and call her name.

Debra echoes through the house.

There is no answer.

You don't pretend to understand what happened, but you do spend the next few days camped out at the Starbucks next to FirmFit, and shopping at Whole Foods for more groceries you don't need. Debra has no cell phone so she has no way of getting ahold of you unless she somehow memorized your number. Which you doubt, somehow.

You are not a guy who covets panties, but you carry Debra's in your pocket. For luck?

By Monday, you're back at Rudy's.

"What can I get you?" asks a woman who is not the usual Monday night bartender.

You order a Tecate and two tacos, although you don't feel much like drinking or eating.

"Everything okay?" the bartender asks after you don't eat or drink much of either.

You nod, noticing you are, once again, one of a handful of single men scattered around the place.

A few minutes later, when she is at your end of the bar again, one of the nearby randos asks the bartender if she's seen a woman who seems to be looking for someone.

She laughs. "Tonight and every night."

"I'm actually looking for a specific friend who may have come in asking about me," the guy says.

"Named?"

"Debra."

Your gut rumbles. More so when another dude three stools

down glances up from his drink too.

"Blonde with a rocket bod and a problem husband?" the bartender asks.

"Sounds like the one," the guy says.

Dude Number Two all but nods.

"Not tonight," the bartender says. "I highly doubt I will."

"Why's that?" the guy asks.

"Because she and her hubby's sick game finally caught up to them."

Sweat breaks out at the nape of your neck.

"Sick game?" the guy repeats, maybe for all three of you.

"The one where she cries about her marriage to some poor sap and then lures him out to that big black truck she drives and Lord knows where else so her creep of a husband can watch them have sex."

The low rumbling in your gut is now registering on the Richter scale.

"We were taking bets around here about how long it would be before one of the men decided he needed to defend the poor girl's honor. Not that she had any."

"And someone did?" he stammers.

Your hands are too shaky to pick up your beer and take the drink you now need. Badly.

"Punctured his tires, apparently," she says. "The truck rolled off an overpass, and they're both pretty bad off."

"Oh God," he says. "That's awful."

"Are you still sure you're looking for that Debra?" the bartender asks. "Because, if you are, I'll bet the cops are looking for you."

PRETZEL LOGIC
dbschlosser

The guys who come back the first time, they always say the biggest difference outside is the silence at night. They can't sleep because it's too quiet.

The guys who come back a second time, they generally ain't too self-aware. They say the biggest difference outside is the sensations. The food, it tastes so much better. The girls, they so much juicier. The air, it don't smell like week-old socks all the time.

Only one guy came back a third time when he was inside. That guy just scored himself a third strike with whatever he could pull off quick and easy that was barely a felony. That guy said the biggest difference is that everyone thinks there's a big difference between being inside and being outside. But there ain't.

I ain't never going back.

The red-blue strobe in his rearview mirror pulled his insides down. Adrenaline roiled him, and he tasted it at the back of his mouth. In his throat, electric and sour. He hit the blinker, searched for a polite excuse for whatever he might be told was the reason for the stop. *DWB*, dressed up like a burned-out bulb. *Yes, sir. No, sir.* An expired tag. *Thank you, sir, may I have another.*

He put the Kia in park. Rolled down his window. Spun the volume on WJAZ to zero. Put his wallet and phone on the dashboard. Put his hands at ten-and-two on the wheel, fingers flung wide. Waited.

"Driver." A woman's voice through the speaker. "Step out of the car and place your hands on the hood."

His head sagged. He took a deep, slow breath. He complied.

The cop was young. If not a rookie, close. She'd be scared.

"Spread your legs," the cop said as she approached. Her hand rested on her pistol. "And don't move."

"Yes, ma'am." He couldn't read her name tag.

The cop started a frisk. "Plates say this car is registered to a Randall Baxter. That's you?"

"People call me Bax." Her frisk wasn't very thorough. "Yes, ma'am. I'm Randall Baxter."

"You prove that?"

"Yes, ma'am." Bax nodded toward his wallet. "My license is there. On the dashboard."

The cop reached through the open window. "Don't move," she repeated. She pulled the license and held it up to compare the photo to Bax's face. Replaced the license in the wallet, the wallet on the dashboard. "You know why I pulled you over, Mr. Baxter?"

"No, ma'am."

"I'm going to search your pockets. You got anything sharp in there?"

"No, ma'am."

"Nothing that's going to stick me?" The cop groped his back pockets, then started to crowd him, almost embracing him as she reached into his front pockets.

"Ma'am—"

"Shut up." The cop got up close and personal. "You hear me, Mr. Baxter?" Raised her voice to a shout. "I said shut.

The fuck. Up." Spun him, backed him up against the side of the little SUV. Reached inside his jacket to search his inside pockets, then dropped something small and hard in the chest pocket of his shirt.

"Ma'am, I—"

The cop silenced him by grabbing bunches of his jacket in her fists, pulling him close. "Your code is Brooklyn," she whispered into his face before she shouted, "I told you to shut up."

"But I din't do nothin,'" he shouted back. Then he whispered, "Brooklyn."

Bax's day had started like most days: coffee, eggs with bacon, and strawberry jelly with sourdough toast at the counter of the diner on the dividing line between the suburbs and his city. Flirting over the newspaper with Venetta, the morning-shift manager. Who'd let him take her out a couple of times. Who'd refused a dinner date at his pal Napoleon's locally famous supper club until he started going to Sunday services with her, her daughter Margaret, and her mom. Who'd squinted up half her face when he'd offered the vaguest possible interpretation of his work.

He recognized the flash off his kid brother's blinged-out shoes in the parking lot. Recognized his boss's Lexus SUV.

"Imma take that booth over there," he told Venetta. "Don't you come wait on me."

Venetta started to speak but stopped when he shook his head once.

Bax slid into the booth before his boss's enforcer, Owsley, opened the passenger door for Reamer Kline. Bax's balls unshriveled a tiny bit when Owsley, so big that the SUV listed toward the side he sat on, didn't follow Mr. Kline toward the diner door. Bax knew Owsley's kind from his bit. Knew Owsley enjoyed the beat-down he put on Russell to persuade Bax to fix for Mr. Kline.

Mr. Kline waited at the diner's door until Russell figured out it was his job to open the door.

Bax saw some sullen fear in his brother's eyes and wondered what it was about this time.

Mr. Kline motioned for Russell to slide into the booth first, opposite Bax, so Mr. Kline could contain Russell. "Your idiot brother said I'd find you here." Keep the kid from rabbiting.

Bax narrowed his eyes. Gave his brother a hard stare. "I'm sorry it couldn't wait until I got to the shop, Mr. Kline." Waited for the waitress to serve coffee. "What do I need to fix for him now?"

Russell snorted a protest.

"Shut up, Russell." Bax and Mr. Kline said it at the same time.

Russell stared at the wall. Slouched lower.

"Your idiot brother went and got all...entrepreneurial." Mr. Kline waved off menus. "Managed to sell some—property— that already had a buyer."

Bax remained silent. Raced through Mr. Kline's lines of business to assess what property Mr. Kline might be talking about. "Is it property we can get more of?"

"It is not."

That ruled out cars and parts, some drugs, and girls. It left knock-off Japanese whiskey and—

"All them FNs," Russell said.

Mr. Kline's backhand across Russell's face flashed so fast Bax might have missed it if not for the split that opened in the middle of his brother's lower lip.

"Russell," Bax said, "you keep your own counsel for the rest of this conversation." He pushed his napkin across the table. Motioned for Russell to use it to stop the bleeding. "Mr. Kline—"

"I know you thought you'd work off Russell's debt in the next two, three years."

"Is this fixable?" *Or just more debt?*

"I sold that property to the originally interested party."

"The gentlemen from San Leon."

"Exactly." Mr. Kline paused while the waitress refilled his coffee. "And your brother somehow managed to secure a commitment to buy from the—how did you say it? The gentlemen from Tyler."

Bax covered his face with his hands. Cursed silently into his palms. *Decades more debt.* "I'm sorry, Mr. Kline." *Lifetimes.* "I—well, I'm just very sorry."

"Now, Bax, you don't need to apologize." Mr. Kline moved his hands like he was giving a benediction. "I know young Russell here is just a half-brother. So I can assume he acquired his extraordinary stupidity from his father, not yours."

Bax kicked Russell under the table to prevent his protest. "Yes, sir, Mr. Kline."

"Is this fixable, you ask." Mr. Kline wrapped his hands around his coffee mug. "All the ways I can think to fix this involve throwing your brother to one or the other of the two motorcycle gangs currently waging war over which will control Texas."

Russell's face melted from sullen fear to absolute terror.

Bax kicked him again. "Let me think on it for a bit, Mr. Kline, if you will."

"You can understand why I'd like to find a more successful resolution." Mr. Kline twisted the big nugget-looking ring that had opened Russell's lip. "Can't you, Bax."

"Yes, sir."

"But our time is short. Thanks to young Russell's commitment, now both parties expect delivery within two days."

"Two days, Mr. Kline."

Bax's boss nodded with his whole body. He pulled a long wallet from inside his jacket, opened it, and fingered through the bills. He tugged out a fifty. "That Miss Venetta is quite a catch, Bax." Folded it under his saucer. "You take good care of her."

***

Bax hustled his brother out of the diner as soon as Mr. Kline's Lexus turned at the end of the block.

"Russell, how you find this much trouble to get into?"

Russell threw a dismissive hand toward the sky. "Man, get off my shit. I just—"

"*Your* shit?" Bax dope-slapped Russell. "I'm carrying that Wells deal you oughtta got dead for, and you talk at me about your shit? You tell Mr. Kline the woman I'm seein', and you talk at me about your shit? How many times I got to tell you 'bout impulse control?" Bax didn't flinch as Russell reared back to retaliate for the dope slap. "You need to think before you swing on a man."

Russell sprawled himself on the smoker's bench, his ridiculous shoes pointed at Bax. "The Cossacks—"

"Shut up." Bax swiveled his head. "You stupider than I gave you credit for, you start name-checking the guys gonna peel your skin off."

"They reached out to me." Russell admired the rings on his left hand. *"They.* Reached out. To *me."*

"Why you think they did that, Russell? 'Cause you the brains of this operation?"

Russell puffed out his chest.

"Or 'cause you the likeliest to fuck up the deal the Bandidos already done for what both of 'em want?"

Russell's face blanked. His head tilted.

"Jesus, Russell." Bax rubbed his palms across his fade. "Go back to the shop. I got to think. You just—just—"

"Gimme your keys, then."

Bax shook his head. "Call you a Lyft. Or hoof it. Just sit in my office. Don't touch nothin'. Or do nothin'. Watch some *SportsCenter* or some shit like that."

"But—"

"Don't you do nothin' or say nothin' till I get there."

***

Venetta's one arched eyebrow told Bax about all he needed to know. He showed her his palms as he straddled his regular counter stool.

"You told me you was going straight after your bit."

"I am."

"Well, I know who that was you was talking to." Venetta raised her other brow. "And people going straight don't spend a lot of time with Mr. Reamer Kline."

"I'm—that was my kid brother. With us."

"The one you did the bit for."

Bax had told Venetta most of the truth about his stretch downstate. He hadn't done what he pleaded to, but he'd pleaded to it to keep his brother out of the system. "Russell fell in with a crew belonged to one of Mr. Kline's lieutenants while I was doing his time. And he—he ended up owing Mr. Kline some."

Venetta turned her back to him. She started wiping the little spring-loaded pitchers of syrup. "I'm still listening."

"Mr. Kline, he got to me the day I landed at the halfway house. Told me I could pay Russell's debt if I fix—if I fixed up one of his businesses."

"Why you work so hard for Russell?"

Bax hadn't told her any of the truth about that. Not really. Just that doing Russell's bit had been the right thing for both of them because he'd done some stuff he hadn't been caught for, that he should've gone away for. "Russell, you know, he came up without a dad. He ain't had nobody to show him how to be a man. And he's my only family now."

Venetta let him keep looking at her back.

"Since our mom passed."

"I don't want no Mr. Reamer Kline in my diner."

"I don't want that neither." Bax thought carefully about his next move. Moves. Thought that what he really needed was time to think about motorcycle gangs and what they wanted with the shipping container that filled a not-too-noticeable hole in the salvage yard he ran for Mr. Kline. "Can I finish my breakfast here?"

"I saved it for you." Venetta turned and slid his plate across the counter. "But it gone cold."

In the diner's parking lot, the cold half of his eggs riding heavy and low in his belly, Bax opened the Kia's tailgate and lifted the floor panel covering the spare tire. He pushed the sidewall of the tire until it gapped away from the wheel, reached inside the tire, and fished around until he grasped his most recent burner. Flipped it open and tapped at the tiny keypad: Hudson. U GOT any friends in DC.

Bax bundled the phone among his newspaper and other trash from his car and stuffed all of that in the stinking, oozing can at the bus stop.

The lady cop had pulled him over between the diner and the salvage yard. Berberian had never responded to a text so fast. The DC ask must have lit a fire under someone important. Bax thought about how he might leverage that as he triple-checked that he'd deactivated all the sounds and shakers on the burner the lady cop had dropped in his pocket.

He found Russell in his office BSing with the guy who knew how to take apart Audis. Bax told the Audi guy to get gone with a chin twitch, then kicked Russell's feet off his coffee table. "Thought I told you not to say nothin'."

"I weren't saying nothin'."

"Russell, you want to get out of this alive, you need to understand that don't say nothin' mean don't say *nothin'*. To *nobody*."

Russell turned this over in his mind for a few moments. "Even you, that means."

Bax felt the growl in his throat. "You know what, Russell? That's the best idea you've had in a long time." He played out the strategy a few moves, imagined all the ways Russell could fuck it up. "Here's your rule: unless you're answering a question I ask you, you don't say nothin' to nobody."

"Even Reamer?"

Bax shook his head. "That man's always Mr. Kline to you. And if he say something to you, the only options you got to reply are yes, sir and no, sir."

"What if—"

"Yes, sir or no, sir. Or answering my questions." Bax paused at the door to the bathroom. "You keep your mouth shut, maybe I can keep you breathing."

In the bathroom, Bax checked his burner.

Brooklyn. 1415 the park.

The park was Berberian's code for the commercial laundry where Bax took the salvage yard's floor mats.

Brooklyn, he tapped back to Berberian. OK.

Bax ordered Russell to collect anything going to the laundry and load it in the salvage yard's F-150. He went out to get chop suey for his crew and get rid of his most recent burner.

After lunch, Bax stuck Russell's phone and his desk phone in a metal locker behind a padlock, then locked Russell in his office and told the Audi guy to make sure no one went in or out.

"This is Parker," Berberian said. "FBI."

Parker was a tiny thing, wiry and coiled. She looked like a kid sitting at the IKEA table in the laundry's back room. She wore a wedding ring with a diamond that looked the size of a bottlecap.

"I'm Bax." Her handshake told him she punched above her weight. "Randall Baxter."

"Berberian tells me that you're his meal ticket," she said.

Bax didn't tell her that he couldn't care less whether it was Berberian's ticket he punched or hers. He knew only that if ratting on someone guaranteed that he'd never go back inside, he'd rat on anyone with a pulse. "I try to take very good care of Detective Berberian," Bax said.

"And why is that?" Parker said.

Bax felt her grip again, but more like it was around his neck. He glanced at Berberian.

"Bax is a man with a—" Berberian said.

"My brother—his name's Russell, and Russell's my only family—my brother made some mistakes when I was in prison," Bax said. "He screwed up a fentanyl deal for one of Reamer Kline's lieutenants. Cost Mr. Kline a lot of money. When I got out, Mr. Kline told me I could make up that money for him or watch his man Owsley kill my brother."

"So you're out to get Reamer Kline," Parker said.

"No, ma'am. I got no particular interest in Mr. Kline. But he's got a very particular interest in me. And I got no interest in going back to prison for whatever he's up to. But a lot of interest in keeping my brother alive."

Parker checked Berberian. "What's Reamer Kline's interest in you, Mr. Baxter?"

"Bax did a—"

"I did a bit for my brother. I stood up. Kept my own counsel. Mr. Kline, he likes people who know how to stay loyal. And I ain't had much school, but I'm pretty good at making sure things run smooth."

"You're just a good citizen."

"No, ma'am." Bax forced the gentle smile he'd perfected to soothe the warden's mind when it was troubled by uppity negroes. "But I didn't much enjoy my time in prison, and I planned to go straight after I got out. Mr. Kline, he gave me no chance to go straight. What I do for Detective Berberian, it's about the only thing I can do to bend the curve back."

"And you obviously know how this game is played."

"I'm always trying to learn." Bax maintained his smile. "Ma'am."

That seemed to chill her out a bit, and she was silent.

Berberian couldn't abide silence. He said to Bax, "Why'd you ask me to call in the feds?"

Bax locked eyes with Parker. "You're aware of a shipping container from FN Herstal that the police in Los Angeles didn't get?"

The silence flattened and got heavy. Parker rapped her knuckles on the table twice. "Excuse me." A third time. Then she left.

Berberian took her chair. "Bax, what the—I mean, chop shops and drugs, right, but—shit. How did Reamer Kline get hold of—I don't even know what FN Herstal is."

"It's Belgian. I can't pronounce it—it's French, like, Fabric National. They make guns for the Army, but also for cops."

"LAPD?"

"Crazy full-auto shit. Looks like the goddam Terminator. One a those half-sized containers packed high and tight—"

Parker returned. She leaned against the door she'd just closed, tapping her phone against her chin. "Can you describe the contents of this shipping container you claim to know something about?"

"That, and more." Bax had grown used to people taking his word since he started fixing for Mr. Kline, and he forced himself to swallow his frustration. "I can give you the numbers off the side of the container, plus who wants to buy it."

Parker's phone made a Charlie Brown teacher noise. She held the phone to her ear, then said, "Hang on." She tapped the screen and put the phone in the middle of the table. "Mr. Baxter, could you—"

"Bax, please, ma'am."

"Sure. Bax, could you tell us the numbers on the container?"

Bax recited the digits he'd memorized, and then described the shipping seal his Jaguar guy had cracked. "It's a twenty-foot container. I ain't taken everything out of it to know the complete inventory, and Mr. Kline, he ain't showed me the manifest. But the one crate I did take out had four rifles, and there's a hella lotta crates in that container."

"How did Reamer Kline come into possession of this container?"

"The driver traded it. To buy his daughter out of Mr. Kline's stable in Memphis."

A voice came out of the phone: "You know where it is?"

"And who's bidding on it."

Parker said, "Bidding?" at the same time her phone flashed a text message.

Bax pretended he hadn't seen the message—MAKE THE DEAL—and said, "But I need something."

Bax returned with the three dozen Krispy Kremes that Berberian brought to the meeting to cover for why he'd been gone so long. His crew tore through the doughnuts so fast that only one was left by the time he unlocked Russell from his office.

When Russell started to whine, Bax said, "I ain't ask you no question."

Russell stuffed the entire doughnut into his sneer.

Bax pushed him into his office. "I got to go back out again tonight."

"You ain't locking me up—"

"The hell I ain't. The only question is, you want it to be here, or you want me to put a man on you at your room."

"Man, what you got to—"

"To save your life, brother." Bax grabbed Russell's shoulder. "You and me, Russell, we all each other got since Mom passed."

"Since my dad got killed."

Bax chewed his lower lip. "He weren't no kind of man for you to follow."

Russell threw off Bax's hand and started building up to something furious.

"No." Bax pointed at the couch. "I'm full up to here listening to your bullshit about how great your daddy was. I'm sorry you only had our granny to show you how to be a man, because she didn't have it left in her to tan your hide the way she did mine." Bax continued pointing until Russell finally sat. "Once was all it took."

"And look where you ended up."

Bax enclosed his fury in the safe he'd learned to build in prison, the lockbox that earned him a little grudging respect from the guards and privileges in the library, the commissary. He slowly, quietly closed his office door and turned on his brother. "I did your bit so you could stay in school. I ended up finishing my diploma in prison. You couldn't even finish your diploma in my old school. And when you started running with Ducornet's crew instead, you fucked that up so bad that I ended up in a whole 'nother prison when I got outta the first one I went to for you."

"Hey, Bax, I—"

"You shut the fuck up, boy, and you listen to me. Where I ended up is putting my life on the line to make sure you ain't skinned alive by the most bloodthirsty savages since you pissed yourself when we watched that chainsaw movie."

Russell looked out the window.

"So if I tell you I got to go back out and you got to choose where Imma lock you up, the only thing you say to me is here, alone, or in your room, with a babysitter."

Russell dug at the carpet with his toe. "I got Xbox in my room."

***

"Yes, sir, Mr. Kline." *Another burner.* "Since Russell introduced competing interests, I think we should keep you as far away from this transaction as possible." *Another boss.* "Russell handed his party off to me, and if you'll hand your party off to me, I've got a solution that will satisfy both." *Another deal.* "But I'm moving the product to a third-party location to limit your exposure."

Bax's crew was used to overnight hours, and the chop suey followed by Krispy Kremes had left them feeling like they'd finished a Thanksgiving meal, maybe Friday leftovers, so the grumbling about breaking the container into two truckloads for staging across town was good-natured, and no one asked him why they had to rustle up the lumber to build as many empty crates as they had crates full of guns and then pack them with recycling scrap picked from the yard to match weight.

The warehouse wasn't exactly abandoned, but the ownership had transitioned into the nether regions of not quite Southland Beverage's and not quite Bank of America's. The liquor distributor had built its warehouse across the state line. A single building that could ship into either state and comply with each state's different regulations and taxes and laws about selling on Sundays. A single building with a concrete wall that sat atop the legal and geographic boundary between the big, mirrored loading bays facing northeast and southwest and overseen by a dispatch room that could look at both sides simultaneously even though neither side could see the other.

And later, at the pizza joint where he bought pitcher after pitcher of Captain Jack to cloud his crew's faculties and memories, when a thick-necked, tatted-up crewcut set a burner on the counter between the bathroom sinks in which they were washing and said, "Your code is Queens.,

Bax said, "Tell Parker I owe this to my brother."

***

Bax hadn't known how Reamer Kline would keep his finger on the deal's pulse.

He'd known Kline would take his advice to stay away from any potential dispute between the Bandidos and the Cossacks, because they were as likely to set one another on fire as they were to rape the other's women or blow up their clubhouses. He'd also known that Mr. Kline's distance came with conditions, with remote sensors, that could get complicated.

So it was a relief, and some luck, when Kline sent only Owsley. Owsley alone probably was the best he could've hoped for. Just one extra guy would make everything easier to manage, but Bax knew Owsley only as a type—powerful, mean, not too smart, but singularly focused and therefore clever about what he applied his singular focus to.

As he had when he put Russell out of commission for five weeks to persuade Bax to fix for Kline.

Since then, Bax made a point of having as little to do with Owsley as possible. Bax figured that probably ended up as a wash: as much as he didn't know Owsley, Owsley didn't know him.

"We gonna be up here," Bax told Owsley, pointing at the dispatch room on the diagram he'd drawn. "The glass ain't bulletproof, but we laid a bunch of sheet steel on the floor and against the walls, so if anyone starts shooting, just get down. There's a door to the outside, down a flight of stairs, and we already hid a car there. There'll be plenty of concrete between us and the warehouse, and I've got a couple of guys watching it tonight to make sure no one scouts us before the deal goes down."

"Clean getaway." Owsley nodded. "Your guys strapped?"

"My guys are labor, not muscle." Bax rotated the diagram. "I'll have one on each side to meet the buyers. The Bandidos come in from the northeast side, the Cossacks from the southwest. Once my guys get them in the warehouse, you and me, we'll take over from the dispatch office and my guys take off."

Owsley nodded. "You strapped?"

"I'll have a nine on my hip and a thirty-eight on my ankle. You?"

Owsley opened his jacket to show twin shoulder holsters. "I carry forty-fives here and a thirty-two in my crotch." He grunted. "They never frisk your package."

"Smart." Bax had learned there weren't many things a dumb guy liked more than to have someone tell him how smart he was.

"What about your idiot brother?"

"I don't let him carry."

"He just hurt himself."

Bax forced him himself to laugh along with Owsley. "You have no idea."

Bax had braced Russell twice—once before Russell went to sleep, once after he woke up—to make it sink in.

"You got one job," Bax told him the night before. "You stand behind me and look mean. The less you talk, the meaner you look."

In the morning, over coffee in the kitchen, missing his eggs with bacon and jelly with toast and Venetta with him, Bax said, "What's your one job?"

"Stand behind you and look mean."

"Good. And how you look mean?"

"By not saying nothin'."

"Very good. Now Imma tell you your second job."

"All right." Russell beamed. "What you—"

"Shut up." Bax opened the cabinet above the refrigerator and lifted out a big, round tin of Danish cookies that had gone stale and hard years before. He wiggled the lid off, lifted out the first layer of cookies, and removed a .38 pistol. "This a Ruger LCP." He pointed it at the wall, at a framed poster he'd bought at Big Lots, a black-and-white photo of a coastline he didn't know where. "When you squeeze the grip—" a red dot appeared on the poster, "—it's got a laser pointer. Now you do it." Bax handed the gun to Russell. "And don't point it at me."

Russell squeezed and released the laser pointer a few times. "This my second job?"

"If anything goes down, you point this at Owsley and pull the trigger before he starts doing the same to you."

"Wait—Owsley?"

"You keep pulling the trigger till ain't nothin' coming out of that gun."

"Owsley gonna be there?"

"Don't matter. Nothing gonna go down."

Russell started to fit the gun into his pocket.

"Gimme that back." Bax extended his palm.

"I thought—"

"Gotta load it." Bax took a magazine from the tin, slapped it in, and racked the slide. "You think Imma let you wave around a loaded gun in here?"

Bax had set up Berberian's most recent burner to text Queens go when he pushed just one button, but he had to wear a jacket loose enough to keep the flip phone both open and hidden. He felt like a damn fool in one of Russell's pimped-out hip-hop jackets.

When Owsley gave him a critical glare, Bax jerked his head at his brother. "It's his OG jacket." Rolled his eyes. "Told me he'd feel better if I wore it."

"That coat, all his shiny banger shoes—he must be joking."

"I don't even know where he gets those shoes. But I'm his only family."

Owsley nodded, then shook his head.

"I hear you." Bax extended his fist for a bump and was gratified when Owsley did the same.

"I got the boys from Tyler," the Audi guy said through the radio. "Two blue box trucks and a white Escalade."

"Tyler is in the house," Bax replied. "Any sign of San Leon?"

"I think they missed the turn and gotta come back around." The Jaguar guy, his only other labor outside, was on the northeast approach. "Two Ryder trucks just went by on the—yeah, here they are. Two yellow moving vans and a—ah, shit, they got like a minivan." Laughter on the open channel. "A black Chrysler."

"Good. Don't make fun of their minivan, right? Get them backed up to the docks. Tyler at four and five, San Leon at fourteen and fifteen."

In the dispatch office, Bax couldn't hear anything outside, but he felt the bumps as the trucks hit the loading docks. "Tyler good?" Bax said into his radio.

"One truck at four," Audi said, "and one truck at five."

"San Leon good?"

"Fourteen and fifteen," Jaguar said.

Bax pushed the buttons that opened those doors. The Bandidos' and Cossacks' rented trucks were lower and smaller than the big rigs the docks had been built for, and sunlight mixed with the overhead fluorescents. A breeze swirled crispy leaves through the Cossacks' bay.

Bax told Audi and Jaguar to let the dealmakers through the staff doors on each side. "Then you guys head back to the shop. Clock in Russell when you get there, and then make sure that container we emptied out is completely shredded."

Moments later, the Bandidos' and Cossacks' leaders entered their respective loading bays. Audi and Jaguar pointed their buyers at Bax perched in the dispatch office. They could see him, but neither could see over or through the concrete wall on top of the state line.

Bax hit the speaker switch for the loading bays. "I'm Bax. We talked last night. Up here are my associates, Owsley and Russell."

Cossacks and Bandidos began drifting out of the box trucks. They carried shotguns and rifles. A couple waved wicked-looking machine pistols. Half established a perimeter, half trained their weapons on the dispatch office.

"This look like the deal we talked about?" Bax said through the speaker.

The Cossack flashed two thumbs up. The Bandido said, "You hear me?"

Bax thought about his response, how he could respond without betraying that he was talking to two people instead of just one. "I can hear you when you talk."

The Cossack said, "This looks like what you said," and the Bandido said, "Looks like what we agreed to."

"Like I told you when we talked, you can grab any crate to check the contents are what you expect." Which would work as long as neither gang moved more than three stacks of crates and found the scrap filler.

Two men on each side slung long guns over their shoulders and approached the stacked crates. The Cossacks grabbed the closest crate on top. The Bandidos moved one stack of crates, then another.

"When you've confirmed the contents," Bax said, "then you'll show me your side of the deal."

He waited to see if the Bandidos would dig deep enough to get to a filler crate. He grasped the hidden flip phone, positioning his finger on the SEND button.

The Cossacks opened their crate before the Bandidos chose a crate from the third stack.

Bax waited until both crates were open. While the guys pulled out sleek, ray gun-looking rifles, horsed around with them, put them back.

"I showed you mine," Bax said. "You show me yours."

The Cossack whistled. The Bandido spun his finger in the air. Cossacks hauling rainbow-striped rectangular nylon duffels emerged from their truck. Bandidos dragging black rollaboard suitcases strolled in from theirs. Both opened their luggage to show bundled stacks of cash.

Bax pushed SEND in the same motion as he raised binoculars to look at the Cossacks—

"What the fuck you looking at over there?" a Bandido shouted.

That's when the windows shattered, when Bax yelled "Get down," when his ears popped and his eyes dazzled from flashbang grenades, when he heard men yelling over gunfire, "US Marshals—drop your weapons," when men started shrieking, when Owsley started for his shoulder holsters, when Russell painted a red dot on Owsley's midsection, when Bax bellowed, "Russell, what did you do?" when bullets clanked and plinked on the sheet metal, when a spurt of blood stained Owsley's shirt and Owsley fell to one side and drew his other pistol.

"Russell," Bax shouted what he'd rehearsed, springing at his brother, pushing him through the door to outside, drawing his pistol, "you traitorous piece of shit!"

Bax fired three, four, five shots over Russell's head and kicked the door shut behind him.

Russell was half over the railing when Parker grabbed his belt and hauled him back onto the landing.

Bax grabbed his brother's head, shook it. "Russell, listen to me." Got his brother's eyes. "This is Parker. She's going to get you out of here." They flinched as bullets pierced the transom behind them. "You're getting a new life somewhere else."

Russell's eyes got big, then rolled a bit as he pissed himself.

"Are you kidding me?" Parker muttered.

"Go," Bax said. "I'll tell you this now because I got to go in for Owsley and I won't see you again. Ever." He planted a kiss on Russell's forehead. "I'm sorry, brother," he whispered. "For everything."

***

Bax crouched low outside the door. "Owsley," he shouted. "You hear me? Imma open the door."

No response.

Bax cracked the door. The crescendo of explosions and gunfire shocked him, knocked him back. The smell of gunpowder and smoke covered the smell of Russell's piss. The plinks on the sheet metal had stopped as Bandidos and Cossacks concentrated their fire on the feds. He peeked in, saw Owsley on his side, leaking blood, one pistol trained on Bax.

Bax ducked. "Owsley—can you move?" Owsley didn't fire. "I got the car. I can get us out of here."

Owsley rasped, "That idiot brother of yours shot me."

Bax didn't tell Owsley that he'd loaded only a single round in the Ruger he'd given to Russell, figuring close range and a laser pointer would get Russell in the general vicinity of Owsley's bulk without being fatal.

"He set up Mr. Kline," Bax told Owsley. "That must be what his whole thing with the other gang was about." Bax crawled through the door. Owsley's gun arm had dropped. "He set us up and I killed him for it, but now I gotta get you out of here."

"I don't—" Owsley yelped. "I can't make the stairs."

"I'll carry you."

Owsley spit up some blood when he laughed. "You're as big an idiot as your brother if you think you can carry me." Then he passed out.

Bax turned down the volume on the TV news coverage of the gang-war gun battle when Mr. Kline came out of the bedroom and closed the door. Behind it, Owsley lay in a queen-sized bed that he made look like a twin, breathing raggedly after the horse-farm vet pulled out the .38 slug and sewed up a couple of holes in one of his lungs.

Bax had held Owsley's hand through the surgery. His joints ached from the crushing grip.

"Owsley says you saved his life," Mr. Kline said.

Bax moved the morning's newspaper off the couch so Mr. Kline could sit. "He's heavier than he looks."

Mr. Kline chuckled, then grew solemn. "He also told me that you made sure your brother won't be assisting the feds he sold us out to."

"I'm real sorry about him, Mr. Kline." Bax let the real emotion of never again seeing Russell show on his face. Leak from his eyes. "After all you done for him—"

Mr. Kline patted Bax's knee twice. "It's not lost on me that you did a lot for your brother, too."

Bax wiped his eyes. It wasn't beyond the realm of possibility that Mr. Kline knew what he'd gotten away with, what he'd stood up and done Russell's time for. But he knew better than to acknowledge it, than to give Mr. Kline even more power over him.

"However, I must be absolutely confident we're covered on that flank. I can blame Russell to the Cossacks, but my assurances to the Bandidos have been met with some…skepticism."

"Yes, sir. When Russell shot Owsley, I put four in his chest and he went over the railing onto the ground. After I got Owsley out, I put another in his head and put his body in the trunk. I can show you a picture on my phone." Parker's people had made Russell look like a chainsaw victim in the movie that had scared the piss out of him.

"Not for me, Bax. But the Bandidos might ask."

Bax put back the phone he'd started pulling from his pocket. "I drove Owsley here, to your ranch to see the doc, and then drove the car with Russell's body out to that quarry in Jefferson County. Wrapped the body with canvas and chain, like we do, and sank it separate from the car."

"Like we do."

"Yes, sir."

"I'm out both the guns and money I expected to get for the guns."

"Yes, sir, I understand that I'm still in your debt." Bax waited for Mr. Kline to acknowledge showing his belly and got a small nod. "I did hold out one crate of those guns for you."

Mr. Kline's mouth twitched to the right.

"The feds are telling the news that it was between the Bandidos and the Cossacks."

"I believe we shall find that sinking that driver in the quarry will pay greater dividends than I originally anticipated."

Bax flinched inside. Maybe Berberian could find out whether the driver's daughter was off the streets in Memphis. "The feds say the Bandidos stole the guns, and the Cossacks ambushed them while they were breaking down the container for distribution."

"Certainly, that's not the story your brother fed them."

"I figure that's their cover for flipping Russell, because they ain't know I killed him." Bax shrugged. "But the closest they can get to you from him is me. And I know how to keep my counsel."

Venetta didn't take much care when she tossed his plate of eggs with bacon and jelly with toast on the counter.

Bax folded the paper he'd brought with him from the horse farm. "I missed you yesterday," he said.

She leaned over the counter, one hand planted deliberately over the front-page photo of the still-smoking, bullet-riddled warehouse. "I 'spect you musta been pretty busy yesterday."

"I finally got it through my brother's head that he needs a fresh start somewhere else."

"Mm-hmm."

"Spent the day packing his things, and then put him on a bus to Houston. He got a cousin there who can help him get established."

"You said you's his only family."

Bax chewed on a slice of bacon. "I think I said he's my only family."

Venetta looked like she might raise an eyebrow, but she didn't. "Now that he gone, you gonna tell me the rest of that story?"

"You gonna let me take you to the supper club on Saturday night?" Bax finished his eggs, appreciating they were still hot.

"I have never met Napoleon, but that ain't our deal."

Bax nodded. "My mom—she was Russell's mom, too, you know—when I came along, she was a working girl. After I arrived, she got on a different track. Started waiting tables in a diner."

"Really."

"This diner." Bax smeared strawberry jelly across his sourdough toast. "I bussed tables here, for tips, after school, when I was eight, nine years old."

Venetta perched on a stool behind the counter and took her hand off the newspaper.

"But Russell's dad, when she took up with him, he wanted her earning more. After Russell come along, he hooked her on dope so he could turn her out."

"Gonna put his baby momma on the street."

Bax wiped his mouth. "So I killed him."

Venetta cleared his plate and ran a towel over the counter. "You did Russell's bit for what you done that you ain't got caught for."

Bax took a twenty from his wallet and laid it on the counter. "I don't need no change."

Venetta extended his paper. She didn't let go of it when he tried to take it.

Bax looked at Venetta's hand. Its firm grasp on the news.

"Not Saturday night," Venetta said. "But you can take my daughter and me out for lunch after Sunday services."

GREEN EARRINGS
Bill Fitzhugh

Eddie Katz and Bumps McPherson were sitting in a booth in the back, nursing their coffee. Not exactly a meeting of peers, what with Bumps having decades more experience and the reputation to match, which wasn't to say Bumps looked down on Eddie. He didn't. Bumps was an old pro, but Eddie had done some impressive work in his limited time, and Bumps gave him that. The way Bumps saw it, he and Eddie were more-or-less in the same game, the reputational difference was due simply to their choice of specialty. Bumps suspected that was why he was here.

"I appreciate you meeting on such short notice," Eddie said.

Bumps shrugged his thick shoulders like it was nothing. "I don't mind. It's not like I work during the day or anything. What's up?"

"Baubles," Eddie said with a twinkle. "Baubles are what's up." Eddie slipped a piece of paper from his jacket, unfolded it, smoothing it on the tabletop. He slid it over to Bumps and tapped it smack in the middle, an item torn from the local paper with a couple of photos.

On the left was an old publicity shot of Tootie Washington, a young beauty from Tarrytown, New York, who took a train west in 1935 and became a brief but bright flame during

Hollywood's glory days. She made a few dozen films under contract with MGM in the '40s. Being a famous beauty, she'd married well, and more than once. Sharp as a tack, Tootie made some good investments, real estate mostly, and by the time her career ended she was filthy rich.

"Oh, man, talk about a blast from the past," Bumps said.

"You've heard of her?"

"Are you kidding? She was something else. A real dame."

"I never heard of her," Eddie said with a shrug. "But here's the thing—"

"Wait." Bumps held up his hand. "You've never seen *Sorry, Angel*?"

Eddie shook his head. "Guess I missed it."

"You should track it down, it's a classic," Bumps said. "Caper-gone-wrong picture. Mobster sets her up to take the fall for a heist he's planned but she turns the tables. Great stuff. And she got Best Supporting for *The Look in Your Eyes*." He gazed off to the distance. "Or maybe just nominated, I forget."

"Doesn't ring a bell."

"Before your time I guess," Bumps said. "Anyway...." Bumps put on his glasses and leaned in for a closer look at the other picture. "So what do we have here?"

"Like I said, baubles." The twinkle returned to Eddie's eyes. "Turns out this Tootie Washington had a thing for jewelry and the money to indulge it," Eddie said. "Burmese rubies, a lot of diamonds, and the infamous Green Earrings of Altamira, two eleven-carat emeralds set in a rare design of jade from the Motagua Valley."

Bumps poked his lower lip out in appreciation. Pointing at the picture he squinted and said, "What's that?"

"A Greek medallion," Eddie said. "Second century, banded agate in twenty-four-karat gold."

"Very nice. The dame had taste." Bumps pushed the article back across the table. "Why you telling me? Looks like it's right up your alley, assuming Old Tootie lives in the Hudson Valley these days."

"Well that's just it, see? She doesn't. She died about ten years ago in Beverly Hills. But because she came from around here, The Hudson River Museum's doing a retrospective of her career, showing a couple of her movies, and putting this collection on display." Eddie coughed into his napkin before continuing. "You know me, Bumps, I'm a second story man. I need your expertise on this one. Museum security ain't exactly in my wheelhouse."

"I appreciate your thinking of me, Eddie, but I just boosted some rare manuscripts from the Harbor Gallery up in Boston. I'm planning to lay low for a while."

"This is a pretty big haul, Bumps, you wanna maybe think it over?"

"Nah, I'm feeling itchy about it, you know, like they're watching me."

Disappointed, Eddie nodded his understanding. "I get it. Not going to do either one of us any good if that's the case." He coughed into his napkin again. "But look, Bumps, here's the deal…I got, uh, I got a situation."

"What sort?"

"The sort where I'm dying."

"What?"

"Cancer."

"Oh, man, that's tough," Bumps said, leaning back in his seat just in case it might be contagious. "I'm sorry to hear it."

"Yeah, thanks. And the bastards just tripled the price of this medicine I take. So I really need this score. You know, sort of a life and death thing."

"Damn, Eddie, I hear ya. And I wish could help you out, I really do," Bumps said. "But the timing's just bad. Like you said, if they're watching me, last thing you need is to get caught in that net."

"Yeah, no, I get what you're saying. Just bad luck, I guess."

"Except maybe...here's an idea. What if you just go for the jewels? Smash and grab. If you get away with it, you're golden, right? If you get caught, they'll probably send you up to the Regional Medical Unit at Fishkill. Get your treatment on the state's dime."

Eddie waved it off. "Thanks, but I think I'd rather be cashed out altogether."

"Don't blame you," Bumps said. "It was just a thought."

They sat there for a while, Eddie coughing into his napkin now and then until he folded up the newspaper clipping and tucked it in his pocket. "Listen, Bumps, thanks again for meeting with me. If you think of anybody who might be interested, somebody you trust, let me know. I'd appreciate it." Eddie slapped a five on the table and left.

A couple of days later, Eddie was back in the same booth, this time with his pal Freddy Johnson who everybody called Peanut owing to the fact that the shape of his head made you think the doctor had used the forceps wrong during delivery. The two had met while doing a stint at Otisville Correctional, Eddie for burglary, Peanut for aggravated battery after he got drunk and stabbed a guy during a fight over a hamburger.

Eddie and Peanut were violating their parole by virtue of their proximity, but neither of them really worried about that sort of thing. They knew there weren't enough hours in the day, let alone a good motivation for an underpaid parole officer to go snooping around trying to catch one of their files in a violation. So Eddie and Peanut were having a late breakfast, brainstorming potential scams and whatnot.

Peanut was thumbing through the sports section, grunting every now and then about what he considered bad draft picks and stupid trades. Eddie was checking the local news in the *Hudson Valley Post*. The feature story, detailing an erosion problem in a local township, failed to seize Eddie's attention.

Below the fold, however, was a headline that gave him pause. After taking it in he whispered slowly, "That son of a bitch." The way he said it almost came across as admiring.

Peanut folded a quarter of the sports page down to look at Eddie. "Can you narrow that down some?"

Eddie stabbed a finger at the headline: *Hudson River Museum heist: Cold and daring! Gem Collection Stolen During Film Screening.*

Peanut glanced at the article. "Wow. Two-point three mil? That's a nice take."

"No shit! That's why I was eyeing it."

"You? I thought you were strictly residential. What was your plan for the security system?"

Eddie told Peanut about his meeting with Bumps, ending with a complaint about how you can't trust anybody these days.

Peanut got a big laugh out that. "What makes you think it was this Bumps character?"

"Who else could it be?" Eddie slapped the tabletop. "That rat bastard. Hell, I even told him I was dying and needed the score!"

"You're dying?"

"No! But he didn't know that."

"I see what you mean about you can't trust anybody."

"'I think I need to lay low for a while,' he said. 'I'm feeling a little itchy that they're watching me.'" Eddie shook his head sadly. "Son of a bitch played me like a cheap ukulele."

"That's one way to look at it," Peanut said. "But think about it this way. Let's say you're right, say this Bumps did it. So what? That's what you wanted him to do, right? He got past the security and got the goods. That's exactly what you asked him to do. But he wouldn't have known about it without you. Now you've both done your part, so all you have to do is go get your cut. Just confront him, man to man. Fair's fair, after all."

"The man wasn't willing to help a dying friend, what makes you think he's going to do right and cut me in after the fact?"

"Well, first of all, you're not dying."

"Yeah, but he doesn't know that! I think that's the thing to keep in mind."

"Fine, so why not just go steal it back? Just do your thing, cat your way in, grab your cut, and cat your way back out."

"Yeah, one problem with that," Eddie said. "Bumps told me one time that he keeps everything in one of those biometric gun safes."

"Bio what?"

"A biometric safe. Like your phone, you know? Your fingerprint is the key to get it open."

"Eww," Peanut said. "That does add a layer, don't it?" They sat silently for a moment before Peanut continued, "Okay, so you have to force him to open it, which means a threat of violence. But it can't be you since I assume he wouldn't let that slide. And you'd spend all your days looking over your shoulder."

"You got that right. He can be a moody bastard."

"Okay, so *I'll* do it," Peanut said. "He doesn't know me from Adam, right? And I've got a sawed-off 4-10 a man can't say 'no' to when he sees it up close."

Eddie mulled that for a second. "What kind of split you have in mind?"

They stole a van that night. Eddie drove over to where Bumps lived, parked a few houses down. The lights were on and, as far as they could tell, Bumps was home alone. Peanut had his shotgun and a black ski mask in his lap. They were sitting there with the windows down, a couple of sirens wailing in the distance, when Peanut said, "What if he won't answer the door?"

Eddie hadn't even thought of that. As he tried to come up with an answer he noticed the sirens. He cocked his head to listen. "Are those gettin' closer?"

"Sure sounds like it."

A second later the first flashing lights rounded the corner behind them. A fire truck going full tilt.

Eddie stuck his nose out the window and sniffed. "You smell smoke? I don't smell any smoke." He looked around for flames but saw nothing.

More lights coming from behind, this time an ambulance.

The fire truck blew past them before stopping at a forty-five-degree angle, blocking the street half a block down. The ambulance stopped in front of Bumps' house and a pair of EMTs jumped out, grabbed their gear, and ran to the door.

All Eddie could muster was, "What the fuck?"

There was nothing else to do so Eddie and Peanut just sat there as the first EMTs disappeared into the house. A second later, a black-and-white arrived as the remaining EMTs dropped wheels on a gurney and rolled it inside.

"You gotta be kidding me, I mean this is fucked up." Eddie pointed toward the house. "Go down there and see what's going on."

Peanut left the sawed-off and the ski mask and made his way up to where the fire department guys were talking to the cop. "Hey, fellas, I'm a neighbor, live over there." He pointed vaguely behind him. "What's going on? Is Bumps okay?"

"Don't know," one of the firemen said. "No word yet."

The fireman turned when he heard the gurney's wheels clattering over the threshold. "Oh, here we go."

It was a man with oxygen strapped to his face, but Peanut could tell whoever it was, he wasn't breathing. No one was doing CPR, and they weren't moving with any urgency as they loaded him into the back of the ambulance.

Peanut talked to the EMTs for a minute before heading back to the delivery van to tell Eddie, "I don't know what the man looks like, could you see if it was him?"

Eddie nodded. "That was Bumps all right. What'd they say?"

"Heart attack."
"That's it?"
"That and condolences."
"Oh, you gotta be kidding! He's dead? Did you ask where they were taking him?"
"Why would I ask that?"
"Because...." Eddie slowly shook his head. "Just get in."

They followed the ambulance to Mid-Valley Regional Hospital and waited in the parking lot. They figured there would be some paperwork and who-knows-what-else before they put Bumps in the fridge.

"You don't think they'd do like an autopsy or something?"

"Eleven-thirty at night, on some fat bastard had a heart attack? Seems unlikely," Eddie said. "But what do I know? Let's just give 'em a few minutes."

In the meanwhile, they went in to get a lay of the land, see where the exits were in case they needed to beat a hasty retreat. While they were poking around, they decided to grab some surgical scrubs so they'd blend in better. The supply room they found was locked, but the hospital laundry was open.

Eddie watched the door while Peanut foraged through one of the laundry carts. "Eddie, what're you? Like, a medium?" He held up a blood-stained top.

Eddie shook his head. "We gotta put those on top of what we're wearing. Get me a large."

"Good thinking." Peanut found a large one and tossed it to Eddie.

"Ewww!" It was moist. Eddie looked at it, holding it at arm's length. "Oh, Jesus, what *is* that?" He threw it back at Peanut then wiped his hands on his pants. "For chrissakes, get me something that doesn't have part of somebody's liver on it!"

Peanut found another top, the stains all dried on this one. He sniffed it, figured it was okay, and held it out it to Eddie.

A few minutes later they were following the morgue signs to the basement. It was near the end of a hall. They stopped outside the swinging doors. The lights were off so they eased in and flipped the switch, triggering a couple of buzzy fluorescent tubes.

Peanut sized it up. "It's smaller than I expected." A porcelain autopsy table stood in the middle of the room with an articulated dome lamp hovering overhead, a sink and some cabinets off to one side, and six stainless steel morgue drawers off to the other.

Peanut found Bumps in the second drawer he tried. "Bingo!" He looked at Eddie. "Now what?"

Eddie lifted the sheet about midway down and took Bumps' right hand. He looked at it for the longest time before he said, "Damn."

"What's the matter?"

"I don't know what finger he used for the thing."

"Well, was he right-handed or left?"

"Pretty sure he was right-handed," Eddie said. "Most people are, but who knows if he used his index finger or thumb or what?"

"That's a good point." They stared at the hand for a minute before Peanut said, "I guess we just take them all, huh?"

"I guess we have to."

Peanut went to the other side of the room and rifled through the cabinet of autopsy tools until he found a pair of rib cutters that looked good for lopping off fingers. "Here, try these." He handed them to Eddie who opened the blades and put them at the base of Bumps' thumb. He hesitated longer than seemed necessary.

"What're you waitin' on?"

Eddie looked around the room. "Get me a trash can or something, to catch the blood."

"Oh, good idea," Peanut said. He came back with a wastebasket and a plastic bag for the fingers. "Okay, go for it."

Eddie hesitated again, pulling the rib cutters away from the thumb.

"Now what?"

"Well, I'm just thinking," Eddie said. "What if it's a whole-hand sort of thing, not just a fingerprint reader? You know, palm and all?" Eddie held his hand out, fingers spread wide. "Like they have in those Bourne movies and shit."

"Hadn't thought of that," Peanut said. "I suppose it's possible. What do you think?"

"I think we better just take the whole hand," Eddie said. "That works either way, right?"

Peanut tapped a finger to his temple. "That's good thinking," he said. "As a matter of fact, now that you mention it, we might as well take *both* hands, just in case, right? We don't want to have to come back if it turns out he used his left ring finger or some weird shit like that."

"Yeah, we definitely don't want to have to come back." He handed the rib cutters back to Peanut. "These won't do for taking the hands. See what else you can find."

Peanut went back to the cabinets and selected a large bone saw. "This ought to do it," he said. "You want to saw or hold him still?"

"Don't matter to me," Eddie said with a shrug. "I'll do it." He used his foot to position the trash can underneath. "Grab him at the knuckles, will you? I guess I'll just cut through the wrist, unless you got a better idea."

"No, that seems like the best place," Peanut said.

As he started to saw, both men got a little squeamish and Peanut looked away. It took more effort than either of them expected and Peanut lost his hold on the knuckles a couple of times. There wasn't much blood but what there was was thick and slippery. And the harder Eddie sawed, the more Peanut leaned away from what was going on.

When the blade finally cut through the last tendon, the release of tension sent Peanut stumbling sideways into the wall.

He lost his grip on Bumps' hand, launching it across the room where it landed with a slap, palm down on top of the dome lamp. It looked like a wounded starfish.

"Jesus, Peanut!"

"Relax, I'll get it." Before he could take a step, Eddie saw a shadow at the threshold of the doors.

Eddie jabbed Peanut with an elbow. "Somebody's coming!"

One of the doors opened. A custodian, about thirty, stood in the doorway, surprised. "Oh, hey, I didn't think anybody was here," he said. "I was going to turn out the light."

Eddie kept the bone saw out of sight. "No, we need it," he said. "But thanks. We'll get it on our way out."

Peanut glanced at the dome light and saw Bumps' hand starting to slide slowly down the slope. He nudged Eddie but Eddie was more concerned about the wary look on the custodian's face, the one that said he knew all the doctors on the night shift and didn't recognize these two.

The custodian tapped the photo ID on his shirt. "You two have your ID badges?"

"Uhh, 'fraid not," Eddie said. "See, they brought us in on short notice. No time for IDs and whatnot."

The custodian didn't seem to be buying it. He stepped closer and said, "Who *are* you?"

Eddie glanced nervously at Peanut then back at the custodian. "I'm, uh, Dr. House and this is, uh...." He snapped his fingers a couple of times. "Dr. Quinn." After a nervous smile he added, "We just met."

Peanut smiled and nodded agreement.

The names seemed to register with the custodian, like he'd heard them before but couldn't place when or where. "Okay, so what's going on?"

"That's a fair question," Eddie said. "But this is strictly a need-to-know situation, so..."

"It's a federal matter," Peanut added.

Eddie shot Peanut a look. "We've said too much already."

GREEN EARRINGS

The custodian gestured at their hands. "Shouldn't you be wearing gloves?"

They looked at their hands then back to the custodian. "Damn right we should," Eddie said. "And normally we would, but, again, they ordered us to do this ASAP, so the mucky-mucks upstairs don't start firing anybody who slowed down the process, if you get my drift."

Peanut tried not to stare and give it away but Bumps' hand was slipping further down the dome light like a man on sloped ice who couldn't get a grip. At its current rate it was going to drop onto the autopsy table any second.

The custodian really didn't want to start looking for a new job, so he started looking for an excuse to get out of there. He said, "Did you say this was a federal matter?"

"Oh yeah, national security situation," Peanut said.

Eddie looked at his partner in disbelief but realized he had no choice but to jump on the bandwagon. So he glanced around the room before he whispered, "Terrorism." He hoisted Bumps' stump for the custodian to see. "This is strictly off-the-record. We're forensics specialists with the...uh...FBI...."

"CIA," Peanut said simultaneously.

After another glance at Peanut, Eddie said, "Like I said, we just met, and they, and by 'they' I mean the FBI *and* the CIA, they uh, sent us down to see if we could determine how this man lost his hand." He wiggled the stump a bit for effect.

"We think it was ISIS," Peanut said. "His head was probably next."

"Whoa," the custodian said, taking a step backwards.

"Whoa is right," Eddie said. "Anyway, the sooner we get to the bottom of this, the better, so if you don't mind...."

The custodian held his hands up. "Oh yeah, those ISIS motherfuckers are crazy," he said. "Good luck!" He turned and left.

Peanut ran over and caught Bumps' hand as it slipped off the light. He dropped it into the plastic bag.

"Let's get this other one and scoot in case that guy checks with security," Eddie said.

Peanut picked up the trash can to move it to the other side. He paused, looking into the container. "Not nearly as much blood as I thought there'd be."

"Yeah, right? Weird," Eddie said. "Grab the knuckles."

They got the other hand off in a hurry, put Bumps back in the fridge, then slipped out a side door.

The cops had locked things up at Bumps' house so Eddie was picking the back door. Peanut stood watch, holding the sack of hands.

They found the safe in a guest room closet.

"Wow," Peanut said.

"You're not kidding, look at the size of that thing."

It was a big sucker, five feet tall, twenty-five bolts, a five-spoke chrome handle, and a state-of-the-art biometric entry system.

Eddie studied it for a second, then pointed at the large square screen. "Good thing we took the hands, 'cause that is definitely a palm scanner." He scratched the back of his head and said, "I say we start with the right hand."

"Sounds good." Peanut pulled Bumps' right hand from the sack and looked at it. "Think I should wipe the blood off?"

"Are you kidding me?"

"What?" Peanut was taken aback. "It's all over the palm. It might screw up the scan if it's covered in blood."

"Not that," Eddie said. "This." He pointed at a small oval lens above the palm scanner.

"What is it?"

"It's a problem is what it is. It's for iris recognition or retina scan, I don't know which, but we can't get in the safe with just the hands."

They stared at each other for a moment.

GREEN EARRINGS

"Oh, man, you mean...."
"You got a better idea?"

Eddie and Peanut had stared at Bumps' head for the longest time before Eddie said, "I guess I'd rather just take the eyes."

"Me too," Peanut said as he poked at one of them. "Got any idea how you pop one of these out a socket?"

"Hell, anybody can get one out of the socket," Eddie said. "The trick's going to be getting them out without damaging them. They need to be in good shape for the scanner to recognize."

"Maybe use a spoon or something like that?"

Eddie looked at the cabinet across the room. "You see anything over there that looked like an eyeball spoon?"

"Not really, no."

Eddie yawned and checked his watch. "I say we just take the whole head. That way the eyes won't get screwed up."

Which is how they got to the point of decapitating Bumps.

Peanut had his hands on either side of Bumps' head as Eddie worked the bone saw back and forth through the neck. After a minute, Peanut said, "Eddie, I think I'm going to puke."

"Jesus, Peanut, you better not! I can't stand that smell! If you puke, then I'll puke and that'll make you puke more and...just don't breathe through your nose."

"Look, Eddie, hands are one thing but I didn't sign up for this."

Eddie stopped sawing and let out a long-exasperated breath. "If you'll recall, this wasn't the original plan. And I don't like it any more than you do, but I *do* like the idea of getting my hands on the jewels inside that safe and this is the only way I can think of to get 'em, so unless you have a better idea...buck up!" He continued sawing.

Peanut was going green around the gills. "Ohhhh," he moaned as Eddie started in on the spine. "I can't take much more of this."

"Close your eyes. We're almost done."

A few more strokes and Bumps' head came right off.

"Thank God," Peanut said. He tucked the head in the crook of his arm like a football. "Let's get out of here." He got to the door and stopped. He looked at Eddie. "What're you waiting for?"

"What is wrong with you?"

"What do you mean? C'mon, let's go."

Eddie stared at him. "You can't just stroll out of here with a human head tucked under your arm like it's a fucking cantaloupe."

Peanut looked at the head, then at Eddie. "Oh, jeez, you're right, sorry. I don't know what I was thinking."

"I get it. It's late, we're both a little punchy." Eddie gestured for Peanut to follow him. He walked to the counter by the sinks. "Let's see if it fits in here."

"That's not big enough, is it?"

"Let's try it." Eddie popped the lid off a big red sharps container and held it while Peanut tried to push the head inside.

"See? It doesn't fit."

"Turn it around, try it neck first," Eddie said, and it slipped right in. "There we go." He gave Peanut a fraternal chuck to the arm. "Now let's get out of here."

"Hold it still," Eddie said. "I can't get the eyelid to stay open."

"It's slippery!" Peanut had his hands on either side of Bumps' head as he lined it up with the biometric lens. "Maybe we could use a safety pin to hold it open."

"Just hang on, we're almost there."

"Well hurry up, this thing's heavier than it looks. It's like holding a greasy bowling ball. Oh shit." Peanut lost his grip and dropped the thing. "Whoa!"

"Jesus, Peanut!"

"I told you, it's slippery. You wanna try holding it?"

"No, you're doing fine."

Peanut picked up the head and aimed the eye toward the lens again.

"That's perfect, right there. Just hold it…hold it.…"

The red light above the lens came on. Something clicked and Eddie said, "Yes!"

Peanut set the head on the floor, watching as Eddie spun the five-spoke handle counterclockwise until the twenty-five bolts retreated. Then he swung the heavy door open.

"Woo hoo!" Peanut kicked the head out of the way. "Let's see those earrings!"

The two men peered into the safe.

"What the hell is that?"

They leaned in for a closer look.

"It damn sure ain't jewelry."

It was, in fact, a large, erect, anatomically-exaggerated cock, a strap-on dildo known as the SD III by Yokahama.

Leaning against the base of the thing was a small envelope graced with the words "To whom it may concern" written in neat cursive.

Eddie removed the card inside. He read it aloud, "Whoever you are, you don't get whatever you came for. But here's your consolation prize. Take it and go fuck yourself! Love, Bumps."

JOSIE
Stacy Robinson

I sat in my father's '67 Riviera, pressing my frozen hands to the vent in a vain attempt to warm them. December 24th, 1977 had dawned icy and cold, the sun hidden behind a heavy blanket of gray. My sister's bus wasn't due for another ten minutes, but my mother had insisted I get there early to pick her up.

It was always about Josie.

Always.

My extremities were in danger of frostbite by the time the bus from Syracuse pulled in. I slowly climbed from the Buick, shaking one leg, then the other, to get the blood flowing as the travelers disembarked. When she finally appeared, one of the last to get off the blasted bus, my heart leapt at the sight of her. It was certainly a blessing that I had been the one sent to get her—the sight of his oldest daughter in leopard-print leggings, sky-high, blood-red heels, and a faux-fur jacket twice her size would've likely sent my father to the hospital. My mother would've died on the spot.

Josie smiled wide with lips that matched her shoes, the tortoise-shell Foster Grants she pulled from her eyes revealing gold and bronze lids ringed in heavy black. Throwing her head back, she laughed as she skipped across the pavement, flinging her arms wide and wrapping them around me in a hug that I didn't want but couldn't live without.

"Oh thank *GOD*, Pattie. I never had a chance to change and thought I was *doomed*." Her crimson mouth left its mark against my cheek with a violent smack. "Take me somewhere I can get into some different clothes, won't you, Baby?"

I cringed at the nickname but nodded.

"Can't believe Daddy still has this old wreck. Surely he can find something better *some*where." She pulled a compact from her purse and flipped it open as I started the car and pulled out of the lot onto Roosevelt. "I'm gonna need a bathroom. Momma and Daddy can *not* see this. But *Christ*, what a night!"

I made a face. Josie noticed.

"Still swallowing their bullshit, Baby?" my sister said. "It's all a bunch of lies, told by aging, desperate white men. Just like everything else."

"Where should we go? A lot of places are closed today."

"Take me to Donovan's. On Fifty-seventh."

"That's ten minutes in the wrong direction. And I'm not eighteen yet, Josie. They won't let me in."

"Won't be a problem. I know the bartender there."

I didn't bother arguing. Instead I turned the car in a large arc and headed back to the west, glancing wistfully down our street at our warm, comfortable house as we passed.

"Will they even be open at this hour? *Today?*" I grumbled.

"They will be for *me*." She laughed. For a moment, I wanted to smack her. To strike that sexy, confident grin right off her face so hard, it never bloomed again. But I couldn't.

Truth be told, I adored her. Just like every other rube who fell under her spell. But unlike them, I hated her, too. And the hate was winning.

* * *

I perched against the brass rail of the bar as if it might break, trying to avoid eye contact with the three or four patrons who felt getting drunk before noon on Christmas Eve was an acceptable thing to do.

Miraculously, Josie emerged from a bathroom just a few minutes later, her face scrubbed clean of the war paint, her obscene clothes changed to a soft sweater and blue jeans, a pair of simple white sneakers on her feet. She looked like the young girl she was, someone in the first wave of womanhood instead of the sophisticated wildcat that had walked in. And yet, every gaze in the bar was directly on her as she strode down the hallway.

Fucking Josie.

She slung her bag over her shoulder. "Told you it wouldn't take long."

"Whatever," I muttered, then turned and walked back out of the bar.

I climbed into the Buick, waiting only a moment before reaching over and popping the lock for her. She opened the door, the frigid hinges groaning as she climbed in and slammed it shut. "*Problem*, sis?"

"I don't know why we had to come here. If Mom and Dad had any idea—"

"But they don't." Her tone made it clear she intended it to stay that way.

"It's *Christmas Eve*, Josie. And you have me taking you to a *bar*. And the way you were dressed—"

"You shouldn't always judge books by their covers, *Pattie*," she cut in. "Didn't anyone ever teach you that?"

"Only you," I mumbled.

We walked into the house to the chorus from "White Christmas," Bing crooning his heart out for all he was worth. Mom came rushing in from the kitchen, throwing her arms around

Josie so hard she squeaked like a dog toy. I rolled my eyes and walked past them and up the stairs, the sounds of Mom's nervous, excited prattle fading mercifully as I retreated down the hall. I walked into the bedroom I'd shared with my sister for all of my life—save the last few blissful months—closed the door and threw myself across my bed. I glanced over to Josie's side of the room, left perfect and untouched since she'd left.

Fuck Josie.

We had just finished dinner and started to clear the dishes when Josie announced her intentions to "pay her respects" to the neighborhood. My mother's face dissolved into a deep frown, the first time her expression had altered from pure joy since Josie had walked in the door.

"Surely you can visit your friends later," she said. "Besides, Mass is in just a few hours and you shouldn't be late. Father Nolan will be so pleased to see you."

"I'll be there, Ma," Josie said with a sigh. "Just want to pop round and see the girls beforehand. I'll meet you at St. Sebastian's before the candles are lit."

My mother looked ready to argue but clamped her mouth shut, acquiescing to the force of will that was my sister. Josie planted a quick kiss on her cheek and another on my father's brow as he settled into his Barcalounger.

"You comin', Pattie?"

I nearly dropped my plate.

"Uhh...yeah. Just, uhh, gimme a sec."

I tossed the dish into the sink, the resulting clatter sending my mother into a fit of protest as I bounded upstairs. A quick glance in the mirror told me all I needed to know. It didn't matter what I wore or how I did my hair or if I fixed what little makeup I had on. I'd never hold a candle to my sister, who seemed to shine with a light of her own. She was a live wire, throwing off sparks in every direction.

I settled for changing my shirt for a sweater and jogged back downstairs, lest my sister change her mind and leave without me. We slipped on our coats at the door, leaving to the sounds of our mother imploring us to be on time and presentable. We burst into giggles as we raced for the Buick, and I felt the old familiarity of sisterhood creeping back under my skin.

"Now for the *real* fun. Head toward Fifty-eighth and we'll see what trouble we can find."

I nearly slammed on the brakes in the middle of our street.

"I thought we were going to see Nadine and Georgie and them," I stammered. "That's what you told Mom."

"Yeah, that's what I *told* her. And we ain't makin' it to Mass either, Baby. But Mom will get over it, so relax."

"Josie, Mom will lose her *shit* if we're not there. She's been at the church all week, helping set things up. How's it gonna look if we don't show up?"

"Like I said...she'll get over it." Josie huffed. "You *have* to let go of this 'good girl' thing, Pattie. You'll be outta the house soon and you need to be ready for reality. Life isn't as safe and perfect as you want it to be."

I almost asked her what she meant but realized I didn't *want* to know. Instead, I obediently steered the car in the direction she'd requested, hoping against hope I could manage the situation *and* my sister.

We hit Fifty-eighth and found ourselves amongst a rowdy crowd. Irish never need an excuse to drink, but a religious holiday—*the* religious holiday of the year—was always a favorite. This Christmas Eve was no exception. Every bar on the strip was packed.

"Just where *are* we going?" I finally asked.

"Donovan's. I need a drink."

"Let's just go to the coffee shop. There's bound to be some people there."

"Yeah, but not the *right* people. Grow up, Pattie. Or drop me and go to church. Your choice."

We found a lucky spot and pulled the Riviera in, the car's groans echoing my own sentiment as the engine idled to a stop. I turned to my sister, frantically trying to find the words to convince her this was a bad idea, and saw Josie frozen in place, her hand immobile on the door handle, her face contorting in fear and hatred.

"Josie, what is it? What's wrong?"

She didn't answer me, just sat there, staring in horror at a group of men gathered outside Donovan's doors. One man in particular seemed the focus of her gaze—tall and swarthy in jeans and a black leather jacket, handsome in a devilish, Harrison Ford sort of way. A cigarette dangled from his lips as he shouted at his friends about something. A baseball game, I think. I wasn't really paying attention, all my focus on my sister.

I'd never seen her so freaked.

"*Josie*," I tried again. "What's going on? Do you know that guy? Who is he?"

"He's no one," she spat. "He's *nothing*."

The guy turned toward us, cupping his hands around his Zippo's flame to light his cigarette. He raised his eyes and I saw the moment they locked onto Josie. A disturbing smile spread across his lips.

Then he started to laugh.

"Get us out of here," my sister hissed. "Just get me away from here."

"Okay," I said. "Okay, Josie."

I cranked the ignition and was pulling away from the curb just as the man started toward the car. As crazy as the whole exchange had been, I almost lost the wheel when I saw Josie steel herself against his approach, her right arm and leg braced against the window and door as if to keep him out, her eyes wild and wide, like prey who's spotted a predator.

"What the *hell*, Josie? You're scaring me."

"Shut up for a second, will you?!" she screamed. "Just shut UP!" She was shaking now, her red lipstick smearing as she wiped the back of her hand across her mouth and started to cry.

I turned my eyes back to the road, just kept driving in long, slow loops around town in silence until her sobs stopped. I finally pulled the car over in front the elementary school and shut the engine off. Eventually, she sighed and turned to face me.

"I don't want to talk about it, Pattie. I'm sorry, but I just *can't*. Besides, there are things you're just better off not knowing. Trust me."

I stared at her, partially mad, mostly worried.

"Can you just take me to St. Sebastian's instead? It'll make Mom happy. And it's what you wanted anyway."

"Yeah, you're right. It *is* what I wanted. And we'll go. But this conversation isn't over."

I drove us to church as Josie fixed her makeup in the mirror. By the time we arrived, she was glowing and pristine, a supernova in human form.

We entered the sanctuary just behind a large group of stragglers. We weren't necessarily *late* for Midnight Mass, but being one of the few days that *all* of Woodside became suddenly devout, Christmas Eve services were always packed to the rafters. I searched the room, dazzling in the light of a thousand candles, and found our parents up front, next to the deacon and his wife. I saw my mother craning her head around, eyes frantic and searching.

I waved and she saw me, a look of relief—then another of irritation—crossing her features. I pointed to the pew in the back row and watch my father nod, then shoved Josie into it and sat beside her as my father corralled my mother and turned her attention back to the cross. Josie was quiet, stiff, her gaze foggy and distant. But to her credit, she repeated all the usual phrases dutifully and completely, standing and sitting and kneeling as directed, a non-believer giving a commanding performance of piety and devotion.

As we all knelt for the final devotions, my heart seized at the sight of my older sister bowing her head in supplication, her hands folded together so tightly her knuckles went white in protest. I reached out a hand and placed it on her back. We stayed like that, melded together, even while the priest wished us all the merriest of Christmases and sent the congregation on its way. Even as our parents stumbled past, my mother reaching for us both, my father pulling her away and through the open doors.

It was silent in the church, all the parishioners gone, before Josie lifted her head and unclasped her hands. Her eyes were ablaze, fiery red with the sting of unshed tears. The delicate blue that normally shined so bright seemed lost in the chaos.

"Josie," I whispered.

"Patricia Ann, I want you to promise me something, and I want you to mean it. Okay?" She all but choked out the words.

"Tell me what's going on, *Josephine Mary*, and maybe I will."

She almost smiled then, the corner of her mouth quirking northward just a fraction before returning to a hard, straight line.

"I just...I want you to be safe, to be smarter than I was...." When she stopped there, her words fading like the incense, I *lost it*.

"What in the holy hell are you *talking* about?"

Even my sister's eyebrows arched at my blasphemy, and in God's own house, no less. On the holiest of days.

We broke into hysterical laughter, clutching onto one another to keep from falling to the floor. The moment didn't last long, but it was enough: cathartic, cleansing. Years of doubt and distrust seemed to evaporate, and suddenly, I wanted nothing more than to be as close as we had been. I took Josie's hands in my own and squeezed.

"Just say you'll be careful, with yourself, with who you *are*," she said. "Don't give that to *anyone*, you hear me? You keep that just for you, Pattie. *Promise me.*"

"I—I promise, Josie," I stammered. She fell into my arms and wrapped her own around me, squeezing tight. I returned the hug with everything I had, hoping she'd feel what I meant, what my words had failed to say.

The next few days passed in a blur. Christmas, in all its tinseled glory, came and went, and we spent the week that followed in relative peace and quiet. Josie remained pensive and subdued, giving in to Mom's requests without so much as an eye roll. Our mother was thrilled. I was terrified.

It wasn't until Friday, the 30th, that I saw even a spark of the Josie who'd snuck out of her window, night after night. The Josie who was a human embodiment of a living, eternal flame, ready and prepared to set fire to anything and everything around her.

We were in the supermarket, walking each aisle as we collected the things on Mom's list. Turning a corner, we collided with a trio of boys, their own cart a myriad of beers and cheap snacks. One of them was a guy from school, a tall, lanky kid named Liam who'd lived the street over since we'd been in kindergarten.

"Hey, Pattie," he said, his smile shy and charming. "Enjoying break?"

"As much as I can, stuck in Woodside." I glanced at my sister and saw her staring hard at one of the other boys. Liam's older brother, Michael. He'd been in her class and was a larger, broader copy of his sibling. Gorgeous, actually.

"Hey, Michael," she nearly giggled. "It's been a while."

Michael shrugged his shoulders and gave my sister a coy smile. "Yeah…it has. Lookin' good, Josie."

"You too, stud."

The third kid, the one I *didn't* know, stood there looking at Josie with the strangest expression. Like he recognized her, but didn't know how.

"You guys coming tomorrow night for New Year's?" Liam asked. "Party starts up at Rockaway, around ten."

I hadn't taken my eyes off that third kid, still peering at my sister. As I began to answer Liam, a massive grin spread across the guy's face and he clapped his hands together in glee, like a toddler at a birthday party.

"Holy shit, it's *you*!" he said to Josie. "I've seen your pictures! *Niiiice*, girl." He began to laugh.

I was instantly reminded of a braying donkey.

Josie had gone the color of ash—pale and silvery and so, so fragile. Michael launched out a fist and caught the donkey on the arm, hard. It shut the stupid animal up, but the damage had been done.

Gripping the back of my arm, Josie hauled me away from our cart and down the aisle as fast as her legs would go. We were out the front door and halfway through the parking lot before I could stop her.

"*JOSIE*," I hollered. "The cart! Mom's groceries—"

"I don't give a *fuck* about Mom's FUCKING GROCERIES!" she screamed. Tears streamed through her mascara and down her cheeks in sooty, ragged paths. "I can't go back in there, Pattie, I *can't*!"

She was trembling, shaking, her eyes wide and terrified. The same way she'd been outside of Donovan's on Christmas Eve. When she'd seen *that guy*.

"Where the *fuck* is the car?" she yelled, turning in rapid, manic circles.

I grabbed her arms and held them tightly at her sides.

She struggled, then stopped and stared at me.

"*Josie...*"

She seemed to crumble at the way I said her name. "Can

we just find the car?" It was almost a plea.

I turned her loose and scanned the parking lot. Dad's Riviera was only an aisle and a few spaces away. I unlocked the door and let Josie in. She sank into the cracked upholstery like a hot bath, her body nearly prone in the seat, like she was trying to disappear.

"I screwed up, okay? I screwed up *so bad*." She burst into fresh sobs and hid her face in her hands.

"*How?*" I asked. "How could anything be *this* bad?"

"It just is," she said. "And you're not going to that fucking party."

I lost it.

"I'll go if I fucking *want* to, Josie. I'm not a kid anymore. I've got my own life, my own friends. And if I want to go to a goddamned New Year's Eve party, I'm damn well going to!"

"You'll lose yourself if you do," my sister whispered. "Lose a part of yourself you can't get back."

"*How?*" I was sick of her double-speak. "Don't you think it's time for the truth?"

She stared at me hard, then took a ragged breath.

"Last year, on New Year's...a guy took pictures of me, you know—" she made a vague gesture with her hand, "—*doing things.*"

"What guy? And what *things?*"

"The guy we saw at Donovan's. And bad things. Things that would kill Mom and Dad if they knew. Things I can't ever take back. *Sex stuff.*"

"Jesus *Christ.*"

She cringed as if I'd smacked her. "I don't know how it happened. I mean, it wasn't like it was my first time drinking. Or even being with a guy. But I got so *smashed* at the party, and then...suddenly I wasn't on the beach anymore. I was on a boat, and it was out on the water, and I was on this mattress on the floor, naked. And there was this guy...on top of me. And Paul, he was in the corner, taking picture after picture with that fucking Polaroid. I wanted it to stop, but I couldn't scream, couldn't move my arms to push the guy off me."

She looked up at me, her eyes wide, staring. "I was so scared. Just kept telling myself that it would be over soon, that I just had to get through it. And then we were back at the dock and Paul was helping me out of the boat like he *gave a shit* and it all felt so...unreal. Like it hadn't really happened. A few days later, Paul saw me in the park and told me I'd better do everything he said or he'd mail the photos to Dad at the garage. I can't even begin to explain what he put me through. I couldn't wait to get out of Woodside and away from him. I wouldn't have even come home for Christmas but Susan Richards told me he'd gotten a job down in Philly so I thought it was safe. Fucking *Susan*!"

Yeah. Like it was Susan's fault.

I'd never seen my sister like this. Frantic, wild—damn-near unhinged. And the story she'd told me. It sounded like she'd been slipped something, and I told her so.

"Doesn't matter," she moaned. "He's still got those fucking pictures and me, naked with my legs spread, is all anyone is ever going to see." She threw an arm across her eyes and howled. "I wish I was dead. Or, just...*gone*. Just fucking disappear and be someone else."

I cranked the ignition hard then peeled out of the parking lot and into the street. Josie sat up in her seat. "Jesus Christ, Pattie. What the hell?"

"I'll tell you what we're going to do. We're going to get those fucking pictures back and teach that asshole a lesson."

She scrambled to put on her seat belt as I took a corner wide, the tires squealing on the pavement. "Now *you're* scaring *me*."

"Good," I growled. "It's about fuckin' time."

Josie wasn't happy with the plan we'd worked out by the next morning, but even she could see it was our best—and maybe *only*—shot. She was sure Paul still had the pictures, and that they were most likely on the boat. He actually *lived* on the wreck, dealt drugs out of it, too. He'd never leave it unprotected. I'd just laid it out for her: how our only option was to get on the boat somehow and find them. Or better yet, get him to give us the pictures himself.

We got everything we wanted, but making it happen cost us. By the time we got back to Mom and Dad's that afternoon we were a pair of zombies, silent and vacant-eyed.

We'd found Paul easily enough—sitting on a barstool at Donovan's. She'd done all the talking—I had stayed by the door, trying hard to look bored and irritated. At one point, his attention turned toward me, and I had to suppress a shudder at the smile he gave me. The guy really was a grade-A creep.

Paul agreed to the transaction readily enough. Oh, he'd scoffed at first, told Josie to go to hell. But the idea of defiling Josie's little sister at the stroke of midnight on New Year's Eve—it was just too good an offer to resist. She told me later it took everything she had to keep from punching him in the throat.

"We don't have to do this," Josie said. "*You* don't."

"Like hell I don't."

"We can figure out another way."

I snorted.

"What if he won't hand over the photos?" she said. "What if—"

"There are a *thousand* 'what ifs.' We can't think that way. We show up at the boat, he'll give you the photos and we get out of there. And if he doesn't, then I'll find them like we talked about and *take* them. It'll be fine."

"So what...you get on the boat, and *then* what? What if he tries to hurt you?"

"I'll hit him in the head with one of Daddy's crowbars."

She blinked at me, speechless.

"Look, I can handle it. He'll underestimate me *and* you. *That's* how we win."

JOSIE

***

Mom and Dad would be spending the evening at their friends' house, celebrating with Dick Clark on the TV and cheap champagne in plastic glasses, so we were free to do what we wanted.

We headed toward Rockaway just after eleven. We could see the bonfires on the beach from the footpath that ran along the shoreline, heard the sound of drums and a few guitars drifting up from the sand. Even from where we were, we could see the coolers of alcohol and the kegs of beer, bodies swaying with the music and the flames. Michael and Liam were down there, with the others. I wanted so *badly* to join them, to dance around the bonfire, light and easy and free of the weight that sat heavy on my shoulders. But there would be other parties. Tonight was about saving Josie.

We found the dock, and Paul's boat, just before midnight. Josie squeezed my hand, then started down the creaking wood. I followed her faithfully, though every hair on my head was standing on end. I'd been the one trying to convince Josie it would all be okay, but now—I wasn't sure of *anything*. Just as Josie reached the end of the dock, the door of the boat opened and a shaft of yellow light poured out. Paul appeared, a self-satisfied grin ruining his otherwise-good looks.

"Finally. Thought you two got lost. Cutting it a bit close, aren't we?"

"Knock it off, Paul. We're here, as agreed. Now hand over the photos."

"You think I'm stupid, Kelly? Un-uh. Your sister comes aboard, spends some time. When I'm done with her, I'll give *her* the photos."

"No. No way," Josie shook her head. "Photos *now* or we're out of here, Paul."

"Your call. But I've been looking forward to this all day, so if you reneg now…. Maybe I'll just mail 'em to Daddy. Not like they're much good to me now, anyway."

Josie's hands balled into fists at her sides.

"It's fine," I caught her eye as I stepped around her. "It'll be *fine*."

"Well, lookee here. The younger Kelly sister, all grown up."

I swallowed hard. No point in covering it. I *wanted* him to think I was scared.

"Come aboard, darlin'," he said. "I won't bite. Unless you ask me to."

I forced a smile onto my lips and looked back at Paul. "I just might."

"Hear that, Josie?" He laughed. "Little sister is going to be just fine. You can leave."

Desperate to look back, I trained my eyes on Paul and took his outstretched hand instead, climbing over the railing and into the boat, the dip and sway of the ancient vessel mimicking the swell in my stomach. I had to duck my head as I entered the cabin. One lamp illuminated the cramped space so well, it had me blinking like mad to adjust my eyes.

There wasn't much to the place—a filthy, uncovered mattress in one corner, a small propane stove and metal basin in another. No cabinets or dressers—nothing suggesting a hiding place.

Fuck.

"You look like you could use a drink," he offered, shutting the door behind him.

I gave my best shy smile and shook my head no. "Josie gave me plenty on the way here."

"Bullshit. You're freezing and a little something will fix you right up."

He poured a healthy dose of some kind of brown liquid into a stained water glass and handed it to me. I thought about what he'd done to Josie and wondered whether he was arrogant enough to try the same shit with me. It didn't matter really. Disgusted as I was—*scared* as I was—I knew I was going to have to drink if Paul was going buy my act.

I tipped the glass back and started to take a small sip to appease him, but it wasn't enough. He raised a hand and tilted the glass back until the alcohol sloshed down my throat. *Whiskey*. I'd never be able to smell it on my father's breath again without remembering this moment.

"Thatta girl," he purred. "Get nice and warm, darlin'."

He leaned toward me and I tensed.

"Re-laaax. I'm a *nice* guy."

I swallowed hard, willing the bile back down into my stomach. I didn't need to look behind me—there was nowhere to go but the dirty mattress and I would've rather died than sit on it. I pasted a smile on my face and looked up at him.

He looked annoyed. "Why *are* you here? You want some of this, don't ya? Your sister certainly dug it."

He closed the distance between us in a breath, leaving me no time to do anything but put my hands up. He batted them away like he was swatting at a fly, then grabbed me with both hands, jerking me toward him. I had just started to scream when the door to the boat swung open and my sister charged through, arms raised above her head, a crowbar in her hands, her eyes ablaze. Two quick steps and she'd brought the tool down, hard, across the back of Paul's head. The blow knocked him flat to the floor.

"Jesus *Christ*! You killed him!"

Josie snorted, then kicked Paul once, hard, in the ribs. He made a strangled sound, half grunt, half moan. She looked satisfied. "I *wish*. He's just knocked out." She kicked him again. "Did you find them?"

"I've been in here thirty freakin' seconds."

"Then start looking. He won't be out for long."

"I was mostly kidding about Daddy's crowbar, you know." I stepped to the side but kept my eyes on the prone figure on the floor.

A crash from the corner containing the bed brought my

head around. Josie had flipped the mattress on its side and was rummaging around on the deck beneath. "Jackpot," she murmured. When she turned around, she was positioning a small, black cube between her feet.

"What *is* that?" I asked.

"It's a toaster. It's a fucking *safe*, Pattie. Jesus. Now help me open it before the asshole wakes up."

"Why don't we just take it?"

Josie stared at me like I was some kind of moron. "You really want to boost this guy's cash? His *drugs*?"

She had a point. I grabbed the crowbar from where it lay next to Paul and handed it to her. She shoved the chiseled end into the crack and starting prying. The metal did nothing but groan in protest. The safe was more formidable than it seemed.

"God *damn* it!" Josie shouted, bashing the safe over and over.

Paul stirred at my feet and I jumped a full foot in the air. "*Josie*," I hissed. "He's waking up!"

"Shit. We'll just have to take the whole thing and figure it out later. Get on the dock and I'll hand it up."

I edged my way around Paul and toward the door, my eyes locked on my sister. She'd thrown the crowbar down and grimaced as she hauled the safe across the deck. I stumbled through the door and over the railing of the boat, clambering awkwardly onto the dock. Josie was just coming to the railing by the time I got turned around, the safe no longer in her arms.

"Josie, *c'mon*. Give me the safe and let's get out of here!"

But she said nothing, just stood there, looking at me, the oddest expression on her face.

"What the *fuck* are you doing?" I squealed. "We've gotta go. *Now*."

She gave a small shake of her head, then walked to where the boat was tethered to the dock. Picking up the rope, she started to unwind it from the mooring, but still, she stared at me, her eyes wide, her lips pressed tightly shut. My stomach dropped as I watched her hands, the calm, methodical way they moved sending a wave of panic through me.

"What are you *doing*?" I pleaded. "Where's the safe? Why aren't you getting off? Josie, *please*!"

The rope free now, she dropped it at her feet, then used one arm to push the boat away from the dock. I stared at her in horror, too stunned to vocalize my protest. When the boat had drifted a few feet from the platform, I finally found my voice.

"We're almost there, Josie. Just get off the *fucking boat!* What the fuck are you *doing*?!"

"He'll never stop," she called. "Never."

And then she smiled at me. There was love and gratitude and the intimacy of a shared lifetime in the expression, an arrow straight through my heart. "It's okay, though. I couldn't have gotten this far without you. But the rest of it?" She shrugged that shrug I'd seen a million times and smiled again. "It's something I have to take care of alone."

The boat continued to float further and further away, my heart seizing in panic with each inch. She turned from me and walked to the stern, where the controls lay. It was a simple layout; throttle, ignition, that was it. A flick of a switch and the press of a button, and the boat's engine fired to life, the craft leaping forward in the inky water.

My sister's gorgeous auburn hair streamed behind her as the vessel moved quickly toward the mouth of the cove. Her chin raised in defiance, she looked every bit the avenging angel, full of the fire and glory of God—the embodiment of a raw flame. She looked—

Immortal.

I shouted out, panicked, calling her name, but she did not look back, and she did not answer me, her slight frame growing smaller as the boat headed for open water. Then, as I watched her move across the deck, the flames appeared—

posies of bright red and orange, like flowers tossed at her feet.

"*JOSIE!!!*" I screamed, but the boat was already moving around the curve of the shore and out of my sight. *What was happening? What was she* doing? But I knew. Deep inside, I knew, though my mind raged against the knowing. This had been her intent all along. Our "plan" had been nothing but a way to keep me distracted and feeling useful.

Fucking Josie.

I sprinted back down the dock, then flew as fast as my two feet would go down the path that followed the shoreline, making for the mouth of the cove and the stretch of beach beyond. I could barely see the ground in front of me but I kept running, my lungs burning, my muscles screaming for me to stop. I burst from the trees and scanned the water, desperate to spot the boat, begging God and all his angels to help my sister get back to me.

It came into view a moment later, the front of the boat still slicing through the water, the back half nothing but an angry mass of flame and oily black smoke. I'd just started to cry out my sister's name when it erupted in a massive fireball, a shock wave of heat and force that seared the flesh on my face and knocked me backward. The boat was underwater in moments, my hopes sinking along with it.

I fell to my knees on the sand. A wave of agony washed over me, so overwhelming I thought my heart might explode. But I didn't die—I stayed horribly and stubbornly alive.

The police ruled it an "unfortunate accident" which was best for all of us, I suppose. The truth was, I wasn't entirely sure how much I should tell them about what had happened. She'd killed a man, after all. Even with the drugging and blackmail, it was still murder. She couldn't have come back even if she'd wanted to.

They scoured the waters, trying to pick up what was left

by daylight, but only pieces of Paul's charred remains were ever found. The authorities determined my sister's body had simply floated out to sea, given the full moon and tidal patterns just outside the cove. Just two drunk kids on New Year's Eve—a tragedy, but nothing more.

Mom and Dad spiraled into a deep depression, too heartbroken to challenge the official ruling. "No piece of paper's gonna bring our daughter back," they say.

But I know different.

I know that one day, when the accident—and Paul—have been all but forgotten, she'll come waltzing through the door, smiling like a Crest commercial and lighting up our world like the flame she is.

Someday—Josie's coming home for good.

DO YOU HAVE A DARK SPOT ON YOUR PAST?
David Corbett

Hello—yes, you in the doorway. Please step inside, and kindly close the door behind you. The glare is dreadful, and it's so insufferably hot outside. As you can see, we in here prefer things refreshingly dark. Why else name the place The Forest of the Night?

Here, please, take a seat. May I offer my services without running the risk of intruding? I fear you may find it difficult to make yourself understood to the gentleman behind the bar, the ringmaster of our little circus here—now, now, Pepe, don't grunt at me like that. We all know how you love your reputation.

Might I suggest you try the gin—or what we know here by that name. On Mizar 5 it is the only spirit not designated toxic by the *regime du control*. Justifiably so, I'm afraid, given the wretched state of our water. Blame the mining operations all along the cordillera for that. But don't let me dissuade you from whatever libation you might prefer. Pepe will be happy to poison you in any manner you please.

Come again? Ah, good, gin it is. Pepe? Please, one gin for our impressive stranger, and freshen my glass as well. I can't help but confess I love the amber glow it kindles within me. When the stars begin to weep and bleed and the rains wash away the coppery dust, I like to walk the streets in the glimmer of Pepe's gin, warmed by its confidence, ambling here and there and talking to myself interminably—yes, like now, here with you. Again, forgive me. As I meant to suggest at the outset, however, my jabbering is not meant to annoy but to inform.

First, allow me to introduce myself. For now, you may refer to me as Tyger. I will educate you in a moment concerning how I am known in this humble little watering hole. There is a certain fluidity of names here, if only because Pepe, day by day, assigns them as he pleases.

See? He has delivered your drink and designated you as Zombie. No, I am quite sure he was referring to you, not the beverage. Shall we drink to that? Good. Well then: Be born again, my friend!

Please, take no offense. Zombie is a relative honorific. You should hear what he calls those he finds genuinely distasteful. Yo-Yo. Scurvy Brother. And those are the gentlest of the lot. It is only with time and the establishment of trust—or in very rare cases, real human fondness—that one ascends to the level of Angel, like those beautiful ladies to our right.

Or, most esteemed of all—other than Pepe himself, of course—there in the corner, see him? The somber, bedraggled creature slumped in the shadows with the sabre? That, my friend, is Slinky Redfoot. If I were you, should you need to pass his table on your way to the house of office, I would give the man some space.

Ah, it is all a bit confounding and mysterious, I can tell from your expression. Allow me to explain.

First, let us return to our host. Look at him. Do you see the scar across his throat, like a second, jagged, menacing smile? He got that collecting what are known here somewhat whimsically as Turkish union dues. Who knows, once you become settled, you may find that particular sideline suitable to your gifts—assuming, of course, you've come here seeking gainful employ.

Then again, perhaps you would prefer the role of chauffeur. I can see in a glance you're qualified. I'm being coy, of course. What I mean is that, should Pepe decide one or another reprobate that stumbles into this place deserves a lesson in common sense, you just might earn the right to, as the saying goes, take him for a ride.

Wonderful expression, offering so many distinct interpretations.

Ah, I see. You believe there has been some misunderstanding, I have misjudged you, concocted some scandalous idea of who you are. But I assure you, I am not one to invest much merit in ideas. When one encounters human misery, cannot it always be traced back to some insidious, intoxicating, even glamorous *idea*?

Besides, let's not dissemble with each other. This is not Alcor 7 or Antares Callisto, with their breathtaking glaciers and bridges of light. You are not here because of your tender voice and gentle bearing.

This is a terminus, far beyond the seven heaven-worlds—the end of the proverbial line. Though there exists a kind of bureaucracy here—the inescapable curse of our kind, propagating regulations even in the void—you will find no policemen. No one cares where you've been or what you've done. Life is raucous here, and violent. At least, since they discovered Procyon ore, and we've experienced what the speculators and their plug-uglies like to call a boom.

Now all is madness, chaos—freedom! People shout to stay alive, while an endless queue slithers outside the Café D'Escargot to watch Yvette perform her infamous Can-Can-Jacques. Others sooner or later wander in here, and enjoy the unique ambience and fellowship to be found in the Forest of the Night. You would not be here if you were not suited to the place.

Besides, look here at the register—you see? Your name. There, at the bottom. Well, yes, it is the name provided to you by the *regime du transport*, but nevertheless—there it is. If you would, please, do us the pleasure—sign in.

There. Very good. Another formality dispensed with. Let us raise our glasses once more. To Pepe's latest zombie—be born again, my friend!

I agree, it is truly wretched, the gin. But trust me, no one survives the alternatives.

You're absolutely right. I have digressed. I was introducing myself and I should get on with it.

As I said, you may call me Tyger, which is a humble alternative to the lofty moniker our dear Pepe has seen fit to bestow on me, or the one I suffered before coming here. Back on Vega Regulus, I was sometimes referred to as the Butcher of Lambs. You've heard of me? No? Please, I am not so vain as to be offended.

Whatever harshness of climate one encounters here, it is nothing compared to the suffocating desolation on that haunted rock. Unless you are far more ignorant than you seem, you may know at least of that planet's miserable tempests of blinding dust, the ruthless glare of its twin suns, the near-worship of the Waterlings—children with the gift of finding underground aquifers.

The Cult of the Lamb remains very powerful there. The exarchs forbid any woman with child not to bring it to term, for fear the aborted fetus might possess that ineffable aqueous gift. Yes, of course, once a child is found to lack any such talent, it's routinely left to die out in the drifting wilderness, or enslaved to the exarchs, but what creed lacks such hypocrisies?

I can see you do not agree with that glib assessment. Good. Neither did I after a fashion, which explains my fate.

The insidious logic the exarchs employed in enforcing their decree was this: at the very instant of conception, every infant acquires a fully formed and immaculate Imago Deí. Every fetus is an uncorrupted vessel of divine innocence—thus their status as Little Lambs. At least, that is how they are regarded up until the moment of birth, when the stinking corruption of existence begins to sink its claws into the suckling's mind.

Please excuse the hyperbole—I am trying to be faithful to the scriptural gibberish of the canon in question.

It wasn't just the hypocrisy that outraged me, however. Nor was it even the fact that I had been one of those abandoned newborns. Child of parents too poor to manage the extortionate tithe that would allow them to raise me, I was left out in the wind and sand as soon as the exarchs decreed I possessed no talent for sniffing out hidden springs. Some nomads found me, a withering scrap of flesh and noise, and kept me alive—just long enough to be viable for sale right back to the very same jackals who'd left me to die.

Twenty years of bondage to those mincing, mendacious priests ensued. There are those who would argue that slavery endured for such a long time could only be a choice. Not even a child would submit to such misery, they argue, but each day of his life would plot his escape.

Do you think that was not true of me? Not just each day, but every hour, every minute, every second, I never stopped contemplating ways to break my chains, to flee into the thundering dust come nightfall.

We all heard the rumors—colonies of runaways, renegades, freemen, out at the farthest limits of the wasteland. Even if those rumors proved untrue, the dream of the lie was powerful enough to induce many of us to think of nothing else but making a run for it.

If you doubt me, I will show you the scars, even more impressive than Pepe's, testament to the lashings I suffered each time they found me and dragged me back.

No, slavery is not a choice. It is an affliction, my friend, a plague. Just because you must lie there awhile, endure your fever, regain your strength, that does not mean you surrender.

As long as you cling to even the slightest hope, there is nothing of choice in your chains.

I say all this merely to convey to you my state of mind as I reached maturity. I was not angry—anger is for idiots. I prefer instead to think of my mindset as one of singular focus.

First, however, I was sold to a merchant who specialized in soothing emoluments and protective sheaths, a lucrative trade in that realm, as you might imagine. I accompanied him from terminal to terminal, module to module, checking inventory, demonstrating merchandise like a living manikin. I kept very, very quiet the entire time, paying close attention to everything I saw, for I knew even little things might matter later as I chanced to begin the end of my servitude.

Finally, one night, after a particularly lucrative bazaar on the outskirts of the capital, my merchant drifted off into a deep, indulgent sleep. I saw my chance and took it.

I won't bore you with the details of my journey. What is there to say? Blistering sun, choking sand, impassable moraine—plus the nonstop terror of being spotted by trackers and slave hunters and their *Maschinen Hunde*.

The sole unique event? My encounter with Slinky Redfoot, the disheveled character there in the corner I pointed out earlier. He, too, as it turned out, hoped to escape civilization. Fortunately, Slink found my begging not to be killed on the spot compelling enough to oblige. Ah yes, he possessed his greedy sabre even then.

Together we made our way across the eternal trackless nowhere, until scouts for a band of auroch herders discovered us near death, lying side by side in the shade of a volcanic outcrop. Were we, at long last, saved? Ha! Once again, we became chattel to be bargained off, but this time to privateers who saw our merit as crewmen.

As vassalage goes, it wasn't half bad. We learned the finer points of pillage, plunder, and stealth. And it was during that time, when we were carrying away not just booty but the wives and daughters of wealthy men, that the general designs of my revenge took shape.

I spoke before of the intoxicating glamor of ideas. Well, what was the most intoxicating idea on that planet?

Care to guess? No?

But I've already told you: *Innocence.*

The more I contemplated my vengeance, the more I realized it was not the exarchs or their toadying acolytes I needed to destroy but the Imago Deí itself—their vision of an uncorrupted soul that quickened into existence at the moment of conception. That was the very core of their claim to power, the holiness they pretended to worship and defend.

Now, I can hear you asking—but how does one murder an idea?

I assure you, that baffled me as well for no short period of time, until I realized it was not a belief but its believers that frame the problem. To say an idea has died is simply to recognize the faithful have fallen away. But how? Why?

I could not hope to prove that innocence does not exist. It's like telling people all but the most minute fraction of their bodies is empty space. So what if it's true?

No, I would accomplish nothing by trying to prove the idea was wrong. Instead, I would show what inevitably happens if the idea is absolutely, indisputably correct.

I already told you of how Slink and I learned, under the purview of the pirates, how to make off with rich men's wives? Well, I simply began to freelance, with a much narrower specialty. I abducted only *pregnant* wives.

I snuck into their modules, subdued them with a concoction called Imlach's tincture, threw them over my shoulder—trust me, given their condition, this often proved far more challenging than it sounds—and made off into the night.

Slink met me at a designated rendezvous in the desert, an abandoned underground shelter built during the Hermit Rebellion. It was there, in our subterranean hideaway, that his expertise with the sabre proved not just impressive but invaluable.

Never before has the term "surgical precision" been more apropos. Doctor Redfoot's skill with his blade would prove the envy of any pediatric surgeon in the universe.

Using the imperial infirmary's own library, we immersed ourselves in how to go about the business, and the black market supplied what additional materials we required. After I took care of cleansing the mother's body and administering the sufficient amount of morphoria for the pain, Slink, with the utmost care, opened the unconscious woman's belly, making an incision not dissimilar in shape to Pepe's scar, but wider, rendering access to the womb. He nicked away the umbilical cord and all the other mess, lifted the tiny shriveled thing from its fleshy reticule, then carried it outside and flung it out into the bush for the raptors and vermin to finish off. How is that for the death of innocence?

What is that, Zombie? You spoke too softly for me to make out your words. Did I hear you call me a monster? Ha! Believe me, I have been called much worse, for much better cause, as you will learn if you simply allow me to continue.

After perhaps a dozen such procedures—and no, we did not abandon the mothers, but stitched them up, took them to a safe spot, and notified their clansmen where they could be found—I composed my manifesto, explaining the how and why of what I'd done.

I explained that I was simply honoring the theology of the exarchs, taken to its natural limit.

Since it is the Imago Deí that lies at the center of that doctrine, and its perfection lies beyond dispute, I argued that it is not the preservation of the child that matters but of its immortal soul.

And since there is no way to guarantee that the soul will not become corrupted after birth—indeed, that is all but guaranteed—to preserve that ineffable innocence, and to grant it the eternal salvation in the presence of the Almighty that—so the exarchs teach us—is the very purpose of our existence, one must do everything in his power to prevent that corruption. The mortal flesh must be sacrificed for the sake of its eternal essence.

By carrying out this mission, was I not, in the absolute fullest sense, living up to the core premise of the exarch ethos? By committing not just murder, but its most unforgivable incarnation, I was condemning my own soul to eternal damnation. But was that not exactly what the exarchs demanded? *For the holiest among us gave up His life so that we might live.* Words to that effect, I'm quoting by memory. How much more poignant, more commendable, if it was not mere mortal existence I gave up, but my very soul.

The point: I accepted my fate, the absolute certainty of eternal punishment, so that the truly innocent might ascend into the light to sit with the Almighty in Paradise.

Of course, this served to enhance the condemnation I received, elevating me from mere murderer—or monster—to blasphemer, heretic, infidel! The Butcher of Lambs.

Accordingly, the intensity of the search for me and any accomplices—they feared I might stand at the head of an army—intensified as well. Search parties by the dozens rushed out into the wilderness to hunt us down. Suspects were summarily executed without the formality of questioning. Meanwhile, every woman even suspected of being pregnant got locked away and put under guard, so that access became not just a question of difficulty but recklessness. Slink took that as a challenge, but my point had been made.

No, I was never mistaken for a god or even revered as the holy man I made myself out to be. No one suggested I wear the sacerdotal fez. But I'd made my mark.

Soon the responses to my manifesto began to appear, anonymously at first, then more audaciously, pointing out that my crime was only too predictable given the exarch's regime. I had simply taken their logic to its most obvious conclusion. And are not all the atrocities known throughout the universe premised on an idea taken to its logical conclusion? Divine right, the invisible hand, national honor, master race—mere stupidities, until put into action with their natural endpoints in mind.

It wasn't long until the absolute power of the exarchs began to crumble. The burgher class, the clerks, the traders, and in time the laboring multitude rose up and demanded "reforms"—meaningless in the end, but that's the march of justice for you. Child slavery remains in place, for example, though I hear its current incarnation is nominally more benign. Rape is strictly forbidden against anyone younger than ten. Long before any such changes took place, however, Slink and I had made our escape, courtesy of the selfsame pirates who had schooled us so well.

Speaking of the devil—I see Doctor Redfoot has risen from his place in the corner and chosen at last to join us. Pepe, too, hovers nearby. Cozy, no? I'm sure Slink merely wants to make sure I'm not improvising too outrageously—and notice how the Angels have slipped across the room. Did I not mention the need to grant the man and his sabre some space? As for Pepe, I believe he would like to share with you the unique sobriquet he bestowed upon me when I arrived at his doorstep not all that long ago.

To him, I am not merely Tyger of Vega Regulas, ex-slave, privateer, heathen killer of innocents. Nor has he even once referred to me as Butcher of Lambs. Not at all. To Pepe, the Rajah of Erase in the Forest of the Night, I am born again as the one and only Godwhacker.

Who would guess that this pitiless brute could be such a wit? I mean, again, look at that face. Would you ever mistake him for a phrasemaker?

Which leads us at last, now that I have fully identified myself, back to you. I'm sure we would all enjoy hearing from you and you alone the exact nature of your business here.

Now, now, Zombie, don't be modest. I have already admitted to being coy. Do I need to confess to every false impression I may have created? Your reputation precedes you. How else would your name have appeared on Pepe's register?

So—no more suspense. How do you propose to kill me?

ON YOUR KNEES TOMORROW
R.T. Lawton

I opened my pocket watch.

"Tell you what," I said, "according to house rules, you got exactly fifteen minutes to cover the bet, else you forfeit the pot."

Junior glanced around at the other players. He wasn't finding any friendly faces. Understandable, since his daddy owned a lot of the town here in Canyon City and threw his weight around pretty heavy to get whatever he wanted. Couldn't blame Junior for trying, though. He had some serious cash on the table.

"Hollis," he said, turning to the man on his left, "loan me some money. You know Dad's good for it."

Hollis grimaced like he'd bitten into something sour.

"Dunno, Junior, your dad's been a little slow lately on covering your debts. Looks bad on the bank books and gets me in a bind with him if he doesn't okay the loan first."

"Sounds to me," the man to Junior's right said, "like Milo's not too happy with his youngest son's overspending these days."

Junior turned to the speaker, a tall rail of a man, and said, "Del, you certainly enjoy having all the legal work my old man sends your way."

Del pulled off his glasses and rubbed them industriously on the tail of his bowling shirt. "Milo's gonna send business my way whether I loan you cash or not. Giving you poker money is liable to just piss him off."

One by one, Junior looked at the other men around the table. They either avoided his eyes or shook their heads no. Most people in Canyon City considered Junior to be a form of toxic waste, but since they did business with his dad, they had to be careful what they said and did around the old man's boys. And, that went double for around his namesake.

Not me.

I was a hired hand at a ranch in the mountains north of town. No family and no ties aside from the job. I could, and would, move on any time I wanted. No loss to me.

I didn't kiss anyone's behind.

"Clock's running on you," I said as I tilted my wide-brimmed Stetson back on my head. "You're still ten grand light."

"Don't rush me, Jack." He looked at me, frustration leaking out around the edges. No doubt his daddy had taught him to use that particular tone with "the help."

"I know you've got nothin'." He stood up from the table and pulled his cell phone from a shirt pocket. "I'm gonna call my brothers. Either Mike or Marty can bring me enough cash to keep you from buying the pot," he said as he moved to the far corner of the room to make his call in private.

He could say whatever he wanted, even reach out to whoever he wanted. All the same to me. I had just put him in a deep hole, and we both knew it.

This was table-stakes poker. Time and money were slipping away from him.

I watched him press in some numbers and talk for a while, getting aggravated toward the end. Then he glanced at me, disconnected his call, and tried a second number. When he returned to the table, he didn't look happy.

"Either of 'em coming?" I asked.

"They're too far out of town right now. Hold off for an hour and they'll both be here."

"My watch says you got five minutes to come up with another idea. Best put your mind to thinking."

Junior took off his Broncos ballcap and rubbed his forehead. Then he looked down at all that money in the middle of the table.

"How about this?" he said. "I'll throw in one night with Candace."

The rest of us all turned to look at the long-haired blonde perched at the bar. Bright red cowboy boots with one boot heel hooked on the barstool rung. Cutoff blue jeans short enough to show off those long legs to good advantage. The flimsy white cowboy shirt she wore with the top three pearl snaps undone was at least one size too small to qualify as decent for the local church league.

I tried not to stare at her for any longer than what might be considered as sociable.

She licked her lips and sucked on the straw in her drink as if there were nobody else in that back room with her at this road house out on the highway west of town. She knew exactly what effect she was having on her audience.

"You can't trade her off for a night like you own her," I started off.

"Sure I can," he said. "She'll do whatever I tell her or else."

She must've figured out we were talking about her, because at this point she turned her full attention in our direction.

I shook my head. "One night for the ten thousand you're short? I don't think so."

Truth was, I was tempted.

"What do you want then?" asked Junior like we were dickering on a horse for sale.

"Cash or collateral," I told him.

"That's what I'm doing, Jack. I'm putting up Candace as

collateral."

I took a longer look at her. Then I decided to call his latest bluff and float a counterproposal, just to see what he'd do.

"Let's make it permanent, Junior. Kinda like writing up a bill of sale for that shiny new pickup out in the parking lot, if'n I was buying it that is and the truck didn't belong to your daddy who merely lets you drive it."

Now it was Junior's turn to look over at Candace.

Didn't take him long. He came right back at me. On a piece of scratch paper, he wrote out a bill of sale of sorts and threw it on top of the money piled in the center of the poker table.

I snatched up the paper and read it. Yep, the boy was giving up full title to her. I didn't think the paper had any real legality to it, but I shrugged and put it back in the pot anyway.

"Okay, you're on."

With a grin, he threw his cards face up on the table.

"I call."

Three aces and a couple of throwaway cards was all he had.

With a bigger grin, I laid out my winning hand, all black cards, same suit.

"You lose," I said.

The stunned look on his face was worth the long hours I'd spent in this smoke-filled room. The way the game with these fellows had been going, I'd gradually won more and more money all night long, till I was looking at more than a year's worth of wages setting in front of me in the middle of the table. Now, it was all in one pot. There was enough here to tide me over for a long time, if I didn't get crazy with it. Naturally, the prospect of having bragging rights over Junior just added to my pleasure. This was truly the land of milk and honey.

I shoulda seen it coming, though.

Junior's expression overflowed with rage. He balled his fists.

"You cheated."

I stood up, a few inches taller than him, even if you didn't count the cowboy hat I was wearing, leaned both of my fists on the table, and slowly shook my head.

"Don't look at me. The only cards I touched were the ones I was dealt. Your buddy here, the lawyer, did the dealing for this hand. If you got any argument about how the cards came out, then take it up with him."

Junior glared around at the men still seated. Then he pushed his chair over backwards and stomped out of the room.

The place was silent for a few seconds after the side door slammed shut.

"Congratulations, Jack," Hollis said as the room started to come back to life again. "Looks like you're the big winner tonight."

I stuffed the money in my jacket pocket and grabbed Junior's bill of sale for Candace. She watched me walk over and kept her eyes on mine as I unsnapped a front pocket on her shirt and gently stuffed the bill of sale inside. The backs of my fingers lingered against her softness on the other side of the cloth. I grinned at her.

"You're a free woman. You can do what you want."

"What if I want to come with you?"

"Then we'll have to discuss possibilities."

"I'll get my purse and jacket."

I walked over to the poker table and picked up my drink to finish it off. Still had my back to the door leading out to the parking lot when Candace called out from behind me. "Something you ought to know, Jack."

I turned to where she stood at the window, watching whatever was going on outside.

She looked my way, eyes wide. "Junior just took a rifle out of his pickup and he's headed back inside."

Chairs scraped on the hardwood floor as the other players quickly scrambled out of the way. Seemed nobody wanted to be standing too close to me at this moment. The only man who didn't back up right away was Hollis. Pretty brave for a banker, I thought. With his right hand, he reached under his sport coat, around to the back of his waist and pulled out a snub-nosed revolver. He laid it down on the table in front of me, barrel pointed at the parking lot door.

"It's a three-fifty-seven Magnum," he said. Then he put my right hand over the gun.

"You just made a fool out of Junior," he continued. "So, there's no doubt in my mind that he now intends to kill you."

Hollis took his hand off mine.

"The gun's unregistered," he went on. "I mostly carry it for personal protection, me being a banker and all. There's six bullets in the cylinder, but you should only need one if you're any good at all." Then he too stepped away to get out of the line of fire.

Junior came busting through the door rifle barrel first, with the butt plate already up to his shoulder.

I didn't wait to hear what his intentions were. The revolver barrel seemed to automatically center on his chest as I yanked hard on the trigger. Twice. The explosions sounded louder than hell in this confined space.

Junior got pushed back a step, spun sideways, tripped over his own feet and went down hard. Blood spray dotted the wall behind the place he'd been standing. A thick redness started pooling on the floor.

I didn't move.

Del came over to my left side and gently pushed the revolver down until the barrel pointed at the table. I glanced at him, but the lawyer's focus was over on the floor where Junior lay moaning.

Hollis walked over and knelt near the wounded man.

"Shouldn't hurry your shots like that, Jack. You pulled them both to the right. Must've had your finger too far onto the trigger. You got him once along the rib cage, and the second one took him in the shoulder. I expect he'll live…if we call an ambulance before he bleeds out. With all the blood on the floor, that might be a likely possibility."

Hollis stood.

"You might want to vacate the premises before the sheriff gets here. I'm assuming you know who donates most of the money for the sheriff's re-election every four years? They won't hang you tonight, but your odds don't look good for a future. Oh, and take the gun with you. You could need it later."

"What for?" I managed as Del hustled me toward the door.

"Milo may not be happy with some of the things his youngest does, but he's still protective of him. Plus, you heard Junior say that Mike and Marty will show up sometime soon. Those two boys of Milo's are not exactly what you call rational in these types of situations when it comes to family. You'd best not be here when they arrive."

"Hey, this was self-defense. You all saw that."

"True," replied Hollis, "but most of your witnesses in this room got businesses in town to take care of. They don't want to get crosswise with Milo, so you can't depend on them not to hedge their bet when it comes to testifying in a courtroom."

I stopped in the doorway and turned to the lawyer.

"Del, what's your take on this?"

"Book law is on your side, Jack, but Milo's wife—Junior's mother—is the judge's younger sister. You might want to take that into consideration. My advice is to leave town and keep on going."

I was hesitating, with half my mind already in my pickup and headed down the road, when Candace grabbed my arm and maneuvered me into the parking lot. A cold damp wind blowing down from the foothills brushed against my neck. I shivered with the chill, but she seemed to be focused on other things.

"Which truck's yours, hon?"

"The black one."

It was parked about three spaces away from Junior's red pickup. His driver's door hung open and the interior light was still on. Funny how you notice some things at a time like this, things that don't mean nothing in the wider scheme. Then, how you overlook other items, until you happen to think back on them later.

Candace turned loose of my arm at the rear of my truck, and I made my own way to the driver's side. I opened the door, got in and put the key in the ignition. She slid in on the passenger side and closed her door.

"I don't want to hurry you, hon," she said in her soft voice, "but they've probably called the sheriff by now."

She leaned over and rotated the key to start the engine.

This was all happening a little fast for me, but the wail of distant sirens out on the highway gave me the sudden urge to get moving. I shifted into gear and stepped on the accelerator.

With the sirens getting louder on my left, I cranked the steering wheel to the right, got onto the highway and headed into the darkness.

"Where we going, hon?"

I glanced at my gas gauge. The needle stood at a lot less than a quarter tank. For right now, I wasn't going far.

"There's a convenience store down the road a couple of miles. I'll gas up and you can call a friend to come get you."

"What do you mean?"

"I mean things have changed. I gotta get down the road fast. There's no room for extra baggage on where I'm going."

"You're calling me baggage?"

"Hey, don't take it personal."

"And, you're actually going to dump me at a gas station on the highway, like I was nothing?"

In the blackness of night, the bright lights of the convenience store glared up ahead on the right. This was gonna have to be fast. Gas and go. No time for sweet words and holding hands.

"Look, Candace, Junior's brothers are gonna be about half-crazy over this. If they find you traveling with me, there's no telling what they'll do to you. So, I'm doing you a favor by dropping you off, getting you away from me."

"Doesn't appear that way to me. Tell you what, I been wanting to leave this town for a long time, head for Vegas, or maybe California. That wasn't possible with Junior and his heavy-handed ideas of what a relationship should be. So, take me with you as far as the next state and I won't take it personal about you wanting to dump me here."

I pulled off the highway, into the store lot and stopped at one of the pumps. Reaching across Candace's lap, I opened the passenger door.

"I'm going inside to pay cash for the gas. Don't be here when I get back."

She sat there, mouth open, staring at me.

"It's for your own good."

Then, I took the keys and left her sitting there with the door open. Whatever I said must've worked, because when I came back outside and walked up between the two gas pumps, she was gone. Both doors on my pickup were standing open, but no sight of Candace, only a note from her to me stuck under my windshield wiper.

I plucked the torn scrap of paper out from under the rubber edge and read the feminine scrawl.

Shouldn't have dumped me, Jack.
When it's all done, I'll be the one smiling,
while you'll be on your knees tomorrow.

I wondered what she meant by that. Then I noticed my pickup was setting lower than usual.

The bitch had slashed my tires and used my own Buck knife to do it. The knife that I usually kept in the middle console was now laying open-bladed on the front seat. I walked around to the other side of the truck. Both tires on this side were flat, too. So much for a quick drive out of town.

I glanced around. The lot was empty. I closed the blade on the knife and stuck it in my hip pocket. The revolver was still secured in the back of my belt and had been since we'd left the road house.

Four bullets remained in the chamber. They'd have to do.

I had my jacket and my hat. Didn't appear there was anything else of value left in the truck to be worth taking along.

My options were limited. The old geezer running the convenience store was the only other person around. He must've had somebody drop him off at work and pick him up later because there were no other vehicles on the premises. But even if he had one, the grouchy old codger wasn't going to close up shop to give me a ride, and there wasn't anyone I could call on short notice to come get me.

I knew it wouldn't be smart to start walking on the highway and maybe get caught in the brothers' headlights. Besides, nobody was passing by at this time of night to bum a ride with even if I did stay on the highway.

With the Arkansas River and the Royal Gorge to the south, there was no way for me to go far in that direction without being cornered. My only hope for salvation was to head north into the mountains. Maybe buy a ride off some rancher up there.

I started walking.

The ground quickly sloped up behind the convenience store. At least with almost no roads back here, anyone trying to follow me would also be on foot. My problem was I was wearing custom-made boots with riding heels and them things aren't made for walking very far or very fast. Within four miles of humping up and down hills and ridges, through patches of scrub oaks, rocks and pine trees in the dark, I was pretty well wore out.

Coming out of the scrub brush at the top of one long climb, I paused on the edge of a brown-grass meadow partway up in the high country. At the far end of all this frost-tipped buffalo grass stood a barbed-wire fence and an old weathered barn with an open hayloft door facing the meadow. I caught my breath and watched for a while. There was no house on the premises; no livestock or other animals wandering around the place. This would do until morning. I could keep an eye on my backtrail from the hayloft door.

As I stepped out of the shadows and onto the muddy, half-frozen dirt, my right boot rolled on a piece of uneven ground. Just enough for an ankle sprain, nothing too serious, but it kept me from walking further than the barn for now.

At the fence, I put my left palm between the barbs on the middle strand of wire and pushed down. With my right, I pushed up on the top strand, slid my left leg through, then my right, without hooking my jacket on the barbs. Squeaks came from the rusty wire when I turned loose and stood up on the other side.

I entered the barn through an open double door on the far end of the large building. An old green tractor squatted in the middle of the dirt floor. Three empty horse stalls stood against the left wall, with a couple of storerooms on the right. Everything gave off a feel of long disuse. I climbed up the wood ladder into the loft and found a cozy spot in front of a stack of hay bales where I could look out over the meadow. Loose hay scooped up around me was old and dusty, but it helped insulate me from the chill night air where my exhaled breath hung in small clouds before disappearing. Drowsiness started working around the edges of my mind.

I fell asleep thinking about how things had gone at the road house. Junior was partially right. Someone probably had cheated that night, maybe more than one person, but it wasn't me. Of course, I wasn't going to complain when I was winning. But now that I thought about it, most of the times when I won, either the banker or the lawyer had dealt those cards. Also, to the best of my recollection, Hollis and Del never seemed to have much invested in the pot whenever those good hands came my way. It was like they were working together and had an idea about the potential outcome in advance.

But why me? Could be that since all the men at the table ran businesses in Canyon City, then the big winner couldn't be one of them. I was the only outsider, thus a good candidate for the position.

And, Junior?

He was the mark.

They'd probably only intended to get the kid in trouble with his dad in order to move Junior out of their hair for a while. But Junior getting mad enough to go for the rifle was a bonus those two took advantage of in an attempt for a permanent solution to their problem. He must've really done something demeaning to get that far on the bad side of these two.

And me, I was the unlucky stiff picked as the fall guy.

Nothing for it now. Settling scores would have to wait.

My last thoughts were of Candace. A pleasant vision in the mind's eye to drift off on, except for the reality of four flat tires leaving me in the lurch. It wasn't her fault the brothers were probably out looking for me, but she didn't need to disable my getaway vehicle out of pure spite. Under other circumstances we probably could've had some fun times together. Maybe I'd have to go back one of these days and give her a chance to make up for stranding me on foot. And then again, maybe it wasn't my brain upstairs doing the thinking. Still, the curves on her body were something pleasurable to dream on.

Sleep—when it finally came—hit me hard.

I woke up gradually in the gray-wolf hours of early morning. The wind had died down to a gentle breeze and it was quiet outside. I laid there for a while, listening to the old barn creak with the change in temperature from cold night to coming day, as my brain went through last night's happenings again. Rolling over onto my side, I looked through the open loft door and back out over the bent-grass trail I'd made on my way to the barn.

Fog drifted along the clump of scrub oak where I had paused a few hours earlier before entering the meadow, but in the pale light of approaching morning I now saw silhouettes just beyond the edge of the grass. Two men in hunting gear with rifles knelt in the shadows of the scrub oaks and studied the tracks of my boots. Other figures stood behind them. Looked like one of them had a dog on a leash.

I inched back from the loft doorway and got to my feet. It was on my mind to go down the ladder and hotfoot it out the other direction, but my sprained ankle had swelled up some during the night. It wouldn't hold me for far. They'd run my slow ass down in no time.

I'd just have to stay here and hope for the best where I had some cover. Using both hands to help me maneuver along the wall of hay bales, I moved to a spot that gave me a good view out the loft door, but kept me out of sight.

Two of the men had moved halfway across the meadow and headed in my direction. Both were armed with long guns. The fog was clearing and I no longer saw men back in the scrub oaks. A squeaking noise down below told me someone was already slipping through the barbed-wire fence. Whoever they were, they were coming fast.

Keeping my back to the loft door, I moved some of the bales on the top row to give me firing portals and protection from any incoming rounds from the opening in the loft floor where the ladder came up. Then I waited. Wasn't anything else to do.

After a while, I heard whispering down below in the barn and then scuffling noises on the wood ladder. Somebody was coming up and there was no way to stop them. It was quiet when they got to the top like they were listening to see if they could find out anything before stepping sideways into cover behind hay bales near the ladder.

More scuffling noises and I could tell another person had climbed the ladder.

"Jack," said a man's voice. "We know you're up here. There's no tracks leaving the barn."

Damn. I couldn't catch a break lately.

"That you, Marty?"

"Yep. Come on out now and we won't hurt you."

Like hell they wouldn't. Marty was the middle brother and almost as sadistic as his older brother Mike. Must've been something growing up in that family.

"Where's the sheriff? I might consider surrendering to him."

"He, uh, couldn't make it. Got other business back at the road house. Told us to see if we could bring you in on our own."

"How's Junior? He die? Or did somebody call an ambulance in time?"

"Just come on out, and we'll talk about it."

I was so intent on Marty that I almost didn't hear his buddy creeping around the far side of the hay bales where I was standing. I barely had time to get a shot off as the man stepped out far enough to get a bead on me. The .357 kicked in my hand and the guy went down. His rifle skidded across the loft floor and got buried in the loose hay.

"Did you get him?" Marty hollered.

"Yeah, I did," was my reply, knowing it wasn't my voice that Marty expected to hear.

"Damn you, Jack!" He fired several rifle shots in my direction before ducking.

In the ear-ringing silence that followed, I heard him holler for someone else to come up the ladder. Then he popped his head up for a look-see.

Through one of my firing portals, I squeezed the trigger and sent a chunk of lead his way, but he dropped down behind his hay bales and my shot went wild.

I could hear him reloading his rifle as he told whoever came up the ladder to "shoot the bastard."

Bullets threw up puffs of hay as incoming rounds laced the

top row of my hay wall. Then the shooter stopped to reload.

"Ow!" I shouted loud enough for them to hear.

"How you doing over there?" Marty threw at me.

"Your man winged me in my gun arm," I replied. "Hurts like hell. Mind if I surrender now?"

"Not at all." Marty sounded pleased with these new circumstances. "Just raise both hands and come on out."

"You won't shoot, will you?"

"No, we'll hold our fire, just show yourself."

I raised my left hand above the hay bales.

"I'm coming out."

"Show your right hand," hollered Marty.

"Can't," I hollered back. "That's the arm you guys shot me in. I can't move it."

"Then throw out your gun."

"It's here on the floor somewhere under the loose hay. You find it, you can have it."

I stood up slowly.

That's when Marty made the mistake of stepping out from cover.

I quickly raised my revolver and blew a hole in the center of his forehead. Must've had just the right amount of fingertip on the trigger this time. At least I didn't pull my shot to the right like back at the road house. He fell over backwards and I ducked as his man started sending rounds in my direction.

Scuffling sounds on the ladder told me another man was coming up to join in the fray.

Didn't think they'd fall for my I-surrender-trick a second time. And there was no sense in me sticking around here much longer. They had the better firepower.

Staying low to the floor, I crawled to the loft doorway, took a quick look outside. No one in sight. I stuck the hot-barreled pistol in the back of my belt, placed both hands on the edge of the loft floor, and swung out into the cold air. It was a long fall. When I hit the hard ground, my swollen ankle exploded with pain. I ended up sprawled in the dirt.

Shakily, I got up on my knees just as Milo and Mike came around the corner of the barn. Both had rifles pointed toward me.

Something whizzed past my right ear as I clawed at the .357 in my belt.

One quick thought crossed my mind as I pulled the gun.
Crap, I only had one bullet.

HARLEY QUINN IS DEAD
James W. Ziskin

"She was cruel. Like she took delight in breaking my heart." Connie rubbed his eyes with the heels of his hands and drew a sigh. "Laugh, she said. Dry your girly tears and pull yourself together, she said. Act like a man, you clown."

Sitting to his right was Jerry Weber, the court-appointed lawyer. A large fellow in a wrinkled suit, Weber had been salivating for a double cheeseburger and fries since before the nice judge ruined his evening by assigning him this client. He leaned his considerable self over and informed Connie in a soft voice that he didn't have to answer any questions if he didn't want to.

"He's right, you know," said Bob Howser, the cop across the table. "You don't have to say a thing. Of course, you don't have to get out of here tonight either. Cooperation is usually the best strategy."

Connie and Weber exchanged looks. The lawyer wiped his perspired brow with a moist handkerchief and offered a silent proceed-at-your-own-peril.

"She didn't even try to deny it, you know," said Connie. "The cheating. She just shrugged and said she was leaving me."

"For Harley Quinn?" asked Howser.

"Yeah. Too bad for her that Quinn had other ideas."

"He wasn't that into her?"

"For sex, sure. Nothing more than that. Of course she thought it was love. Quinn was going to be the one. The one she'd latch onto before it was too late."

The cop squinted at him. "Too late? How do you mean?"

"She's always been terrified about getting old and losing her looks. Figures she'd better find a great guy while she's still hot."

"I've seen her," said the cop. "She's a beauty. How a guy like you ever got so much as her phone number, I'll never understand."

"Yeah, thanks for the compliment. Everyone thinks my pain is funny. I'm sure she'd agree with you now, but she used to think I was the one. When she dumped Joey Grimaldi for me back in high school. Suddenly I'm not good enough. She wouldn't even know a diamond if she held it in her hand."

"And I suppose you're a diamond?" smirked the cop.

Jerry Weber's stomach chose that moment to groan, calling out to the coveted cheeseburger as if to a wayward lover. Howser pulled a pack of gum from his pocket and tossed it across the table.

"Try to keep the noise down, big boy," he said. "I can't hear a word your client's saying." He turned back to Connie. "Tell me about this obsession of hers."

The suspect twisted his lips in disgust. "Her mother did a real job on her. 'Don't wait too long, Paloma,'" he said in a falsetto voice, mocking the girl's mother. "'Don't settle cheap. You'll miss your chance.'"

"You're a funny guy, you know that? You should be a clown or something."

Connie said nothing. Just frowned at the cop. Weber stuffed three sticks of gum into his maw and commenced to ruminate. Howser leaned forward and fixed Connie with a stare. He spoke in a conspiratorial whisper.

"Why don't we get this over with so your friend here can get himself something to eat? Tell me why you killed Quinn."

"I've told you a hundred times. I didn't kill him. He rejected Paloma, didn't he? Slept with her then tossed her aside like a used tissue. Why don't you ask *her* why *she* killed him?"

"She was in love with him. My money's on you."

Connie dismissed the theory with a wave of his hand. "If it hadn't been Quinn, she would've left for someone else. I told you, she's determined to improve her prospects before it's too late. Thanks to her drunk of a mother."

"It's the mother's fault your girl is leaving you?"

"No, not her fault. She hates me—thinks I'm loser—but Paloma makes her own choices. And Quinn looked like the best option."

"And how did you figure out she was cheating on you?"

Connie looked past the cop to a spot on the wall. It might have been a speck of food, the jetsam of a long-ago propulsive sneeze, or perhaps even a squashed fly. Who could tell in the dim light? And who really wanted to know? The main thing was he liked making the cop wait.

"The evidence was there," he said finally.

"What evidence was that?"

"Little things," said Connie, turning his attention back to Howser. "Wouldn't mean anything to you."

"Try me."

The suspect reached for the paper cup before him, swirled the cold coffee around three or four times, raised it to his lips, but then thought better of drinking it. "Like I said, little things. A smear of makeup on her neck, for instance."

"Not your brand?"

"Ha ha. You're the funny one, not me. There were other clues, too. Plenty. Like a beret on the floor of her car. And a pair of white gloves. And she started acting squirrelly. Wouldn't tell me where she was going or where she'd been. And she always had a headache, if you know what I mean."

"Sounds innocent enough," said the cop.

"Like I said, things that wouldn't mean anything to you."

Howser leaned back in his chair and clasped his hands behind his crew-cut head. "Is that why you killed him?"

Connie chuckled softly and shook his head. "Nice try."

"Your girlfriend says you did it."

"She doesn't know anything, no matter how smart she says she is."

"This isn't about her," said the cop, leaning forward again. "This is about you knocking off the guy who stole your girl."

"You have no proof. You've got nothing on me."

Howser pursed his lips and blinked slowly. "Okay, then." He made a great show of pushing his chair back, its legs scraping over the floor tiles, and he stood. Planting both hands at the small of his back, he thrust his hips forward and grunted. "I'm beat. Have a good night, fella."

The lawyer twitched to life. Like Pavlov's dog upon hearing the dinner bell, his salivary glands roared into overdrive. He was already deciding which fixings he would slather on his double cheeseburger.

"Finally," said Connie. "Can I go now?"

"You?" said Howser. "You're not going anywhere, pal. My partner's got some questions for you. And she's not a sweetheart like me."

"He's lying," Paloma said to Sergeant Ernestine Jackson. "He killed Harley. I'm sure of it."

"Oh, we know he's lying," said Jackson, arms folded across her chest as she considered the suspect and his hungry lawyer through the one-way glass.

The door popped open and Howser stepped inside. "Miss," he said, greeting Paloma. Then turning to Jackson, "Tag, you're it, Ernie."

She rubbed her hands together. "Anything I should know? Something I might've missed through the glass? A nervous tick? Is he sensitive about his mother or something like that?"

"He's smart, but, as you know, he's made mistakes. We've already got all the evidence we need. He just doesn't know it yet."

"So you say. I don't like trusting my cases to a civilian jury. Too risky." She studied Connie again through the glass for a long moment, then added, "I'll get a confession before he asks to take a leak."

"Where did you meet this Harley Quinn anyway?" Ernie asked the young man slouching at the table.

Connie pouted, as if he was considering the question for more than its face value. He looked to Weber for a thumbs-up or -down on whether to answer. The lawyer was nodding, even if he wasn't exactly making eye contact with his client. In fact, Jerry Weber was at that moment engaged in an imagined conversation with his phantasmal cheeseburger.

Connie took the nod as permission to answer the question. And why not? There was no evidence against him, after all. He'd read in the papers that the streets had been deserted the night Harley Quinn was run down and killed. No witnesses had come forward. Who could point the finger at him besides Paloma? And she had no proof. All he had to do was stick to his story and he'd be fine. Suspicion was one thing; evidence was another.

"Quinn was a professor at my college," he said but didn't elaborate.

"Let me guess. Besides poaching your girl, he flunked your ass."

Connie said nothing, but Ernie's words stung. Yes, as a matter of fact, he thought. Goddamn Professor Harley Quinn had failed him. Or nearly. He'd given him a D-plus in the history of the Comedia dell'arte.

"Actually, I don't have to guess at all," said Ernie, filling the void in the conversation created by Connie's silence. "We already know he flunked your ass. We checked your school records."

"Yeah, so what? So he gave me a crappy grade. There's book smarts and street smarts. Quinn had neither. He got just lucky."

"Is there a vending machine or something outside?" asked the lawyer, interrupting the exchange he'd been tuning out in favor of his delusions of cheeseburger.

Ernie ignored his question. She was zeroed in on the prisoner.

"So it was your street smarts that told you it was a good idea to run him down with your car?"

"I didn't run down anyone. I already told the other cop that."

"Your car sure has a lot of dents in the fender."

"And did you find any blood? Any flesh? Any DNA?"

"You know we didn't. What did you do, run that heap through a Clorox car wash?"

"Admit it. You've got the wrong guy."

"I think we've got the right guy."

"Then prove it."

Ernie nodded, adjusted her brassiere strap on her shoulder with a smart snap, and settled into her straight-backed chair, wriggling her rear end as if the motion might knead the hard seat into a more comfortable shape. She rubbed her chin as she sized up the subject in front of her. Connie didn't like that. Weber's stomach rumbled again.

"We'll get to that in a minute," said Ernie, referring to proving the case, not the lawyer's gastric rumblings. "Why don't you tell me how you managed to lose your girl to an old man?"

"He wasn't that old."

"Oh, come on," said Ernie, rolling her eyes. "He was at least thirty-five. Ain't that old to you? Of course it is. So he must've been one charming motherfucker to snag a looker like Paloma. How come the college didn't fire him for fraternizing with a student?"

Connie snorted a laugh. "A student? You gotta be kidding. Do you really think Paloma could get into a school like CSPU?"

"It ain't exactly Harvard," she said.

Connie assured her it was top-notch research institution with a storied history and legions of distinguished alumni. Ernie feigned a yawn.

"That's nice. But I'm more interested in how Paloma and Mister Steal My Girl met. Why don't you tell me about that?"

Connie scowled. Knowing Paloma as he did, he wondered how could he have been so stupid. Introduce her to Quinn? What had he been thinking? The guy was famous for turning on the charm and stealing young girls' hearts. He was the strong silent type. Silent anyway. And he was old enough to buy liquor for the undergraduates. How was Connie supposed to compete with that?

He drew a sigh and then, in even tones, he began sketching out the story for Sergeant Jackson. Paloma had visited him at the college. It was homecoming weekend. They'd been dating since junior year in high school. But when Connie went off to CSPU—the first step on his planned meteoric rise to the top—Paloma stayed back in Kansas where she waited tables, biding her time until Connie returned with his diploma and bright future. Or perhaps until someone better came down the pike.

"She's been telling me she's a genius since she was seventeen," he said. "I suppose she's smart enough. But not enough to get into CSPU."

Ernie nodded. "Yeah, you're repeating yourself now. What about how they met?"

"It was last week. There was a student-faculty mixer in the quad," said Connie. "Arranged by Quinn. He was the hip teacher, after all. The cool one who hung out with the students, like he was running his own Dead Poets Society. The girls really dug him, and the guys all wanted to be like him. Be near him. Like we might absorb his charisma."

"I gotta be honest with you," said Ernie. "If you were paying tuition in the hopes of soaking up some of his charm, you should ask for your money back."

Connie glared at her. "You're not exactly Miss America yourself."

"That's it," she said with a laugh. "Get angry. Grow a pair. Speak your mind. Quit being a joker for a minute and tell me the truth. Tell me you ran over Quinn because he rack-jacked your girl."

"I didn't do it. I already told you that. Yeah, sure, I hated the guy for hooking up with Paloma. For pretending to be my friend. And for giving me a D-plus. But I'm not going to risk my future on a piece of lint like Harley Quinn. I'm going straight to the big top."

"Yeah, you still seem like a sorry-ass clown to me."

Connie sulked for a moment before defending himself. "Hey, I'm young. Quinn got lucky early. Earlier than most. That's how it happens sometimes. Some people hit a home run on the first swing, then they crap out and end up as batting coaches. Guys like me, we have a vision for our careers. Our future. Our legacy. I'm not going to teach others. I'm going to leave a mark."

"In your underpants, perhaps."

"I will. Just watch and see."

"Spare me. The only career you're gonna have is pounding out license plates in the state pen."

In the next room, Howser and Paloma watched and listened. She gnawed her thumbnail, and he studied her. She focused on the scene playing out on the other side of the glass with an intensity that struck Howser as remarkable. As if she were the cop and not the girlfriend. He fancied her lips were moving, and not just as she bit her nails. Then she caught him staring at her, and she stuffed her hand into the pocket of her jeans.

"What?" she asked.

"Sorry," said Howser. "You're a pretty girl is all. I apologize if I made you uncomfortable."

She cracked a weak smile. "A little, yeah. But it's okay."

"Can I ask you a question?"

She shrugged. "Sure, I guess."

"Is it true what he told me before in there? About you, I mean. Are you afraid of losing your looks? Afraid of getting old?"

Paloma blushed. "Do I have to answer that?"

Howser shook his head. "No. I was just wondering." He paused as they listened to Ernie grill Connie some more about the student-faculty mixer. After a while, Howser spoke again.

"You know, it's strange that you told us Connie took his car out the night Quinn was killed."

"Strange how?" she asked, thumbnail back between her teeth.

"Strange because his car was spotted on a couple of security cameras nowhere near where Quinn got run down."

"I don't know anything about that. Just that I told him I was leaving him. Then he went out and took his car."

Howser nodded slowly. "Funny kind of car he owns, too. A Yugo. I mean, who owns a Yugo these days?"

Paloma shrugged again. "Sorry. I don't know much about cars."

"They stopped making those pieces of shit back in, what, '92? And they were lemons when they were new. Where the heck does he even get the thing serviced?"

Paloma offered a clueless gesture then turned to concentrate on the interrogation going on inside the interview room.

"And such a conspicuous car," continued Howser. "You don't blend into the crowd in that heap." He clicked his tongue in bafflement. "But it was nowhere near the scene that night. Maybe he's telling the truth after all."

* * *

"Let's talk about cars," said Ernie, and Connie's head nearly hit the table.

Distracted as he was by his cheeseburger cravings, his derelict lawyer noticed nothing,

"You gotta be kidding," groaned the suspect. "We've been over my car about ten times already. I took it out for a drive in the country because I was upset. I was nowhere near the place where Quinn was killed. And there's no blood or anything on it."

"Yeah, that bothered us for a long while. The fact that your car showed up on security cams on the other side of the city. And that there was no brains or blood or nothing. Did you know that you can never really clean up all the DNA when you hit someone? There's always a trace, a drop of blood, some hair somewhere on the car." She let her words hang in the air for a long moment. Then she added, "But not on yours."

"Right," said Connie, beaming at her. "Because my car didn't run over Quinn."

"Oh, we know that," she said. "But I wasn't asking about your crappy little car. By the way, a Yugo? Really? Come on, man. Have some respect for yourself."

"What's wrong with my car? It's a classic."

"Never mind that. I want to know about the car you were driving that night. The one we pulled out of the river this morning."

"I don't know what you're talking about."

"I think you do. It's the little Volkswagen Beetle someone ditched in the river about hundred miles from here. Quinn's car."

"You know, some of those security cameras are pretty good these days," said Howser. "Maybe not enough to show a face clearly in the dark of night. But good enough to see when there are dents in the fender or not. Strange. The first image we got showed no dents. But the second one did."

"That's interesting," said Paloma. "Excuse me, but I'm trying to listen to what they're saying in there."

"Don't fret about that. I know exactly what they're saying. At least Sergeant Jackson's side. And you know the other half."

Paloma reeled around, eyes blazing with fear. "I beg your pardon?"

"What your boyfriend's saying in there. You know the script, don't you? I'm sure you two rehearsed it and practiced it, right?"

"I don't know anything about Quinn's car," said Connie. "I was driving mine."

"Oh, no you weren't. We know it wasn't you at the wheel of the Yugo. It was your pretty little girlfriend, Paloma."

"That's ridiculous."

"Oh, my God!" piped up Weber, reaching under the table. "There's a Slim Jim in my brief case! I forgot all about it."

"Have yourself a banquet," said Ernie. "But shut up, will you? This is the part where I get my teary-eyed confession from your client." She turned to Connie. "Now you. You and your pretty accomplice overlooked two little details. That's how we nailed you."

"We didn't overlook anything, because we didn't do anything."

"Did you know that your girlfriend bashed your crappy little piece of shit Yugo into another car to make it look like you hit something?"

Connie nudged Weber and implored him to say something. Anything legal to shut up the cop. But the lawyer was savoring the Slim Jim with a joy that bordered on the perverted. Acts-against-nature perverted.

"And there's a lonely toll collector who thought your

Paloma was the prettiest thing he ever saw. At least that night. And, since his job is mind-numbingly dull, he's become a car counter. That means he counts makes and models and plays some stupid, I'd-rather-shoot-myself-in-the-head game of bingo with his co-workers. And he won two hundred and fifty dollars when your relic of a Yugo went through his lane. He even took a picture to prove it to his pals."

"Weber, say something!" yelled Connie.

"Keep your hands off! It's mine! You can't have any!"

"We've got a picture of you at the wheel of your boyfriend's Yugo," said Howser. "How does that jibe with your sworn statement that he took the car out that night?"

"I want a lawyer," said Paloma.

"They always ask for a lawyer about this time."

She returned to chewing on her thumbnail. Howser moved in for the kill.

"You and Connie planned the whole thing after Quinn had his way with you then dumped you. You begged your boyfriend to forgive you. Said you'd never cheat on him again. He agreed, but only if you helped him erase his humiliation. Isn't that right?"

"I want a lawyer," she repeated.

"And you decided to stay here with him. Probably even to marry him. And the two of you cooked up this story to cover for each other. You would blame him, he would blame you. You knew his car would be clean. No proof. We'd never make the charges stick."

"Okay. I want to make a deal," said Paloma, changing course. "I'm not spending the rest of my life in jail for a clown like Connie."

Howser nodded knowingly and produced a sheet of paper for her to sign. "I guess the weekend at the college didn't turn out like you planned."

***

"You still can't prove I was anywhere near the scene," said Connie. "I read the papers. There was no one in the street. No witnesses."

"You're right. At least partially," said Ernie. "There was no one *in* the street. But I've got nine witnesses. Eyewitnesses, as a matter of fact. And their stories all match."

"Nine witnesses? That's impossible."

Ernie rose from her chair and pulled a piece of paper from her back pocket. She placed it on the table before Connie and smoothed the folds and the wrinkles.

"I'm gonna need you to sign this confession," she said. "The judge might go a little softer on you and your pretty girlfriend if you do. Go ahead. Read it. You'll find it's all true and in order. And I'll lay odds Paloma's already signed hers in the other room."

"I'm not signing anything. I want to know who your nonexistent witnesses are."

"All right then. I'll tell you. You were careless, friend. Stupid, really. That clown college of yours didn't make you so smart after all. You're going to be one of the most famous—infamous—undergrads Clown Science Polytechnic University ever produced. Even more famous than your mime professor, Harley Quinn. Lost your girl to a mime? That's pathetic, even for a clown. But what I don't understand is why you didn't just club him to death with a juggling pin? Squirt him with poison from your lapel flower? Or sabotage his unicycle on the high wire? What the hell were you thinking taking nine classmates along with you to run him over? Did you really think they wouldn't turn you in?"

As the realization dawned on him, Connie lost the power of speech. He was going to jail, and so was Paloma. He cursed himself silently for his oversight. He'd planned everything so carefully, only to make that one tiny mistake that nabbed him. Why had he chosen death by clown car?

He began to weep. Weber, having swallowed the last of his Slim Jim, set about licking the grease from the inside of the wrapper. Ernie patted the prisoner on the shoulder. At length, Connie composed himself and Ernie asked him one last question.

"I gotta know one thing," she said. "How did you fit ten clowns into that little car? I just don't get it. How the hell did you do that?"

Connie lifted his head and regarded the cop with more vitriol and hatred than she'd ever encountered in a criminal. He fairly spat his words at her.

"*That* is a trade secret."

"You know, this case reminds me of an old song," said Howser, raising a beer to his partner at McNally's.

Ernie rolled her eyes. "Not more of your seventies crap. How many times do I have to tell you I hate that progressive rock you play."

"No, no. Not my usual stuff. I was thinking of an opera I heard once. You know, the one about clowns."

SHOW BIZ KIDS
Brian Thornton

The orderly pulled back the sheet. I didn't recognize the face beneath it.

"Either of you know him?" I said to the two guys flanking me.

Pritzkau, looking green, shook his head.

"Burbridge," Moore, our corpsman, said. "He's an Ops guy. ST, OS, something like that. One of the FNGs we picked up in Guam."

I looked from the paperwork on my clipboard to the remains of Seaman Apprentice Tim Burbridge, laid out on the slab before us.

"He's no ST," Pritzkau, the sonar tech, said. "And if he were any kind of ops guy, I'd have seen him around CIC."

Moore reached over and pulled the sheet all the way back. Burbridge was fair-haired and young—no more than twenty—shirtless and barefoot, a pair of flare-legged jeans the only thing on him other than the tag adorning his right big toe.

There were only two marks on the kid: a long red gash traveling the breadth of his forehead and a partially healed skull tattoo on the inside of his left forearm. I was willing to bet my crow and the stripes stacked below it that the tat had nothing to do with his death.

"What's an FNG?" the orderly said.

"If you gotta ask what an FNG is," Pritzkau said, "you're an FNG."

"I know that CIC means Combat Information Center," the orderly said testily. "That ST is a sonar tech, that OS is short for Operations Specialist, and that although we asked for your Master-at-Arms, we got a Sonar Tech, a Hospital Corpsman, and a Quartermaster, which is some kind of navigator. Where's your Master-at-Arms?"

"Ashore," I said. "I'm the Master-at-Arms for today's duty section, which is how it works on anything smaller than a carrier. And an FNG's a Fuckin' New Guy, Boot." Sometimes with boots you gotta spell it out. "Who found him? And where?"

"Bunch of kids diving off the Shit River Bridge for coins found him."

"That's practically on the base. How did nobody else turn him up before them? They take his clothes?"

"I don't know."

"He have anything else on him other than his ID?"

"He won't know that, either," Moore said. Then to the orderly, "Where's base police? NIS? SP's?"

"Subic base police brought him in," the orderly said.

"This isn't what an accidental drowning looks like," Moore said.

"You can say that again." The orderly crossed his arms and looked triumphantly from me to Pritzkau, and back at me. "What drowning victim has his ID folded up and stuffed down his throat?"

"Think that gash on his noggin killed him?" Pritzkau called over his shoulder, loud enough to be heard over the Jeep's engine as we bounced down the access road in the direction of Pier 6. He was the duty driver, and our ship, the USS *Paul F.*

Foster, was moored there.

"There was no hemorrhaging in the whites of his eyes, and no water in his lungs," Moore yelled from the passenger seat. "He didn't choke on anything, and he didn't drown. Someone smacked him upside the head with something heavy and then tossed him into the Shit. He was dead before he hit the drink."

"And in the Shit River?" Pritzkau laughed. "Gimme a break."

Everyone called this particular body of water the Shit River because of the smell. Even our U.S. Government-issued charts and pubs used that name for it. But the Shit wasn't really a river. Size-wise, it barely qualified as a creek. It was only listed at all because it marked part of the border between the outer perimeter of the Subic NAVSTA and the Philippine territory of Olongapo City.

I had often wondered whether the sages at the National Oceanographic and Atmospheric Administration had designated it a river to avoid giving any wiseacre squid an open invitation to make "up shit creek" jokes.

I attributed it at least in part to Jimmy Carter being president. That shit never would have flown under Nixon, and Ford wasn't around long enough to make an impact at government agencies like NOAA.

While musing on whether the Shit was actually a creek or a river, I had unconsciously pulled out the letter I'd been carrying around unopened in the left breast pocket of my dungaree shirt for the past two days. Now I sat staring at it, as if trying to determine its contents without indulging in the finality of unsealing it.

Moore's voice brought me back. "Say again?"

"I asked what you think, QM2." He used my rank rather than my name. Most of my shipmates did. I was the only second-class Quartermaster on the *Foster.*

I looked back down at the envelope I'd been turning over and over in my hands. "What're you askin' me for?"

"You're the Master-at-Arms."

"*Duty section* Master-at-Arms," I corrected him. "Chief Day's the cop. You'll have to ask him."

"We'd have to see him to ask him," Pritzkau said.

"Oh, we're gonna see him. If Moore's right," I repeated, "this might be an accidental death and it might not. Either way, that kid's dead, and he's one of ours. And *that* is gonna necessitate a fair amount of paper-pushing from our ship's Master-at-Arms."

"He'll just make you do it."

"He may try," I said as I folded my letter. "But I only work for the chief on duty days. And Gorelick outranks him."

Senior Chief Gorelick was the leading quartermaster, and my boss. In the Navy, quartermasters have nothing to do with the Supply department, a fact lost on my Army-veteran father when I first told him I'd joined up. Navy quartermasters are navigation experts.

Moreover, Senior Chief Gorelick and Chief Day hated each other. So I didn't foresee my boss allowing Day to pass off the paperwork on a ship's personnel death—accidental or otherwise—to me. And none of the other duty-section MAAs knew how to do it.

"If Burbridge is...uh...*was* Ops," Pritzkau said, "why wouldn't I see him in CIC, or at least around the berthing?"

"He was already mess-cranking," Moore said. "Washing dishes for the officers up on the second deck, so it's not like you'd ever even see him in CIC. They put him to work up there the day he stepped onboard in Guam."

"Okay, but the berthing?"

"Your berthing's full. They stuck him in Engineering's berthing."

"With the *snipes*?" Pritzkau was from Kentucky, and his accent really came out to play when he was either surprised or scandalized.

"With the snipes," Moore repeated.

"Poor bastard," Pritzkau said, as if Burbridge's actual situation—being dead—was only marginally better than berthing with ship's engineers.

"Was he hanging with snipes?" I asked, impressed by how switched-on Moore was with the goings-on onboard the *Foster*. It was a time-honored truism: people open up around their doctors. Our corpsmen were the closest thing to one.

Moore shrugged and fished a cigarette out of a pack of Old Golds. He offered the pack around. I waved him off. Pritzkau took one.

"A couple of 'em. You know how it is, QM2," Moore said. "FNGs on a new duty station, maybe they get to know each other a bit waiting for their ship, hang together for a while—at least until they start to fit in within their division."

I looked down at the still-unopened envelope in my hand. I refolded it and tucked it back in my shirt pocket. "Sounds like all roads lead to snipes berthing."

"God help you," Pritzkau said around the Old Gold dangling from the corner of his mouth.

Lieutenant J.J. Willis met me on the *Foster*'s quarterdeck just as we crossed the ship's brow. He was the duty section's command duty officer for that day, filling in for the captain and XO, who were both ashore. He looked tired. I knew the look. He was my division officer. I had seen that look a lot.

I quickly filled him in. He removed his ship's ballcap and wiped his sweating face. "Why does shit like this have to happen to me?"

Yeah, that's right, I thought. *This sure is one big inconvenience for you.*

"Guess God just hates you, sir. Is MAC Day back aboard, sir?" I knew the answer already. Still, it was important to fix in the CDO's mind how my first move upon returning to the ship from ID'ing a dead kid was to respect the chain of command and seek to make contact with my superior. "If he is, then maybe we ought to get him up here. After all, he's the expert."

Willis made a face. "Chief Day is still ashore. I've left messages with his wife's sister at the number he left as a contact point when he went on leave, but so far, no dice."

"Captain and XO?"

"Still ashore, too. I've left messages for both of them at the BOQ."

"Anyone check the White Castle yet?" This from the petty-officer of the watch, a loud-mouth boatswain's mate named Davison.

It was common knowledge that when in the P.I., our captain was fond of frequenting a place in town called the White Castle Hotel. A couple of Australians ran it, and the captain knew one of them from 'Nam. There were standing orders from him that, unless the ship was sinking, we were not to disturb him while he was off-ship, regardless of port. Our captain was a work-hard/play-hard kinda guy.

And it was precisely that sort of thing that drove an indecisive twit like my boss nuts. Where our captain was a risk-taker by nature, having won both a silver star and the Navy Cross in Vietnam, our ship's navigator was one of those guys comforted by the rules, considering them guidelines to live by.

Willis turned and stared at Davison. Davison clasped his hands behind his back and looked down at his boots.

I broke the tension by saying, "Mr. Willis, would you wake up the duty Ops department head and the duty Personnelman? I'm gonna need access to some of the kid's files so I can get going on the paperwork."

"I'll pull his medical file," Moore said.

"And I'm gonna need Pritzkau to help me inventory the contents of the decedent's locker and rack, sir."

* * *

I used the master key to open the lock situated just below the middle edge of the dead kid's mattress. Then I reached over and snapped on the reading light over the head of his rack, right above his pillow.

Burbridge's rack was made up neat: sheets clean, with crisp, hospital edges, standard-issue wool blanket folded into a square just like they drilled into us back in boot camp.

"Put out that light!" The voice came from somewhere off to my left.

I ignored it.

Pritzkau cleared his throat, leaned close, and murmured, "Do you *really* wanna roust this whole berthing?"

Snipes tended to be a notoriously unruly bunch when they were awake. A sonar tech—any non-snipe, for that matter—caught in their berthing after lights-out, making enough noise to wake up even a few of them, could expect to be on the receiving end of a pink belly at the very least.

"Kid's dead, Pritz. Can't be helped. This is ship's business, and I'm the MAA, so it's on me. Don't worry," I added as I got a grip on lip of the kid's locker. "Your belly will depart this berthing as white as a full moon."

He grinned in the half-light and leaned in to help me with the lid.

"Goddammit, I *said* to put out that light!"

"Pipe down!" another voice broke in. "Tryin' a sleep, here!"

The lid came up with an audible creak. Before I could so much as flash my light into the locker, I found myself clamped hard on the shoulder and spun around.

"Just what in hell do you two *assholes* think you're doing down here after lights-out?" Engineman Third Class Lynn Glenn snarled.

Like me, Glenn was a duty section Master-at-Arms. Lots of guys tried to get qualified to do it so as not have to stand a quarterdeck or engine-room watch. Most of them didn't take the job very seriously. To them it was considered "cake duty."

EN3 Glenn was one of those guys.

I shone the flashlight full in his face to back him off a bit. He was bare-chested, in just his skivvies.

He raised a hand to shield his eyes and swore loudly.

"Ship's business, Glenn," I said brightly. "You want me to turn on every light you have in the overhead, or are you gonna leave us to it and go back to your rack?"

"You don't get that light outta my face," he said, "I'm gonna shove it up your ass." But there wasn't much behind the words.

"Yeah, yeah, yeah," I said. "If you're not gonna turn back in, shipmate, then *pitch* in." I slapped a new plastic bag full into his broad, hairy chest. "Help us bag up Burbridge's belongings."

"What did Burbridge do?" a third voice, this one coming from the next row over.

"How much trouble's he in?" asked another.

"The worst," Pritzkau said. "He's dead."

That brought a chorus of equal parts shock and disbelief, and the overhead lights went on.

Demands for explanation followed, echoing down the aisles in this berthing that served as home to fifty men. Pritzkau and I found ourselves in the middle of a knot of at least twenty of them. The others must have been out sampling the sins on offer in the fleshpots lining Magsaysay Drive.

"When was the last time any of you guys saw him?" I asked loudly.

"He and Rummage went out to the Pearl of the Quarter last night," someone said.

"Nah, not the Pearl of the Quarter," said another guy. "They closed that place down. New one. Forget the name...."

"Who's Rummage?" I said.

A torrent of speculation poured forth from those gathered around Burbridge's rack as to which of Magsaysay's colorfully named brothels—cum-bars Burbridge might have intended to spend what turned out to be his final night on this earth.

"The Washington Zoo?"

"That's not new."

"Around The World?"

"Nah, a new one. Opened up, like, our third day here, man."

"Goornzee Fare," said a hulking Gas Turbine Specialist I knew only as Mungo. He got an approving round of sounds from the other snipes.

"Another crank," Pritzkau said to me.

I looked at him.

"Rummage. He's another crank."

"How do you know him but you don't know a crank in your own department?"

Pritzkau shrugged. "He's from Kentucky."

"Oh?"

"Paducah," he offered, as if that explained everything.

"Where is he, then?" I said. "Anyone seen Rummage since he and Burbridge took off together?"

"He's crankin' in the morning," Glenn said. "Probably in his rack."

"Get him up," I said. "I need to talk to him." Then I nodded for Pritzkau to get busy bagging up the contents of Burbridge's locker. "And I'm likely gonna need to get statements from a few of you once the watch section changes over in—" I looked at my wristwatch, "—three and a half hours."

"Oh shit!" This from the next aisle over. "QM2! Quick, QM2!"

"You find Rummage?" I called out as I started to move.

"He's in his rack. He ain't breathin'!"

"Asphyxiated," Moore said, pulling the sick-bay hatch closed and locking it behind him.

"How can you tell?"

He pulled back the sheet.

The corpse was on its right side, with its left arm covering its face and its left leg pulled up, knee bent, as if still asleep.

Rummage was a tall, powerfully built kid, with an unruly shock of curly brown hair, clad only in skivvies and a too-small T-shirt.

"Look at that skin tone," Moore said. "Red, like he's sunburned. That's what you look like when you're smothered."

"Like with a pillow?" Pritzkau said.

Moore shook his head. "He got his hands on some of the solvent those guys use to clean up after working on the engines all day, and decided to store it in his rack. Fumes got him. So, like I said. Asphyxiated. If he hadn't stuck it in his locker, he might have killed half the guys sleeping in his aisle in addition to himself."

I rubbed my eyes. "You guys thinkin' what I'm thinkin'?"

"That King Kong here brained his buddy, dumped him in the Shit, and then came home to clean the blood from his cuticles with cleaning solvent?" Pritzkau said.

"I dunno," Moore said. "Those two were tight. Look." He pointed at the corpse's inner forearm. "New skull tat."

"Just like the one Burbridge had on his forearm," Pritzkau said.

"Same spot," I said.

"And not more than a day old," Moore said. "Now, I ask you, what kind of person gets a tattoo with a buddy one day, and cold-cocks him the next?"

I didn't like the *Foster*'s Master-at-Arms shack. To the good, the chief had a radio down there, and that almost made up for the fact that the place reeked of his cheap Texas cigars.

But it was quiet, especially at 0630, so I used it to finish the accidental-death form on Rummage. Yes, the Navy has a form for that. The Navy has a form for everything. Hell, they probably have a "Getting Fished Out From Under The Shit

River Bridge" form, but I settled for typing up a close-enough form on Rummage and attaching it to the preliminary autopsy report on Burbridge we'd brought back from the base hospital.

Then I'd run them down to sick bay where Moore and Pritzkau were still sitting with the dead, waiting for a detail from the base hospital to remove the body. Once I got Moore's signature, I could look forward to more choruses of "Why does this shit always happen to me" from my boss, who was still CDO until watch-section turnover at 0800. Part of the price for getting his John Hancock in all the right places.

And then, after turnover to the in-coming duty Master-at-Arms—and coincidentally, that was EN3 Glenn—I'd rack out for a couple of hours. Or try to.

After that I'd go find Chief Day and get his ass back to the ship. Two deaths, one day? Even if there's no foul play, you need your ship's cop for that.

The problem was that Chief Master-at-Arms Elton Day was a short-timer—less than two months away from retirement. And lately it was showing.

The chief's Filipino wife had family in the area, and apparently he got along well with his in-laws. Even before we'd sighted the coastline of Luzon, the chief made it clear to those of us who served as his duty-section fill-ins that he intended to be scarce while we were pier-side at Subic, and that he was doing so with the captain's blessing. The phrase "We served together in 'Nam" counts for a lot in certain circles.

Which left his duty-section guys to pick up the slack.

My eyes had begun to cross by the time I typed the last line on the final page and unrolled the original and the carbon from the typewriter. The watch had rousted me at 0215, and I had been going most of the night. The stench of the chief's cigars had combined with lack of sleep to give me one hammer of a headache.

I sat there in the sudden silence, scrubbing at my eyes with the heels of my hands, trying not to think of the faces of these two shipmates I'd never known in life. Not since 'Nam, and the riverboats, and all the black stuff that went with it, had I seen such death.

Putting that thought away brought me around to the letter, and I just left that behind, too. *Time to run down signatures.*

As I stood to leave, the hatch popped open, and in walked Chief Elton Day.

I'd last seen Chief Day four days previous. At that time, he'd been in civvies and flip-flops, with a good week's growth of beard. He'd obviously stopped at the chiefs' berthing on his way down to the MAA Shack, because his chief's khakis were freshly pressed, and his beard was gone.

From the first time I'd met him, I'd thought Chief Day looked more like a croupier in a saloon in one of those old-time Westerns than a Navy chief. Maybe five-four in his stocking feet, the chief had a broad build going to middle-aged paunch, a broad, pale face set off by cheeks so ruddy he looked perpetually slapped. And the way he slicked down his close-cropped black hair, parting it deliberately in the middle, made me think of sleeve garters and barbershop quartets and John Wayne movies.

"Ah," he said, "QM2, there you are. Fill me in."

I did.

He began looking through the forms I'd just finished typing before I was halfway through my summary of the events of the past four hours.

"Good job. I can take it from here. The captain and XO are coming in for this, and I've got to debrief 'em."

"Want me to get signatures, or get started on the next-of-kin notification paperwork, call the Red Cross, and so on?"

He shook his head. "Nah, you've put in a full day and it's not even seven yet. Consider us turned over, and go get some shut-eye."

Must have been worried about being seen to not be doing his job after all, I thought to myself as I stretched the kinks from my back. "Okay, Chief. If you say so. Rough night."

"It's not every night some boot FNG kills his buddy then rolls home and offs himself by accident," Day said.

"You think that's what happened?"

"Based on what you've laid out for me, it sure sounds that way. I'll read your report—" he raised it as he mentioned it, "—but that's what my gut tells me."

"Reveille, reveille, asshole!" The words were preceded and followed by a pair of kicks to my coffin locker loud enough to wake me from a coma. I knew the voice. Glenn was getting some of his back.

I sat up on my rack and rubbed my eyes. "What the fuck are you talking about?"

"Chief wants to see ya."

I rubbed my face with both hands. "About?"

"Get the fuck out of your rack and get your ass up to the Master-at-Arms shack. What didja fuck up, big shot?"

He was standing over me, and based on what happened next, didn't expect me to come out of my crouch and head-butt him. My bell rang, and I saw lights, but Glenn was off his feet, on his back and staring up at me with a stunned expression on his face.

"Whoops," I said as I stepped over him. "Sorry about that."

I did what I always did when entering the Master-at-Arms shack. I leaned in, one shoulder lowered in a sign of respect that I happened to know Chief Day liked. "You wanted to see me, Chief?"

"Where are Burbridge's keys, QM2?" Day snapped. He had one of his cigars lit and clenched between his teeth.

"I inventoried everything in his rack and it's all bagged up." I gestured toward the black bags piled in the corner. "I don't recall any keys."

"Lieutenant Preble is losing his shit on me over this," he said. "Burbridge was an EW."

"So?" Then it hit me. "Don't tell me Burbridge had a key to Growth."

Preble ran Combat, which included the Electronic Warfare gang. Their space was commonly referred to as "E.W. Growth," for reasons I had never learned, and likely never would.

"Preble's busy reaming Heithus out about it as we speak." EW2 Heithus was the LPO who ran the EW Gang. As such he was a pretty much constant target of reaming on Preble's part.

This time he might have that ass-chewing coming. "Who gives keys to a secure space like that to a boot who's still cranking and not even assigned to your gang yet?" I said.

"We gotta find those keys."

Glenn suddenly hove into my peripheral vision. "Sounds like a job for the duty Master-at-Arms," I said loudly just as he burst into the shack. It felt cramped with just Day and myself in it. Adding Glenn made it feel downright claustrophobic. The smell of Day's El Supremo didn't help any.

"Glenn, I want you to muster all the restricted men and get them going on a field day of snipes berthing ASAP," Day said. "We're looking for a set of keys, some likely civilian, others ship's issue. Get going."

Once Glenn had gone, Day said to me, "I need you to ask around and find out where those two went in and around town, and see if you can track down those damned keys."

"You're serious? Isn't procedure to just have the MRs recore the locks and issue new keys?"

"Sure," Day said. "And there's the standard inventory of all secret and confidential pubs and equipment. But I need to do my best to make sure no one without authorization saw anything they shouldn't have."

"They fished him out of the Shit. Ever occur to you that they're probably in the mud at the bottom of that cesspool?"

"More than likely," he said.

"So you want me to go try to track down his keys where he might have left them?" I said. "In *Olongapo*? They could be anywhere."

"I don't need you to find them," Day said. "I need you to do your best to eliminate the possibility that they wound up out there in the wrong hands."

"Whyn't you just have the SPs check in every bar while they're dragging the Strip during their rounds? They might as well be good for something."

"Can't be SPs. Preble says Captain wants *us* to do our best to find 'em. Check in with me by 0800 tomorrow."

"That's not much time."

Day leaned toward me and spoke in a whisper. "We're checking the box on this one, okay? I can't trust a moron like Glenn with something like this. So just do what I tell ya and get on this."

"I need to check out with Senior Chief. Let him know I'm not available today in case—"

"I'll handle Gorelick. Ship's security trumps updating charts and pubs, especially since we're pier-side for at least the rest of the month." He lowered his voice. "C'mon. You're a smart guy. Smartest I got. Gonna need a Master-at-Arms after I leave...."

And there it was. The carrot. I heaved a sigh as my thoughts flashed to the charthouse, over the arc of my career, and the letter in my pocket. And then I remembered how, through the babble of questions, speculation, gossip, and outrage being expressed by that group of snipes in their berthing last night, someone *had* said something about where Burbridge and Rummage went on their last night out.

"Aye-aye, Chief."

***

"Glenn don't like you."

Without looking up I kicked a chair toward the tower of muscle standing next to my table. It hadn't taken me long to track him down. He'd been at The Washington Zoo, a favorite snipe hang-out, and one of the seedier of Magsaysay's roadside establishments. The Washington Zoo was the kind of place where you could get a game of Smiles going right out in the open. Usually they were back-room only. A rarity, even for a place as devoid of a moral code as Olongapo City.

I had never played Smiles. I need to actually know the girl sucking my dick in order to make me grin. And I don't usually like that sort of connection obscured by a table top.

It's the romantic in me.

I'd just interrupted one of these very games with an offer of a beer for the guy I'd come to find. I was actually surprised when he came over to my table.

"Feeling's mutual." I nodded toward the open seat.

"Glenn's a snipe. You ain't."

"Glenn's bad at his job. I ain't." As Mungo Cheney considered that, I added, "And neither are you."

He sat.

"Free's free." I gestured toward the cold beer in front of him.

He looked from the open bottle to me, and back at the bottle. "Free's free," he agreed at last, and took a pull.

I'd ordered him a Red Horse, the local beer, several bottles of which were arrayed in front of each and every one of the five other snipes playing Smiles at the corner table. For my money Red Horse drank like mule piss, so I'd ordered a San Miguel for myself.

"I need to ask you about Burbridge and Rummage."

"Why do you care about those two?" he asked.

I shrugged. "My job."

That clearly puzzled him. Mungo had gotten his nickname because of his resemblance to Alex Karras, the ex-football star who famously punched a horse in *Blazing Saddles*. The guy was a mountain. And about as communicative as one. "Chief Day's job. He's the cop."

"Not for long."

He looked uncomprehendingly at me.

"Short-timer's disease."

"Ah, yeah." He nodded. "Chief's give-a-shitter ran out of gas a while ago, I think."

"Maybe that's all it is," I said. "Maybe I just think *someone* oughta give a shit about a couple of FNGs too new to make many friends. You lived with them. You seemed to know a fair bit *about* them last night when we talked in the berthing. Did you know them at all?"

"Nah. Rummage, he was okay, I guess. Plus, he was a snipe. But he was the only real friend that other one, the Ops puke—"

"Burbridge."

"Burbridge—" he repeated and continued, "—had. Him we barely tolerated. Kid had a big mouth. Always running off at it. You know the type. Get him drunk, can't shut him the hell up."

"Yep, I know the type. That happen recently?"

Mungo made a face. "Just the other night. The one where they took off together and Rummage came back alone. They'd already been out drinking all day. Came back to the ship for more money, or somethin', Burbridge was plastered and blathering on."

"About?"

"His girl."

"Back home?"

Mungo took another pull off his beer. "No. Here. Local bar girl."

"He ever bring her onboard? Take any of you guys to her bar?"

It was a custom among many of the squids who hit Olongapo to set up an "understanding" with a local Magsaysay bar girl. She'd get paid, wouldn't have to troll for someone to pay for her every night, and the squid would bring his money and maybe his friends—and *their* money—to her bar every night. That would make the *mamasan*—the house madame—very happy. It had been going on for the better part of the twentieth century and showed no sign of abating in 1978.

"Nah."

"Mention her name?"

"All the time. Melinda."

"He mention where she worked?"

"Bragged about that, too. Said he and Rummage drank for free at this new spot."

"The one where Melinda worked."

"Giggled like a little girl about it." Mungo made the face again. "Then said they had a secret 'in' with the new ownership."

"More than just paying Melinda."

"Claimed he wasn't payin' her, either."

"He say what kind of 'in'?"

"Nah." Mungo took a drink of Red Horse. "He started to, but Rummage jumped his shit and shut him up."

"He ever name this place? I mean, hey, free's free, am I right?"

"Free's free," he repeated. "I told you last night, when we found Rummage dead in his rack."

"Do you remember the name?"

"Can't say it. It's hard to say." He drained his bottle. "I gotta get back." He motioned with his head to the table where the other snipes were busy with their game of Smiles. "Thanks for the brewski."

I nodded and began to pick at the label of my bottle of San Miguel. And then I started to figure in my head the number of bars lining either side the mile-plus length of Magsaysay, and the number of girls there, and then the number named Melinda—assuming that really *was* the girl's name. It wasn't a common Filipino name, but that was cold comfort. Chief wasn't making it easy for me.

A shadow fell across my table and jerked me out of my reverie. I looked up. Mungo towered over me again.

He tossed something onto the table in front of me, and turned on his heel and headed back to the company of his friends, their table, and the girls lurking beneath it.

I looked down. The thing he'd thrown onto the table in front of me was a bar coaster with the words *Guernsey Fair: Olongapo's Newest Club!* printed across it.

As it turned out, I had been in The Guernsey Fair before. Then it had been called Tompopo's. The place had been an institution around Olongapo for almost as long as The White Castle.

I'd been to Subic half a dozen times in my career, the first for two weeks of R&R during my hitch in the Mekong riverboats operation in '68. Back then, everything about the place had seemed fresh and exciting to my callow view.

I'd found the kids diving off the bridge into the Shit hilarious, and had dumped God alone knows how many quarters into its toxic, noxious waters for them to dive for. The bars seemed bright and electric. The girls cute, fun, and so much more to a lonely nineteen-year-old far from home and hungry even for female conversation.

In the decade since, I had become more jaded, and the colors of Olongapo more faded. Or perhaps I was just seeing things more clearly than I had as a teenager. Plus, I didn't handle the heat as well as I once did.

These days I just handed the kids on the Shit River Bridge any change I had on me, and more often than not, many of the dollars in my wallet, too. And while I still went out drinking with the guys in my department, and a few outsiders like Moore, I tended to avoid the bars which featured "Donkey Shows," "Peso Shows," and other feats of sexual prestidigitation.

I pulled the letter from my breast pocket as I walked past The White Castle, with its faux battlements and oddly shaped columns framing its front door. By contrast, everything in The Guernsey Fair was new and gleaming, and clean. Even the *mamasan* behind the bar looked young for the kind of work she was doing.

It was mid-afternoon, so most of the usual crowd were likely somewhere sleeping the previous night off, standing duty on base, or some combination thereof. There was a skeleton crew of girls on shift, no more than ten. Light for one of these bars. They all seemed fresh and new, too. I doubted any of them was a day over seventeen.

I ordered and the *mamasan* opened a bottle of San Miguel for me. Some Bee Gees song was playing on the sound system, and most of the girls were out on the floor in pairs, dancing to it.

"Disco?" I said to the *mamasan*.

She laughed. "It slow. Girls are bored. We play rock later, when white boys here. Soul if more brothas. Depend on crowd." It was amusing to hear a Filipino accent wrapped around the way most of the black guys I knew said the word "brothers," but that was Olongapo for you. Cosmopolitan in the weirdest ways.

"What you looking for, Joe?" We were all "Joe" to them. A linguistic remnant of nearly eighty years of military occupation. Because she was Filipino, it came out as "What you looking *poor*, Joe."

"A girl."

She waved her arm to take in the entire establishment. "We have girls."

"A particular girl."

"You see her here?"

"I don't know her. She works here. A friend of mine... knows her. He asked me to talk to her. Give her a message from him."

Mamasan crossed her arms. "You got name?"

"Melinda," I said hopefully.

"Melinda," she said. "There no Melinda here."

Before I could reach for my wallet, she said, "There *Mer*linda." She spelled it, adding an "r" between the "e" and the "l."

"That could be her. Is she here?"

She peered at me again, this time cautious, not uncomprehending. "Merlinda no bar girl."

"Okay."

"No bar fine. She server only." A "bar fine" was the cut the house took out of a bar girl's price for the night. Merlinda might be a girl who worked at The Guernsey Fair, but she wasn't a "working girl" at The Guernsey Fair.

"I'm not looking for that, *mamasan*," I assured her. "I just have to talk to her." I pushed a ten-dollar bill across the bar at her. "That's for the beer." I pushed another ten across. "That's for the conversation."

"Just talk," *mamasan* said. "No more."

"We'll do it right here. Won't even leave the bar. I'll be sitting in a booth."

"I get her."

The family resemblance gave it away. *Mamasan* was protective of this girl because they were related.

She sat across from me while we waited for one of the other girls to bring the expensive lady drink she had ordered (and for which I had paid), looking nervously from side to side.

Merlinda was short, even for a Filipino, under five feet. Her straight black hair hung down her back nearly to her waist. More "pretty" than "beauty," she seemed out of place here.

And she was definitely overdressed. While shapely, and possessing the right curves, she was the only woman wearing pants in the place. And instead of the revealing tank top which was practically the uniform of bar girls up and down Magsaysay, she was wearing a yellow T-shirt with a stylized Steely Dan logo emblazoned across her breasts.

"Thanks for meeting me," I said. "I know Tim."

She looked blankly at me.

"Burbridge," I said.

Same look.

"From the *Foster*. He said you were his girlfriend."

"Oh! You mean Jamie?" Light accent. And I was relieved that she spoke English, because my Tagalog was pretty awful.

I worked to keep my surprise from showing. "Sure. I only know him as 'Timothy Burbridge.'"

"I think that his first name." Then she said, "He tell me first night I meet him that he go by middle name."

I made a note of that. "Have you seen him?"

Her face clouded. "Today?"

"Well, recently."

"Two days ago. Him and Sean."

Rummage's first name.

I took a deep breath. "I'm afraid I have some bad news."

I've never been much of a judge of female tears, but they seemed genuine. And they were enough to bring *mamasan* running.

After a lengthy explanation in both English and Tagalog, accompanied by a *second* expensive lady drink for the distraught Merlinda, *mamasan* retreated to her perch behind the bar, and I finally was able to ask the questions which needed asking.

"Tim—Jamie—he was your boyfriend?"

She looked over her shoulder at *mamasan*. "Yes. But the

right way. Not Olongapo way."

"No bar fine? No arrangement? No money?"

Her brows furrowed. "No. No money. I like Jamie. Nice man. Not all hands. Talk to me like I am someone, not some-*thing*."

"*Mamasan* told me you're not a bar girl. I just had to ask."

"*Mamasan* my *tiya*." She used the Tagalog word for aunt. "I work here for money, wash dishes. Take drink order only. Save for business school. I know what you think about bar girl."

"No, you don't."

She looked disbelievingly at me.

"Is *mamasan* the new owner? Jamie told other people on the ship that he had an arrangement."

Her brow furrowed again. "No owner. Her sister husband—my uncle—new owner. Very smart. Run thing right. Why you ask these question?"

I explained about Burbridge and Rummage and how I had drawn the duty of filling out their paperwork, and further explained how my boss had sent me looking for Burbridge's missing keys, which had led me to her.

"Sean kill him?" she said at last.

"No way to know for sure. Looks that way."

"Sean, him *saput, hayop,* no like him."

I knew that *saput* meant "uncircumcised," a big insult in Tagalog. I didn't know about *hayop*, and told her so.

"Animal. Outside. Pig. Look around." She reached up with one hand and flipped her long hair in a move that took in the whole bar, the girls, everything. "Sean, *hayop*." She looked like she wanted to spit. "Act like he own everything. Even girl. Just like you."

"No. Like I said. Not like me. We all gotta make our way in the world. I don't make judgments about how people earn their bread."

She gave me an uncomprehending look.

"Their living. Their bread? People gotta eat."

She nodded. "Okay. Not *you*." She pointed at me. "*You*." She waved an arm in the direction of Subic, the base, and all those ships. "*You*, all *Amerikano*."

"You mean squids in general."

She nodded. "Yes." She nodded again, as if to herself. "Not all, I guess. Not you. I see how you come in. Respectful. Nice to *mamasan*. Nice to girls. No judgement. You just here. So, you," she clarified, "but also, not *you*."

I couldn't dispute it. So I thanked her for exempting me, and tried to steer us back to the "arrangement."

She shrugged. "Jamie do something for my uncle."

"Sean too?"

"They work together."

I let that one percolate.

"About his keys...."

"Ship's keys?"

"Yes. And maybe some of his personal ones."

She reached under her t-shirt and produced a thin gold chain from which dangled a religious medal. "This Jamie's. He give to me to keep. Say this—" she raised the medal close enough that I could see it was a St. Christopher's medal, "—the key to his heart. And this." She moved the medal aside, and behind it, hanging off the same chain, was a padlock key. She held it so close in front of my face that I could make out the model number and code stamped on it.

"This—" she tucked everything, chain, medal and key, back under the collar of her shirt, "—the key to our future. That the only key of his I see ever."

"Wow," I said.

She smiled and took a long pull on the straw in her expensive lady drink.

"So he fell hard. You knew each other, what? A couple of weeks?"

"*He* fell. Yes. I barely knew him." The expression on her

face hardened. "I not fall for him. I *like* him. Big-sky dreamer. We very different." She looked away, then murmured, "He could have persuaded me. It would have taken time. But I wanted to let him try."

She turned back around and looked me in the eye. "For that, I cry."

"FR-439, FR-439. FR-439." I repeated the sequence over and over, all the way back down Magsaysay, across the Shit River Bridge, past the base gate guards, on the walk to the pier, up the gangplank, and onto the ship.

The key Merlinda had shown me fit a Master Lock. The model number on it was FR-439. I didn't want to write it down, because I didn't want there to be a written record of it. I wasn't sure why. Something about the conversation had unsettled me, something to do with what she'd said about Burbridge and Rummage and her uncle. Couldn't put my finger on it.

But I knew a Navy-issued padlock key when I saw one. And I had a feeling I knew where to find the lock it opened.

I made my way below decks toward the Master-at-Arms shack.

I needn't have bothered. Glenn was parked in there, smoking a cigarette. I'd forgotten he was still duty Master-at-Arms. "Where's Chief?" I said.

He glowered at me. "Ashore. Back tomorrow."

"Right," I said, as if his mentioning it had jogged my memory. "Let me see the master key list."

He sat up straight in the chief's desk chair. "Why?"

"Ship's business," I said.

"Fuck that," he said. "I'm duty MAA, not you."

"Uh-huh," I said. "How'd field-daying snipes berthing go?"

"Like shit, and you know it," he said. "But we did find the little fucker's keys."

"No shit?"

"I wouldn't shit you, QM2," he said almost mildly. "You're my favorite turd."

"Can I see 'em?"

"The fuck is it with you and keys?"

"Got a bet with Moore," I said. "I say the kid had personal keys on that ring. He says not." I held up a ten-dollar bill, the last one in my wallet. "Cut you in."

Glenn sighed loudly, and I thought he was going to say no just to fuck with me. Then he reached for the MAA lockbox, pulled out a nondescript ring of keys, and tossed them to me.

"You guys have a real problem," he said as he snatched the ten-spot from my fingers.

The key the girl had shown me was a duplicate. The original was one of the keys on the keyring Glenn had shown me.

It was the work of ten minutes to change back into dungarees, scare up some more cash from my slush-fund stash in the charthouse safe, and get down to snipes berthing to find the duty MR. I asked a couple of guys watching a porn tape on the berthing TV where the duty Machinery Repairman was. Turned out he was up in the MR shop, "working."

I found him there. Asleep on his desk. His name was Werner. I knew him a little.

"Why you sleeping up here and not racked out down in snipes berthing?" I said.

He shrugged and rubbed the sleep from his eyes. "They were watching a fuck film. Too loud."

"I don't know you as a guy who'd pass up a porno," I said.

"It was my tape."

"Well, that explains it," I said. "Anyway, wanna make twenty bucks?"

***

I had been positive the key would belong to the padlock on the exterior hatch at EW Growth. How wrong I was. When Werner matched the number to the lock in the Officer's Wardroom pantry, it took me a moment to put it together.

Some kid I didn't know and didn't recognize was washing dishes in the Wardroom galley when I stuck my head in.

"Oh, hey, QM2," he said.

"Hey." I looked past him. "Who's duty cook up here today?"

"It's just me," he said as he opened the drain in the sink. He was a black kid, on the short side, with a boot-camp haircut. "There's only the CDO and a couple of duty junior officers. They've already eaten. I'm just cleaning up."

"Do I know you?"

He grinned. "I cut your hair last week."

I touched the side of my head reflexively. "What's a Ship's Serviceman doing cranking up in the O-Gang Wardroom?"

"Well, the kid who was s'posed to crank up here's dead, as if you didn't know. Chief said I gotta cover, 'cuz I'm on duty. Anyway, whatcha need?"

"I gotta look around in here."

"Oh?" he said as he rinsed out the sink. Then he began to methodically wipe it dry. "What for?"

"Ship's business."

"This anything to do with Rummage?"

I shook my head. "Something else."

"Okay, well, I'm all finished up." He snapped the towel once and folded it neatly. "Can you kill the lights and lock it up when you're done?"

I'd been at it an hour, and one thing was readily evident: that pantry was full of way better food than what I was used to eating on the mess decks down below. But I hadn't found anything worth hiding yet.

Then I remembered something I'd read in a Ship's Security

Circular, which got sent regularly with the standard radio traffic, and which Chief Day was forever hectoring his duty-section MAAs to read. This particular circular went into detail about how drug smugglers had taken to using peanut butter to get their stuff past law-enforcement drug dogs. The smell of peanut butter was strong enough to cover just about anything.

And here I was, staring straight at the largest tub of peanut butter I'd ever seen. The Navy buys in bulk, so this one was larger than a coffee can—easily a five—pound tin.

It was nearly full, and mostly with actual peanut butter. But after I'd mucked around in that container for about ten minutes, I found one pound which wasn't peanut butter at all. It was a brick of a white substance tightly wrapped in several layers of taped and re-taped plastic.

"Odorless and tasteless," Moore said as he straightened up from examining the brick. Lucky for me, he'd been in sick bay when I'd come knocking. "It's pure, whatever it is."

"Any guesses?"

"Coke? Heroin? Don't believe all that guff about corpsmen having all the best drugs. I got a family, so nothing but beer and the odd joint for me. This have something to do with—"

"Do you really wanna know?"

"That depends," he spoke slowly and turned his head to look at me sidelong, "on what your next move is."

"I have to go back out into Olongapo."

"That where the answer is?"

"Something someone said. I gotta follow it up. If it's connected to this...." I trailed off.

He nodded, re-wrapped the brick, wrote something on one of the many pads laying around on top of the chief's desk, tore it off, and handed it to me. "Your receipt. I can hold personal meds overnight in the sick-bay fridge. If you don't pick it up in the morning, I'll have to explain it to my chief, and then he'll turn it in, likely to Day, or to the CDO, depending who he finds first."

Two more stops onboard, one of them to change back into my civvies, and I was back in The Guernsey Fair within a half-hour. Night had fallen, and the overhead lights were low, with the neon and music at full wattage. Bodies writhed all over the dance floor. The place was jumping.

I found Merlinda in the back, loading glasses into an industrial-size dishwasher. She frowned when she saw me.

"More question?"

"Just one."

"We close soon."

"Do they know that?" I jerked my thumb in the direction of the open door.

"Restaurant only. I work for restaurant part of business. I go home when we close. Club stay open later."

"I really do only need one question answered."

She started the dishwasher and turned back to me. "Okay. Then I go."

"You said, 'They work together.'"

She blinked. "Who?"

"That's what I'm asking. 'Who?'"

She stared at me, clearly not following.

"I asked about Jamie and Sean's arrangement with your uncle, and you said they did something for him, and then that 'They work together.'"

"Oh." She nodded, clearly remembering. "Right."

"Who? Jamie and Sean? Is that what you meant?"

"And my uncle."

"The owner."

She nodded and looked past me, out on the dance floor. "He not here. Upstairs. His office."

SHOW BIZ KIDS

* * *

The first stair creaked under my foot, as if in warning. I trod carefully in response, highly conscious of the trickle of sweat pooling between my shoulder blades and running the length of my spine, down to the .45 stuck in the waistband of my jeans.

Couldn't be helped. This time there was no cavalry coming. No SPs. No NIS. No backup.

I almost turned to head back down the steps to the alley and to Magsaysay beyond, to another bar, where I could get good and drunk, and read that damned letter burning a hole in my shirt pocket, and maybe even, assuming there was enough courage to be found in whichever bottle they were pouring from, tell the Old Man what I thought of him and his Navy and their traditions and most especially about "the good of the service."

Then an image jumped up in front of me, brought me up short, caught hold and wouldn't let me look away. It was the face of that first kid, lying pale and stiff and oily on the Subic hospital slab. Then the muscle-bound oaf dead in his rack, face that off-red which Moore assured me comes from asphyxiation.

Put together, their combined ages barely tallied five or six years more than my own. Baby-faced boots like them were supposed to be around long enough to profit from their stupid mistakes.

More faces intruded on my thoughts, kids I knew in 'Nam. Kids I'd served with on the riverboats. Kids who went home in body bags exactly like the ones these last two kids would go home in, and with only a faceless, shadowy enemy and a faceless, shadowy government to fail to answer for their deaths.

I'd been powerless to do anything about them then.

But these last two.

Stupid, selfish kids.

I eased the .45 out of my waistband.

There was a new smell lying in wait at the top of the stairs. One that overpowered all competing odors, wrestled them out of the way so it was the only thing you noticed.

One that gave away the whole game in a flash.

A stench I'd lived with for months.

A reek of cheap Texas cigars.

And just like that, I knew who I'd find behind the only door at the top of the stairs.

I had already chambered a round in the .45, so all I had to do was thumb back the hammer before I rapped on the battered door.

"Come!" a familiar voice thundered from the other side.

I opened the door and did what I'd done a thousand times in the presence of its occupant back onboard the *Foster*. Like I had every time I'd entered the Master-at-Arms shack, I leaned through the open doorway, my head cocked to the side and my right shoulder lowered in what ought to look like my accustomed show of deference.

Only this time the move obscured the loaded pistol I held in my left hand.

"Hey, Chief," I said, breezy, like I would have if I were about to muster restricted personnel before eight o'clock reports, and I'd just noticed he was in there drinking coffee at his scratched and dented little green steel desk.

This room had a desk, too. Only it wasn't green, and it wasn't steel. It was mahogany, slightly smaller than the deck of an aircraft carrier, and there wasn't a scratch anywhere to be seen across its length and breadth. The only two things Day had on it were a phone and an ashtray. And in the ashtray was the El Supremo that had helped me identify him from the landing.

"Hey, QM2," said Elton Day, hands conspicuously out of sight. "You found my product."

"'Product'?" I grinned. "And here I thought it was," I paused and picked one, "heroin."

His left hand came up from his lap and he held it out horizontal, then waggled it back and forth. "Same difference."

"Spoken like a true drug lord."

He chuckled. "What's it gonna take for me to get it back?"

I smiled again. "What makes you think you can?"

"You're here, aren't you? So you've obviously worked a few things out." He craned his neck to look past me. "And you're alone. No SPs. No locals."

"Don't you already have an understanding with the locals?"

He shrugged. "You're here alone. That tells me you're here to deal."

My turn to shrug.

"Come on in. Did you bring the *heroin*—" he emphasized the word, "—with you?"

I shook my head.

"Figured you were too smart for that. Where is it?"

"Never mind that," I said. "Why Burbridge?"

He looked hard at me. "'Why Burbridge,' what? Why'd I recruit him? Easy. He was greedy and that made him malleable, and he had a clearance that allowed him access to EW Growth. Can you think of a better place to hide something on a ship like the *Foster*?"

"No, not that. I'd already worked out the 'why' of that for myself. Why'd you have Rummage kill him?"

"He got cold feet. Was afraid we'd get caught. Worried what his mom would think of him." Day shrugged.

"And here I thought you had him put the solvent in Rummage's rack."

"So they could knock each other off?" Day crushed out his cigar. "You give that kid way too much credit. He didn't have the brains or the guts for a move like that. Once he'd gotten spooked it was only a matter of time before he started talking to the wrong people about it. Tell me, how did you manage to get into Growth and get the smack out?"

"I didn't."

"Stop puttin' me on. It was gone by the time I got in there."

"The kid moved it. Maybe right before Rummage killed him."

"Where to?"

"The pantry in Officer's Country."

He laughed at that, and the hand on his desk came down on his thigh with a resounding *slap*.

"Are you just gonna stand there?" he said. "Make your deal half-in, half-out of my doorway?"

"Where'd you get the desk?"

He smiled. "You like? How'd you know—"

I waved my free hand. "It doesn't really go with the rest of the room."

His eyes flashed left and right. "It's a start. Got big plans for this place."

"Gonna finance it with horse smuggled in from Thailand?"

He laughed. "Are you kidding? The market's not here. The real market's stateside. And as long as there are U.S. ships in this harbor, that's a straight shot back."

"All it takes is another Burbridge, right? Another Rummage?"

"I'm done with kids. Know how many nephews my wife's got? How many cousins? Dozens. Know how many of them are serving on Seventh Fleet ships? Most of them. Shame about Burbridge, though." There was not a bit of regret in his voice. "Rummage was just a combination of a moron and a bad choice. An accident. That's not on me."

"And if he used that solvent to wash the blood off his hands after he brained Burbridge and tossed him in to the Shit?"

"That's why I'm done with stupid, corruptible kids like those two." He leaned forward. "Whyn't you come on in and close the door and we can talk about what this could mean for you?"

"Do I look either stupid or corruptible to you, Chief?"

"I doubt you've ever drawn a stupid breath," he said. "Why do you think I pulled you off the Burbridge and Rummage paperwork and gave it to Glenn? I couldn't take the chance that you'd put too much together too fast."

I didn't feel all that fast or all that smart.

"As to whether or not you're corruptible, well, you're *here*, ain'tcha? So are you comin' in or what?"

I knew why he wanted me in the room. Either to be bought or to be shot. I stepped in, the Colt down at my side, pointing at the floor, and closed the door behind me.

"You think there's any need for that?" He nodded toward my pistol.

"As much as there is for the one you're holding cocked and loaded in your lap."

"Don't you trust me, QM2?"

"I might, if only I didn't know you so well."

He smiled a smile that didn't quite reach his eyes, and put an automatic of a type I didn't recognize on the polished wood in front of him. Then he pulled a cigar from the breast pocket of his loud Hawaiian shirt, and lit up using his ship's lighter.

And then the son-of-a-bitch actually blew a smoke ring.

"I put mine down as a show of trust. Whyn't you do the same?"

"We've already established I don't trust you, Chief."

"Well, what's it gonna be, then? I know you know how to handle that thing. But do you have the stomach to use it on me if I reach for my Cheka, here?" He drummed his fingers on the table just an inch or so from the pistol. "I think I know the answer. I think you lost your stomach for stuff like that on the riverboats in 'Nam. I've read your jacket. I know your kind."

"What do you have on the Old Man?" I said.

"Pictures. Lots and lots of pictures. He's not involved and he doesn't want to know what goes on. As long as they don't get sent to a JAG office, or, worse yet, his wife. Or both." He laughed his non-laugh again. "Speaking of the home fires, you think I don't know what's waiting for you back in the States?"

My thoughts flashed yet again to the letter. How could he know what was in it when *I* didn't know?

"You could have a sure thing right here." He pressed his perceived advantage. "You coulda taken my smack to NIS, but you didn't. I respect that." He gestured toward one of the mismatched chairs across from and facing his desk. "Sit down. You're here to make a deal. I'm a businessman now. Got the desk and everything. And soon I'll have the office for it, too."

"Is that really why you think I'm here? To cut myself in?"

"Yep."

"Maybe I'm here to take you in."

He laughed. "You're not gonna take me in and we both know it."

I smiled a genuine smile for the first time in a long time. Not a put on. The real thing. "You've got me there, Chief. I'm not here to take you in."

He visibly relaxed.

And then I lifted the Colt and put six slugs as close to the center of that terrible Hawaiian shirt as I could. The seventh I put in his head after stepping around that big desk of his to get a clearer shot, since my initial fusillade had knocked him out of his chair.

The club music pulsing up through the floor of his office never even missed a beat.

I set down the Colt and parked one hip on the edge of his desk. Then I picked up the handset of his phone. While I dialed, I reached into my breast pocket and pulled out the letter.

And as the line began to ring, I opened it.

ABOUT THE CONTRIBUTORS

DAVID CORBETT is a recovering Catholic, ex-PI, and former bar-band gypsy who turned to writing because, hell, why not? He is the author of six novels, including 2018's *The Long-Lost Love Letters of Doc Holliday*, as well as dozens of stories, numerous scripts, and far too many poems. Nominated for virtually every major prize in crime-writing, he would hate to ruin things by actually winning one, though having a *New York Times* Notable Book and two joints selected for *Best American Mystery Stories* is kinda sweet, as is the fact that his story "Babylon Sister" was named one of the Top Five Stories for the two year-period 2015-2016 by *Narrative Magazine*.

NICK FELDMAN is a crime writer from Seattle, best known for his series of detective stories about private investigator Mina Davis (*Hungover & Handcuffed*, *Asshole Yakuza Boyfriend*). Nick's work has been taught at Cornell University, and his whiskey-soaked prose has garnered a strong reputation for bringing a more feminist & LGBTQ-friendly bent to the noir genre. His upcoming heist novel, *The Fifth Woman*, is expected out in late 2019, and is expected, primarily by Nick himself, to kick all kinds of ass.

BILL FITZHUGH is the award-winning author of ten satiric crime novels. His debut, *Pest Control* was translated into half a dozen languages; the film rights sold to Warner Brothers; it was produced as a popular radio show in Germany, and as a stage musical in Los Angeles. His most recent book is *Human Resources*. In between, he published eight other comic thrillers and satires. *The New York Times* put him in a league with Carl Hiaasen and Elmore Leonard, calling him "a strange and deadly amalgam of screenwriter and comic novelist." The late

ABOUT THE CONTRIBUTORS

Molly Ivins said, "Fitzhugh is one seriously funny guy." He wrote, produced, and hosted Fitzhugh's All Hand Mixed Vinyl for five years on Sirius-XM's Deep Tracks channel. Fitzhugh recently adapted a Peter Straub short story for PCH Films. He lives in Los Angeles with his wife, two dogs, and a rotating cast of chickens.

LINDA JOFFE HULL writes in different genres with a focus on the hidden dangers of suburban life. Her debut novel, *The Big Bang* was published in 2013. Since then, she has authored the romantic comedies *Frog Kisses* and *Over the Moon* as well as three titles in the Mrs. Frugalicious Mystery Series: *Eternally 21*, *Black Thursday*, and *Sweetheart Deal*. Linda's newest novels as one half of the writing team Linda Keir are *The Swing of Things* and the soon-to-be released *Drowning With Others*.

R.T. LAWTON is a retired federal law enforcement agent, past member of the Mystery Writers of America board of directors and a three-time Derringer nominee with over 130 short stories in various publications, to include *Blood on the Bayou* (2016 Bouchercon anthology), *The Mystery Box* (2013 MWA anthology), *And All Our Yesterdays* anthology, *Who Died in Here?* anthology, the *West Coast Crime Wave* anthology, *Deadwood Magazine*, *Easyriders*, *Outlaw Biker*, *Woman's World* magazine, and 41 sold to *Alfred Hitchcock Mystery Magazine*. He also has six e-collections at Amazon for Kindle, plus distributed by Smashwords for other e-readers. You may have attended one of his Surveillance Workshops at various writers' conferences.

CORNELIA READ is the author of *A Field of Darkness*, *The Crazy School*, *Invisible Boy*, and *Valley of Ashes*. In sixth grade, she also wrote the fictional diary of a child spy who gets recruited by her father to join the CIA and bust an international heroin ring, which was taken to a United Nations conference on gifted children and apparently scared the shit out of the Soviet contingent. She lives in Dutchess County, New York, with her beau and within spitting distance of Bard College, where Steely met Dan. She hopes Trump dies screaming in Gitmo.

STACY ROBINSON is a writer, editor, wife and mother- almost never in that order, but always all at once. The owner/editor-in-chief of The Next Chapter, a company specializing in developing and editing novel-length fiction manuscripts, she makes her short fiction debut here with her story, "Josie". Though Stacy has seen more countries in the world than states in the U.S. (but not as many as she'd like), her roots run deep in Northern California where she was born and raised and is currently growing her own little crop of Lost Boys.

dbschlosser is an award-winning fiction and non-fiction writer and an award-winning editor. He taught higher-education writing and crime fiction, and served the boards of Editorial Freelancers Association and Mystery Writers of America regional chapters. His fiction appears in literary journals and online magazines. His non-fiction appears in global news outlets and industry publications. As a communications strategist, political consultant, and candidate, he has delighted and offended people around the world. A Kansas native, he earned degrees at Trinity University and the University of Texas. After working in nearly a dozen states, he settled the Pacific Northwest with his lovely wife and their dogs.

BRIAN THORNTON is the author of eleven books, including *The Book of Bastards: 101 Scoundrels and Scandals from* *the World of Politics and Power,* and *Honest Abe: 101 Little-Known Truths About Abraham Lincoln.* His short fiction has appeared in such venues as *Alfred Hitchcock's Mystery Magazine,* the late, lamented *BULLET UK,* the Akashic Books anthology *Seattle Noir, The Big Click,* and *West Coast Crime Wave,* which he also edited. His collection of three novellas, *Suicide Blonde,* is due out from Down & Out Books in late 2019. He lives in Seattle with his wife and son and is currently serving his third term as Northwest Chapter president for the Mystery Writers of America. Find out what he's up to at brianthorntonwriter.com.

JEFFREY WEBER has produced over 200 CDs. His projects have yielded two Grammys, seven Grammy nominations, at least seventeen top ten albums, two number one albums and an assortment of other honors. He is the author of You've Got a Deal! The Biggest Lies of the Music Business, and We'll Get Back to You! Even Bigger Lies of the Music Business.

SAM WIEBE is the author of the Vancouver crime novels *Cut You Down, Invisible Dead* and *Last of the Independents,* and is the editor of the anthology *Vancouver Noir.* Learn more or contact him at SamWiebe.com.

USA TODAY bestselling author **SIMON WOOD** is a California transplant from England. He's a former competitive racecar driver, a licensed pilot, an endurance cyclist, an animal rescuer and an occasional PI. He shares his world with his American wife, Julie. Their lives are dominated by a longhaired dachshund and seven cats. He's the Anthony Award winning author of *The One That Got Away, Accidents Waiting to Happen, Paying the Piper, Terminated, Deceptive Practices* and the Aidy Westlake series. His latest book is *Saving Grace.* He also writes horror under the pen name of Simon Janus. Curious people can learn more at SimonWood.net.

JAMES W. ZISKIN, Jim to his friends, is the author of the Anthony and Macavity award-winning Ellie Stone series. He worked in New York as a photo-news producer and writer, and then as director of NYU's Casa Italiana. He spent fifteen years in the Hollywood postproduction industry, running large international operations in the subtitling/localization and visual effects fields. His international experience includes two years working and studying in France, extensive time in Italy, and more than three years in India. He speaks Italian and French.

On the following pages are a few
more great titles from the
Down & Out Books publishing family.

For a complete list of books and to
sign up for our newsletter,
go to DownAndOutBooks.com.

Murder-A-Go-Go's
Crime Fiction Inspired by the Music of The Go-Go's
Edited by Holly West

Down & Out Books
March 2019
978-1-948235-62-4

The Go-Go's made music on their own terms and gave voice to a generation caught between the bra-burning irreverence of the seventies and the me-first decadence of the eighties.

With a foreword by Go-Go's co-founder Jane Wiedlin and original stories by twenty-five kick-ass authors, editor Holly West has put together an all-star crime fiction anthology.

Wear Your Home Like A Scar
Nik Korpon

Down & Out Books
May 2019
978-1-948235-82-2

A clandestine surgeon goes to extreme lengths when she's torn between family loyalties. A con man tries to help his girlfriend escape her pimp, despite what the tarot cards tell her. A drifter hunts down the man who hung her out to dry with a cartel boss. A sicario has a crisis of faith when an old legend stalks him.

From the streets of Baltimore to the comunas of Medellín, the Mexican Sierras to Texas border towns, *Wear Your Home Like a Scar* shows that no matter how deep you cut, you'll never truly leave your home behind.

Sunk Costs
Preston Lang

All Due Respect, an imprint of
Down & Out Books
978-1-946502-88-9

Dan is a con man and drifter who thinks he just hitched a ride back east. Instead, he finds himself going 70-miles-an-hour with a gun pointed at his head. But instead of a bullet, he's hit with a proposition to make some fast money. Soon Dan finds himself deeply involved with misdirection, murder, and the sexiest accountant he's ever met.

The Bad Kind of Lucky
Matt Phillips

Shotgun Honey, an imprint of
Down & Out Books
978-1-64396-002-9

Remmie Miken is starting over after a bad run. He's got himself a crappy apartment in the big city and a job hustling burgers and fries. One night Remmie makes nice with a neighborhood gangster. So begins his quixotic pursuit of a whore-on-the-run and ten grand in cash. Heading south into Baja, Remmie brushes shoulders with lowdown crooks, a Catholic priest, cartel enforcers, a strawberry picker, and a wild-eyed expat.

The Bad Kind of Lucky is a twisted comedic noir that follows Remmie straight into the void.

CPSIA information can be obtained
at www.ICGtesting.com
Printed in the USA
LVHW051026100619
620698LV00004B/660/P